HURT

For my parents, Laurence and Katrina

ALSO BY

Also by Brian McGilloway

The Inspector Devlin Series

Borderlands
Gallows Lane
Bleed a River Deep
The Rising
The Nameless Dead

The DS Black Series

Little Girl Lost

HURT

Brian McGilloway

corsair

Constable & Robinson Ltd
55–56 Russell Square
London WC1B 4HP
www.constablerobinson.com

First published in the UK by C&R Crime,
an imprint of Constable & Robinson Ltd, 2013

A copy of the British Library Cataloguing in
Publication data is available from the British Library

ISBN 978-1-47211-113-5 (hardback)
ISBN 978-1-47211-114-2 (paperback)
ISBN 978-1-47211-115-9 (ebook)

1 3 5 7 9 10 8 6 4 2

Printed and bound by
CPI Group (UK) Ltd, Croydon, CR0 4YY

Friday 9 November

PROLOGUE

The one benefit with getting a school picture taken was that it took so long you missed an entire lesson. Especially when all the other girls in the class were taking forever, fixing their hair, nipping out to the toilet to put on make-up they weren't even meant to have in school. Her mother forbid her using it. 'Fourteen is too young for make-up,' she'd said. Not that make-up would have made much difference, Annie thought.

Annie Marsden stood, watching the group in front of her, their conversation soundtracked by the music leaking from her headphones. If they were aware of her standing behind them, none showed it.

A flash to their left. Up on the stage an old guy, white haired, slightly stooped, was standing at the camera while Nuala Dean preened herself, angling a little in front of the canvas image of a library of leather-bound books, their spines mixtures of red and blue and green. Showing her good side. At least she had a good side, Annie thought.

The line in front of her shuffled forward a space and she moved to fill the gap.

She glanced up only to catch the eye of her physics teacher. He was standing, his arms folded, watching her. Without unfolding his arms, he gestured towards his own ear then waggled his finger at her.

She obligingly pulled out her earphones and pocketed them. The group ahead of her had moved onto the steps of the stage now, their conversation reduced to a murmur as each prepared themselves for their shot.

'Move up, will you!' someone behind her said, and Annie shuffled forward again, pulling her cardigan sleeves further down, gripping their cuffs in her hands. The floor was yellow, she noticed. Assembly hall floors always are. Yellow because that's the only colour of light they can't absorb. Or it's the only one they can absorb. She couldn't remember which.

'Give me a beautiful smile,' she heard the old man say. The girl on the stool in front of him obliged.

'Button up your top button, Annie,' someone said. The physics teacher was standing next to her now. 'Look like you have some pride in your uniform.'

Annie blushed slightly, murmured an apology as the girls behind her tittered at the comment. She struggled to bring the collars close enough together to clasp, in the end gave up and tightened the knot of her tie nearer her throat. She'd told her mum she needed a new shirt in September. Four months later and she was still waiting. Either that or she'd put on too much weight.

'Aren't you just lovely?' the old man said, earning the reward of a smile from Sally McLaughlin.

Annie made her way up the steps, stood, next in line, for the shot, her stomach churning. Sally got up, flicked her hair over her shoulder and strode across and down the set of steps on the other end of the stage.

'Sit yourself down, love,' the old man said.

Annie came across to the stool, edged herself onto it, picked a spot above the photographer's head to look at, waited. He was busying himself with the flash, adjusting the angle.

Hurry up, Annie thought. She was aware that her skirt was pulled up on her thighs a little, revealing the whitened scar of the ladder in her black school tights. She shifted in the seat, pulling at the hem.

'Right, look at the camera, please,' the old man said.

Annie, despite herself, did. She saw a distorted version of herself reflected in the concave of the lens.

'Haven't you the prettiest eyes?' the old man said.

Annie instinctively glanced at the floor, just as the flash brightened the stage.

The wood was yellow.

Sunday 16 December

Chapter One

He'd just got a pint in when the aura started. A quick flickering of iridescence on the periphery of his vision that already made his stomach turn. He shut his eyes in the hope that perhaps it was a trick of the light, overtiredness from the night before. The last thing Harry needed was another late evening, but then he'd promised the missus this for months. A bit of dinner, a few glasses of wine, then down to the pub after for an hour. The tentative re-beginnings of a relationship which had sprung leaks years earlier, but whose gaping holes only became apparent with the departure of their only son to university.

'Empty nest syndrome,' one of the drivers had told him that day as he'd mentioned during break that he had to go out. They'd all been out the night before on a work do; John-Joe Carlin's leaving party. He'd been driving the Belfast–Derry train for thirty-three years, through all kinds of shit. And now, this evening, he was bringing his last train home.

Harry glanced at his watch, could just make out the time beyond the growing intensity of the flickering, his whole field of vision now haloed with shifting ripples of light. John-Joe would be on the final stretch of his final drive, passing Bellarena.

He stumbled back to the table where his wife, Marie, sat, glancing around her, smiling mildly at the other drinkers.

'I need to go home,' Harry said. 'I've another bloody migraine starting.'

Marie tried to hide her disappointment, a little. 'Have you none of those tablets?'

Harry shook his head. 'They're in my work uniform. I left them in the station.'

She tutted, turning and picking up her coat, the fizzing soda water untouched on the table where Harry had set it fifteen minutes earlier. 'Come on, then. I knew it was too good to be true.'

The shimmering had thickened now into a perfect circle of tightly packed strands of light that seemed to encircle his pupil. Harry felt his stomach lurch, swallowed hard to keep down his meal. It really would be a wasted night if he brought that back up.

His phone started vibrating a second before he heard the opening notes of 'The Gypsy Rover', his ringtone. He stared at the screen, trying to make out the caller ID.

'John-Joe,' he said, answering the phone. 'You're done early.'

'Earlier than I'd planned. Something's happened. The train's just died.'

'Where are you?'

'Just past Gransha. Coming in on the final stretch.'

That was less than two kilometres from the station. The train would already have been slowing, rounding the curve at St Columb's Park, then the last few hundred metres in past the Peace Bridge.

'What happened?' Harry asked, shifting the phone to his other ear.

'I don't know. We just lost power. Everything. Can you check it out?'

Harry glanced up at where Marie stood, the keys in her hand, the hoop of the key ring hanging off her wedding finger.

'I'll be right down,' he said.

As he moved onto the tracks, away from the brightness of the station, Harry was grateful for the silence after all he'd listened to in the car. The darkness actually helped ease his building headache a little. The aura had stopped as they'd pulled into the station, though that was perhaps because his attention was diverted into trying to placate Marie. After all, he was well enough, she suggested, to work, but not to take her out for the night. How could he explain that it was John-Joe's final night? That the man needed to get his train home, one last time? She wouldn't understand it. He could see her now, sitting in the car, the heater turned up full, arms folded, tight lipped, her expression pinched.

He could feel the migraine proper begin to build. He tried focusing on the bobbing of the torch he held as he walked the line. He glanced ahead a distance, to his right, at the looming shapes of the trees separating the train line from St Columb's Park.

Power cables ran along the track side, heavy copper, sheathed in plastic. It was to these that Harry turned his attention, for undoubtedly that was the reason for the train stopping. Sure enough, only ten yards ahead, just beneath the Peace Bridge, the lines had been cut.

He dialled through to the train.

'John-Joe? Sorry, man. You're not going to be bringing this one in for a while. The lines have been cut just outside of the station. We'll need to get the passengers bused out. Have you many on board?'

'One. And he's sleeping off a session.'

It wasn't unusual. The Belfast to Derry train was so slow a journey most people took the bus. The line had been promised an upgrade for years. They were still waiting. Maybe, Harry reflected, the cost of replacing the broken lines would be the latest excuse for not doing it.

'Maybe just a taxi, then.'

'How much cable is missing?' John-Joe asked.

'I'm still walking it,' Harry said. 'It's gone until at least St Columb's Park,' he added, shining his torch along the side of the tracks, noting the absence of the thick cabling.

He was moving away from the light thrown off from the street lamps of estates up to his right now, and heading below St Columb's Park itself. The moon hung low over the tops of the thick-limbed sycamores above him. To his left, the lights of the city seemed to wink at their own reflection off the river's surface. Harry could smell the sharpness of the mudflats he knew to be just a

6

few feet away from him, a sudden drop down from the tracks to the river's edge.

Suddenly, ahead of him, he saw something.

'Shit, I think one of them is still here,' he whispered, lifting the mobile to his mouth again.

'Get out of there. Call the cops,' John-Joe said.

Harry squinted up ahead. His headache had gathered now behind his right eye. He felt a wave of nausea, felt the sweat pop on his forehead. He could make out a figure who seemed to be lying on the ground, as if hiding, perhaps hoping that, in so doing, he wouldn't have noticed them.

'Oi! You!' Harry shouted. He tried training the torch beam on the spot where the figure was lying, but even so, his headache had grown in intensity to the point that he found it hard to make out what exactly he was looking at.

'Get up off the tracks,' he shouted as he stumbled up the tracks, his foot catching on one of the sleepers beneath, his hands taking the main force of the impact on the sharp-edged grey gravel between the tracks as he fell.

Cursing, he stood again, retrieved his torch and stumbled onwards. It was clear now that the figure was lying on the train line. It looked like a girl, for the hair was long, brown, hanging over her face. She was lying face down on the tracks, her throat resting on the side closest to the river, her legs supported by the other side, her body sagging into the space between them.

'Jesus, get up,' he shouted. 'You'll be killed.'

7

It seemed a pointless thing to say. The train wasn't going anywhere because of the cables. Besides, lying where she was, she was obviously trying to kill herself anyway. Not brave enough to throw herself in front of the train, she was lying on the tracks, waiting for it to come. She'd picked a spot on the curve so the driver wouldn't have time to brake by the time he'd seen her. In fact, he might not even realize he'd hit anyone at all, until the body was found.

'Come on! Get up, love,' Harry shouted, as he covered the last hundred yards. He wondered if she'd be pleased or sad to find out that the train wouldn't have made it as far as her. Maybe God was looking out for the girl when he sent whoever out to steal the cabling. Mysterious ways and all that.

'Are you all right?' he asked, approaching the girl now. He couldn't tell her age, but she was dressed young: flowered leggings and a hoodie. He noticed one of her baseball boots was lying on the gravel off to one side.

He crouched down beside her, placed a hand on her shoulder. 'You need to get up, love.'

No response.

He left the torch on the ground and, using both hands, gripped her shoulders harder, struggled to turn her over. Finally, she fell onto her back, though in doing so, he knocked the torch onto its side, its beam spilling out onto the river.

At first, he couldn't quite comprehend what had happened. Her head lay unnaturally tilted back, though in the weakening gradations of light thrown from the torch, he couldn't quite see why. It was only when he shifted the torchlight towards her that he saw the gaping wound severing her throat.

Harry struggled to his feet but only managed a few yards before he finally brought his meal back up.

Chapter Two

A flash of lightning bloomed inside the thunderheads far to the east as DS Lucy Black, trailing a step behind her boss, DI Tom Fleming, picked her way along the train tracks towards the arc of light thrown off from the crime scene beyond. A sharp, earthy smell carried off the River Foyle, which was slate grey and choppy in the rising breeze. From the canopy of the trees bordering St Columb's Park, to their right, the crows shifted uneasily on the branches, curious as to the disruption to their night roost.

As they approached the crime scene tape, Fleming flashed his badge at the uniformed sergeant standing at the cordon.

'And Sergeant Lucy Black, also Public Protection Unit,' Fleming added as the man wrote the names on the clipboard he held.

Lucy glanced to her left; the lights of Derry City winked in the shivering water of the river next to the train line as a breeze shuddered down the Foyle valley. The embankment across the water had been pedestrianized and newly refurbished. The increased street lighting meant Lucy could make out the figures gathered across there, watching over at them.

Fleming stood back, holding up the tape for Lucy to duck under it.

'It's a mess up there, Sergeant,' the officer at the tape said.

'I'll manage,' Lucy commented, noting that he had not offered the same advice to Fleming.

As they made their way along the edge of the train tracks, the first thick drops of rain raised dusty plops from the wooden sleepers the tracks dissected. Lucy recognized the figure coming towards them as Tara Gallagher, a DS from CID.

'Hey you,' Tara said, smiling warmly when she saw her. 'I didn't know you'd been called.'

'DI Fleming suggested we should ID Karen. Is it her?'

Tara nodded. 'We think so. She fits the description, anyway. I'll get the boss down.'

Tara lifted her radio. 'Inspector Fleming and DS Black from the Public Protection Unit are here, sir,' she said.

Lucy glanced up to the scene, saw one of the suited figures put away his radio and turn towards them. He lumbered down the tracks. Lucy assumed this to be the new CID Superintendent, Mark Burns, who had been recently appointed as the replacement for the late Chief Superintendent Travers.

Burns had been fast-tracked up through the ranks though and was a very different creature from the late Chief Super, by all accounts. He'd only taken up the post a week or two earlier, following the last round of promotions.

'What's he like?' Lucy asked Tara, nodding towards the approaching figure.

The girl shrugged. 'All right, so far. *Thorough*,' she added, in a manner that meant Lucy couldn't tell if it was intended as a compliment or a pejorative.

'Chief Superintendent Burns,' the man said, approaching them, gloved hand outstretched. 'Tom, I've met before. You must be Lucy Black. I've heard a lot about you.' His eyes twinkled above the paper mouth mask he wore. Lucy wondered just how much he could have heard in a fortnight.

'Lucy can ID the body,' Fleming said. 'She'd been heading up the search for the girl. She knew her a bit.'

'Great,' Burns said. 'Of course. Come with me.'

He held out his hand, gesturing that Lucy should lead the way. 'I'm sorry for the loss. Did you know her well?'

'I'd met her in one of the care homes a few times,' Lucy said. 'Her mother's an alcoholic; Karen would be taken in anytime her mother went on a particularly long bender. She was a nice girl.' Lucy's placement with the Public Protection Unit of the PSNI meant that she primarily worked cases involving vulnerable persons and children. As a result, she spent quite a bit of time in the city's Social Services residential units, in one of which Karen Hughes had been an occasional inhabitant.

'How do you like the PPU?' he asked, as they walked. 'It's a strange posting for a young DS. I'd have thought CID would have been the obvious place for someone like you.'

What did he mean, *someone like me*? Lucy thought. Young? Female? Catholic? All of the above?

'I'd rather work with the living than the dead,' Lucy said a little tritely, though she knew it was not entirely true even as she said it. The dead motivated her as much as the quick. More perhaps.

Burns nodded. 'I'm afraid in this case that will prove a little difficult. There's no doubting which she is.'

They had reached the body now, which lay across the tracks so that the girl's neck was supported by one of the metal rails. It could easily have been mistaken for a suicide attempt, had it not been for the knife wound that had severed her windpipe. A handful of SOCO officers continued to work the immediate scene. One documented the area with a hand-held video, while a second used a digital camera to take still shots.

The girl lay on her back. Her clothes were as described in the Missing Person's alert that Lucy had released just three days earlier. She wore a white hooded top, too long for her, over flower-patterned leggings. The top was soaked in blood now, but the material near the hem still retained the original white.

Lucy couldn't really see the face too clearly. Part of it was smeared in the girl's own blood, the rest covered by the loose straggles of her hair. She could make out, on one side, the soft swell of her cheek, still carrying puppy fat. A smattering of freckles was more vivid now, against the pallor of her skin.

Her hair had also become stuck to the blood that was already congealing at the edges of the wound at her throat. Lucy didn't look too closely at it. No doubt she'd be treated to all manner of post-mortem pictures over the coming days without having to look at it here, too. She resisted an urge to push Karen's hair back from her face, instead gently touched it with the tips of her gloved fingers. 'Jesus,' she said, softly.

She tried to dissociate the memories of Karen alive from the scene before her as she examined the body. 'She used to wear a cross and chain around her neck,' Lucy said. 'It might have been lost when her throat was cut.'

'Any other identifying features?' Burns asked. 'Or do you want to wait until she's cleaned up?'

Lucy lifted the girl's left hand. She noticed that the tips of each of her fingers were scored with deep gashes.

'Defence wounds,' Burns said, watching her. 'She must have tried to grab the knife as he was slitting her throat.'

'He?'

'Most likely,' Burns said.

Lucy turned the dead girl's arm. She wore a number of leather wristbands and friendship bracelets. Lucy recognized them. She pushed them up the girl's arm, exposing the skin of the wrist, finding what she was looking for: a series of criss-crossing scars in broken lines traversed the girl's lower arm.

'That's Karen Hughes, all right,' Lucy said, tenderly laying the girl's hand back onto the grey gravel.

Chapter Three

Burns walked back up the tracks with them to Lucy's car. The breeze off the river had risen now, bringing with it further flecks of rain and a sudden chill that heralded the first grumble of thunder overhead.

'We'll need to get her covered before the rain hits,' Burns said. 'So, what's the story with the girl, then?'

'She's been in and out of care for years now,' Lucy said. 'She'd be in the residential unit for a few months at a time, then out home again.'

'What are the home circumstances?'

'As I said, the mother is an alcoholic. Every time she'd be taken in to dry out, Karen ended up in care. Plus, occasionally, Karen would be hospitalized for self-harming and would be kept in care until her mood stabilized.'

Burns nodded. 'And I don't need to ask about the father.'

The element of the story the media had focused on, despite Lucy's best attempts to keep it all about the girl, was the fact that her father was Eoghan Harkin, a man coming to the end of a twelve-year stretch for murder. He'd been part of an armed gang that had robbed a local bank in a tiger kidnapping which had left the bank's manager dead.

He'd done his time in Magherberry, in Antrim, only to get moved closer to home a few months earlier, to Magilligan Prison in Coleraine. He currently resided in the Foyleview unit there, which prepared offenders for release. As the girl had used her mother's surname, it hadn't been an issue when Lucy had drafted the first press release on Friday expressing concern for Karen. By Sunday, one of the trashier papers had somehow made the connection and ran a front-page story under the heading 'Killer's Girl Goes Missing'.

'Who found her?'

'A poor sod working for the railways,' Burns said. 'He was called in because someone stole cabling. The late train is stuck down at Gransha. Lucky really. The bend she was on, the train would have been straight into her before the driver would have seen her.'

'Was that the point? Lay her on the tracks so that, when she gets hit by the train, the damage it'd do would hide the wound to the throat?'

'Make it look like suicide,' Burns agreed. 'We'd have thought nothing of it with her having been in care and that.'

'Whoever did it knew she was in care then,' Lucy ventured.

His face mask down now, Lucy could get a better look at Burns. He was stocky, his features soft, his jawline a little lacking in definition. But his eyes still shone in the flickering blue of the ambulance lights.

'Maybe.' He huffed out his cheeks. 'Look, I appreciate you coming to ID the remains, folks. We'll be another few hours here at least and we'll have the PM in the morning. Maybe you could call to the CID suite about noon and we'll take it from there.'

'Of course, sir,' she said.

Burns pantomimed a winch. 'And a second favour. Seeing as how you already know them, perhaps you'd inform the next of kin.'

They stopped first at Gransha, the local psychiatric hospital, where Karen's mother, Marian, was being held while she dried out after her latest two-week session. She'd be in no fit state to talk to them for some time. At that moment, they were informed, she was insensible.

As they left the ward to return to the car, Lucy glanced across to the secure accommodation where her own father was a permanent resident. The block was in darkness now, low and squat. Her father had once been a policeman too, but had been suffering from Alzheimer's disease for the past few years. Lucy's estranged mother, the ACC of the division, had sanctioned the man's incarceration in the secure unit following the events in Prehen woods a year earlier.

'Will we get the prison officers to break the news to the grieving father? Or do you fancy a drive to Magilligan?' Fleming asked.

'We'd best tell him ourselves, sir,' Lucy said, deliberately turning up the heat in the car.

It had the desired effect. By the time they were passing the road off for Maydown station, on their way to Coleraine, Fleming was already swaying gently

17

asleep in the front seat. Lucy flicked on a CD of the Low Anthem, turned it up enough to hear without wakening the DI beside her, and let her mind wander.

Chapter Four

Their voices echoed in the emptiness of the visiting room. Eoghan Harkin had been brought in, dressed in his own clothes, evidence of the relaxed regime in Foyleview wing. As he took his seat opposite Lucy and Fleming, he'd already guessed the nature of their visit.

'She's dead, isn't she?'

'I'm afraid so, Mr Harkin,' Lucy said. 'I've just left her.'

He wiped at his nose with his hand, sniffing once as he did so, glancing at Tom Fleming. He raised his chin interrogatively. 'Who's he?'

'This is DI Fleming, Mr Harkin,' Lucy said. 'He's my superior officer.'

Fleming stared at him steadily. 'I'm sorry for your loss, Mr Harkin.'

Harkin accepted the sympathies with a curt nod. 'Where's her mother? Has she been told yet?'

'Not yet. She's in Gransha at the moment. They felt she might not be receptive to the news until morning.'

Harkin accepted this, likewise, with a terse nod. 'So what happened to her? Did she cut herself again?'

'No. We believe she was murdered,' Lucy said.

Harkin initially seemed unaffected by the news then, at once, reached out to grip the back of the chair nearest him. He missed and the prison guard, Lucy and Fleming had to grapple with him to pull him back onto the chair from the floor.

'I'll get him a drink,' the guard said and, crossing to the wall, lifted the receiver of the phone attached there and passed the request along. A moment later, someone knocked at the door and, opening it, the guard accepted a clear plastic cup of water and brought it across.

Harkin accepted it and sipped. 'Sorry, George,' he said to the man, his head bowed. His back curved as he inhaled deeply, then he straightened himself, puffing out his cheeks as he released the breath. Finally, he looked up to Lucy. 'How?'

Lucy moved and sat in the seat next to him. 'The post-mortem won't be till the morning, sir, but it appears she died from a knife wound.'

'A stabbing?'

'Not quite,' Lucy said.

Harkin processed this piece of information, considering all the alternatives. Finally, he settled on the right one, for his face darkened.

'Who did it?'

'It's a little early—' Fleming began.

'You must have some fucking ideas,' Harkin spat, rising from his seat in a manner which caused George to immediately stand to attention again. Aware of his reaction, Harkin raised a placatory hand then slowly lowered himself into his seat again. 'You've been looking for her since Thursday. Where did you find her?'

'On the railway line. At St Columb's Park.'

Harkin stared at the tabletop, his breath heavy and nasal. 'Was it me?' he asked finally.

'What?'

'Was it because of me?'

Lucy shook her head. 'We've no reason to believe so, Mr Harkin. Your daughter hasn't shared your name since she was a child.'

'She still was a child,' he retorted, though without rancour. He sat a moment in silence, before speaking again. 'That trash rag ran the story about her today. About her and me. If I thought it was done because of me, I'd ... You read all this shit in here, educating you. *Sophocles* and that. You know, the daughters die because of who the father was. You start ... you know, you can't help ...' He stared at them, his mouth working dryly, though producing no sound.

Lucy shook her head, but did not express her own thoughts. The girl was missing until the papers ran with the connection to Harkin. Suddenly, she turned up with her throat cut, set up to look like she killed herself on the train line. Except the train never came. They couldn't discount the idea that her death was connected with her father, even if she didn't believe the two things to be related.

'Can you think of anyone who *might* want to get back at you, Mr Harkin?'

'You mean apart from the family of the poor sod I shot?'

'Anyone else?' Lucy continued, silently considering the possibility as one she'd need to mention to Burns.

If there was, Harkin wasn't going to share the information with them.

'When did you last see Karen, Mr Harkin?' Fleming asked.

Harkin looked up at him, then dipped his head again. 'About a fortnight ago. She'd started visiting after I wrote to her a while back. She was here three times, I think.'

'Did she mention anything to you during any of her visits? Anything that suggested she might have been in trouble?'

'She barely knew me. She was four when I went inside.'

His expression darkened suddenly, his eyes hooded by his brows where they gathered. Lucy felt Fleming's hand rest on her arm on the desk. She glanced at him and he shook his head lightly. They would get nothing further of use from Harkin.

'Is there any thing we can do for you, Mr Harkin?' Lucy asked, standing to indicate to the prison officer that they were concluding their visit.

'I'm out of here next Saturday. If you find out who it was, give me half an hour with whoever killed her.'

'Careful, Eoghan,' George called from the corner. 'I'm sorry for your news, but we don't want you back in here again too soon, now do we?'

'Half an hour,' Harkin repeated to Lucy.

* * *

22

The prison officer, George, walked them back out to the main reception area where they returned their visitors' badges, crunching on an apple as he walked with them.

'You found her on the train line?' he asked, clearly having overheard.

'Just at St Columb's Park. There's a dark bend on the line.'

'Oh, I know it surely,' the man said. 'I'm from Londonderry myself. I get that train in the evenings if I'm doing the day shift. When did you find her?'

'Sometime before midnight,' Lucy said. 'A little before that, maybe.'

'The body can't have been there too long then.'

'Why?'

'There's a train that leaves Coleraine about 9.10 p.m. I aim to make that if my shift finishes on time. It gets into the city for just shy of 10. If I miss that, I have to get the late train, hanging around Coleraine till 10.40. It makes it in for 11.30. If the body had been lying for a bit, the 10 o' clock train would have run over it. Whoever put it there must have done so between 10 and 11.30.'

'What about trains coming out of Derry?' Lucy asked.

'The last Londonderry train is at 8.30,' the man replied. 'There's none after that.'

He took another chunk off the apple, chewing happily as he said. 'If you need me to solve the whole case for you, just let me know.'

Monday 17 December

Chapter Five

The smoke was so dense, Lucy could barely see in front of her. She felt the burning in her lungs, the need to take a breath, but she knew she had to resist. Somewhere, below her, the heat was rising, its presence marked by a vague yellow glow from the living room, the splintering of wood as the door cracked.

To her left she saw Catherine Quigg's closed door. The woman bolted it from the inside; Lucy remembered that. She reached for the door, tried to open it. Locked. Raising her boot, she kicked at the spot below the handle where she knew the sliding bolt inside had been screwed. Once, twice, a third boot at it before it too splintered and she tumbled through the doorway into the room. Empty. She didn't stop to think how an empty room might be locked from the inside; didn't find it strange.

Where was Mary's room? Ahead of her, at the end of the corridor. She looked up. Cunningham had fitted a brass bolt on Mary's door too, but on the outside so he could lock her and her brother Joseph into the room when he stayed over with their mother. She fumbled with the bolt. It wouldn't shift. She felt across its length with her fingers, then found the heavy padlock attached to it.

From inside the room, she could hear the muffled cries of the baby, the sounds indistinct. She knew this was because Mary had wrapped towels around the child's head to protect him. She'd used all the towels on him, left none for herself. Lucy hammered on the door.

'Mary? Mary? Can you hear me?'

She heard a reciprocal light thumping from the other side.

'Mary?' she screamed.

She heard the alarm ringing. Finally she thought. After all this smoke and it's only starting to ring. Maybe help would come.

The thumping from the other side seemed to intensify in frequency, though not strength.

'Mary, I'm here,' Lucy cried, tears streaming down her face now.

Suddenly, the thumping stopped.

'Help me,' Mary whispered in her ear.

Lucy looked down to her arms, where she held the baby, Joseph, his swaddling clothes frayed towels, singed and black with soot.

The alarm grew louder, pulling her away from the door.

'Help me,' the child repeated.

Lucy jolted awake, almost falling off the sofa where she'd lain down when she finally got home after 4 a.m. She put her hands to her face, felt the wetness of her cheeks. The tears, at least, were real.

She sat up, glanced across at the clock on the mantelpiece; it was already gone 7 a.m. The sky beyond was beginning to lighten behind the miasma of rain misting the windows.

The house was quiet, save for the creaking of the floorboards upstairs and the occasional rattling cough of the water pipes when the timer switched on the central heating at 7.45. Lucy had yet to redecorate, had yet to see this as her own home, rather than her father's home in which she was staying. She showered, then clattered about in the kitchen, pouring herself out cereal, eating it in front of the TV, watching the news.

She thought again on what Harkin had said, about Sophocles and his being to blame for Karen's death. It seemed unlikely somehow. The man had not been a feature of the girl's life. Indeed, she had jettisoned his surname at the first opportunity, just as Lucy had retained her father's name after her mother reverted to her maiden name, Wilson. Even when Lucy had met Karen, in the months before when she was still in care, she'd never once named her father. It had struck Lucy more than once that they had that disowning of a parent in common. It was, perhaps, why Lucy had been drawn to the girl. That coupled with the fact that, as her mother had quite correctly commented, Lucy had an affinity for the vulnerable, for all the little lost girls she encountered. None more so than Mary Quigg, the girl about whom she had recurrent dreams who had died along with her mother the year previous.

The mother's partner, Alan Cunningham, had been a low level recidivist who the PSNI had arrested erroneously for child abduction. Lucy had managed to prove the man innocent. Upon release, however, Cunningham had gone on the run, but not before ransacking his partner's home, stealing all he could sell from it, then setting the house alight with his partner and her children still sleeping inside. The only survivor was the baby of the family, Joe.

Lucy was at the City Cemetery as the gates opened at nine o'clock. The council worker in the high visibility jacket who unlocked them waved her in, before opening the second gate back.

Lucy drove up the incline to the very top of the cemetery. She knew where the plot was, knew well enough the handiest place to park. She got out of the car, stood and stared down at the river below and across to Prehen, the houses of the estate emerging from the ancient woodland which surrounded them. It was a breathtaking view, even on so bracing a morning.

Locking up the car, she climbed the last hundred yards of the incline to the row where Mary Quigg was buried. Even before she reached the grave she could tell something was wrong. The graveside railings that Lucy had had set around the grave were missing, the only evidence of their absence a thin trench in the soil, a few centimetres wide. The gravestone itself was still intact, fine black marble, with the names of the mother and daughter. However, the bunch of flowers that Lucy had laid there a week earlier were crushed, as if underfoot. The small teddy bear she'd placed on the grave for Mary lay dirtied now, its face pressed against the clay. Lucy could see the muddied ridges of a boot mark on the sodden fur.

She must have been visibly upset by the time she found the man who had opened the gates for her, for his first instinct was to place his arm awkwardly on her shoulder.

'We didn't know who to contact, love. I'm sorry,' he said. 'We found it like that yesterday. They came in the night before and took the wee railings off a couple of graves.'

'Who did?'

The man shrugged. 'God knows. They took the lead flashing off the roof of the church that same night. It was probably the same people. The cops told us there's a gang going about, lifting metal. Its price has rocketed with the recession and that. It's being investigated, but you know the police; God knows if they'll ever get them.'

Lucy shuddered with a mixture of anger and the effort she needed to suppress her tears.

'Look, love. I'll get the grave tidied up for you,' the man said, his hand still on her shoulder. 'Don't be upsetting yourself. I know it seems it, but it's not personal. These things never are.'

Lucy stared at him.

'Of course it's personal,' she said.

Chapter Six

The Public Protection Unit, in which Lucy was a sergeant, had a wide remit, taking responsibility for cases involving domestic abuse, children, missing persons and vulnerable adults, frequently working closely with Social Services. It operated from Maydown PSNI station in the Waterside of Derry City. Maydown was actually a compound rather than a simple station: a range of buildings stretched across a site of about ten acres, housing many of the PSNI units for the city, as well as a branch of the training college. It was surrounded by twelve-inch thick corrugated metal fencing, a vestige of the Troubles that had yet to be replaced. This was not the only visible impact the Troubles had had on the design of the place. Rather than consisting of one large building, which would have proved an easy target for potential rocket attacks, even those requiring a degree of pot luck in the targeting due to the height of the perimeter fencing, the compound was divided up into a number of small blocks, squatting at various points around the station area.

The PPU was Block 5. Lucy parked just outside and went up to the front door of the block to punch in her access code. As she did so, she regarded herself in the reflective foil coating on the door itself. She had cut her hair a few weeks earlier and was still undecided. She'd worn her hair in a ponytail for as long as she could remember until recently; during an altercation with a drunken father whose wife had had enough and locked him out of the house, the man had grabbed Lucy by the hair, pulling her down to the ground and managing a kick that glanced off the side of her head before the uniforms accompanying her had managed to subdue him with pepper spray. She'd lost weight and that, combined with the haircut, made her features thinner than she realized. For a moment, she saw her mother reflected back at her. She turned away quickly, pulling open the door.

Once inside, she headed up to Fleming's office first, but it was empty; having not got home himself until 3.30, Lucy figured he'd slept in. She crossed the corridor to the open area where interviews were conducted. Generally, the people interviewed here were children, so the room was spacious, with plastic crates of toys and a worn red cloth sofa. Two mismatched bookcases sat against the wall, holding a variety of kids' books of all shapes and sizes. To the immediate left of the bookcases sat a video camera on a tripod, which was used for recording the interviews as unobtrusively as possible.

Her own office was on the first floor. She hung her coat over the back of her chair and, standing on tiptoe, peered out of the small window high on the wall behind her desk to where the last of the previous night's raindrops glistened off the barbed wire curling along the top of the compound fence.

As she turned her attention to the room again, she noticed the small red flashing light on her desk phone indicating that she had a message. She dialled in her code then listened to the various options available to access her voicemail. As she did, she glanced up to where the picture of Mary Quigg remained pinned to her noticeboard. Lucy had sworn to herself that it would remain there until she had found Mary's killer, Alan Cunningham.

The message was from a man who introduced himself as David Cooper. He was with the Information and Communication Services Branch, a team specially developed to support operations that involved analysis of computer equipment. Lucy guessed that he'd been tasked with examining Karen Hughes's phone. Karen had been reported missing from the residential unit on Thursday night. Lucy had called at the unit to find that Karen's phone had been left in her room. When she still hadn't turned up on Friday, she'd released the first press appeal and sent the phone to ICS to be examined.

Lucy dialled the number he had left on the message and, when he answered, introduced herself.

'DS Black. Thanks for getting back to me. I've taken a look at this phone and I'm pretty sure I've found something. I'm over here in Block 10. Can you come across?'

Chapter Seven

Designed during the North's Troubles, the various blocks in Maydown Station had not been geographically placed in sequential order; Lucy suspected that, as with the small, high windows, it was an attempt to reduce the likelihood of an attack from outside. If someone wanted to target Block 3, for instance, they couldn't be sure that the third block from the entrance was indeed Block 3. Of course, those attacking the compound probably wouldn't have realized that, so rather than preventing an attack, it would simply mean that the wrong block would be targeted. Someone would still get hurt – just not the intended victim. This thought offered her scant comfort.

Block 10 was at the opposite end of the compound from the PPU, so it took Lucy a few minutes to get across. The man who buzzed her in was tall, carrying a little extra weight around the gut, but not much. His hair was wavy brown, his features even. He wore a black suit over a white cotton shirt.

'DS Black? I'm Dave Cooper. Come in.'

She followed him into an office which sat to the left of the main corridor. Once inside, she realized that, in fact, the room spanned the entire left-hand side of the corridor. His desk, which had been visible from the doorway, sat at the top of a huge room. Along one wall, on a worktop, over a dozen computers and laptops hummed quietly as lists of operating system information ran up the screens.

'I'm afraid I've only started a few weeks ago here, so I don't really know anyone yet,' Cooper said as he led her across to his desk on which sat a large iMac.

'I'm here over a year and I still feel that way,' Lucy said, gaining his smile in reciprocation.

'I'm not sure if that's comforting or not,' he said. 'I've hacked into this phone. Look at this.'

Lucy moved in closer as Cooper leaned in towards the screen, bringing up on the iMac an image of what was showing on the phone's screen. She felt the pressure of him beside her, but didn't move.

When he spoke again, his voice was deeper, quieter, as if in accommodation of her proximity. 'Up until about eight weeks ago, she was using this phone for everything. Texting, calls, the lot. Then she stopped. The only calls she made to and from there are to four different numbers. Here.'

He pointed on screen to the listed numbers. Lucy immediately recognized one as the number for the residential unit in the Waterside run by Social Services where Karen had been resident, and the second as Robbie's work mobile number. Robbie had been Karen Hughes's key worker. He was also Lucy's former boyfriend. Lucy told Cooper the first of these pieces of information.

36

'The other two numbers are also to mobiles registered with Social Services,' he said.

'But she didn't make *any* other calls?'

Cooper shook his head.

'She must have got a new phone and didn't tell them,' Lucy said.

'That's what it looks like. She also stopped using this one for internet access. But I was still able to trace her history from before she changed. I also managed to access her Facebook account. She has about a hundred friends,' Cooper said. 'I managed to trace a lot of them back to the contacts listed on the SIM card of the phone.'

'You've only had this since Friday afternoon,' Lucy commented, impressed.

'The case has changed from missing person to murder. I assumed that took priority over checking bankers' accounts for fraud.'

'I'm not complaining, trust me,' Lucy said.

Cooper smiled as he turned to the screen again. In the wake of the movement, Lucy could still smell the citrus scent of his aftershave.

'She has a number of friends who she's not really in contact with – pop groups and that. And a few fellas who obviously know friends of hers in real life, based on their messages to her on Facebook.'

He scrolled through the friends list and stopped at someone called Paul Bradley. 'Then we have him.'

'Paul Bradley?'

'They became friends three months ago. I've printed out the status comments between them. Here.'

37

He handed her a list of messages which she read through quickly. The first was dated 18 September. Karen and Bradley had become friends and he had thanked her for adding him, which suggested he had made the first approach. The same day, Karen had posted a comment about a band she was listening to, and Bradley had liked her comment. This continued until Karen had, according to her news feed, updated her profile picture two months previous. In the picture, her eyes were not quite meeting the lens, her smile embarrassed. Her hands were clasped in front of her as though crossing one arm over the other.

The message from Paul Bradley simply said, '*Cute pic.*'

Karen's reply had been simply '*LOL*'.

'Laugh out loud,' Cooper said. 'It's one of those—'

'I am younger than you,' Lucy said.

'Do you think?' Cooper laughed gently.

Lucy smiled as she read Bradley's reply. '*Seriously. Cute pic. U R gorgeous.*'

'*HaHaHa,*' was Karen's response.

'That's a standard expression of amusement, both for the younger generation and indeed for my own,' Cooper said.

'That's useful to know, Officer Cooper.'

'David,' he said.

Lucy scrolled on through the wall posts, but no more came from Bradley.

'Is that his only contact with her?'

'Oh no,' Cooper said. 'From then on in, he contacted her through her messages rather than her wall. More privacy.'

He opened her message account and opened the first message. It was posted the same day as the comments about her picture.

Hey Karen, Don't put yourself down. Too many people will do that to you. U look lovely. Don't let anyone tell you different. Friends, family, whoever. WTF do they know anyway? Don't take any shit from anybody. Paul x

'He knows how to impress a fifteen-year-old girl,' Lucy said. She read through the rest of his messages. Many of them commented on music or books he had read, with Karen replying that she loved the same song, or the same author. 'They're remarkably well matched, too,' she added.

'Everything he mentioned there, she had listed as her Likes. It's like he's tailor-made for her.'

About eight weeks earlier, Paul had suggested they should meet. They agreed to do so in the Foyleside Shopping Centre, at his suggestion, at 3.30 on the following Saturday afternoon.

'He chose a public place to meet,' Lucy commented. 'To make her feel safe.'

'Every update she made thereafter to her page is made via iPhone,' Cooper said. 'That seems to have been when she got her new phone. And her messages to him stop completely. So, either they fell out on their first date ...'

'Or they found an alternative method of communication.'

'I assume her iPhone hasn't been found, or I'd have been examining that too.'

Lucy shook her head. 'You can't trace it, can you?'

'I can try reverse tracking it through her account for a number, then try the mobile networks to get access to the records but it'll take weeks, probably.'

Lucy nodded. 'Can we trace Paul Bradley?'

'That might be a little quicker. He says in some of his messages that his mobile is broken, so there's no number recorded for him here. Presumably after Karen got her phone, he gave her a number that she was able to use. I could get a warrant and ask Facebook to give me the ISP address for his activities.'

'And for the younger generation that means?'

'Where he used the internet. His home Wi-Fi or that. We can trace back to the phone line that he was attached to each time he logged on. It'll take a day or two to get, but it is one way.'

'That would be great, David.'

'You're very welcome, DS Black,' Cooper said.

'Call me Lucy.'

'Lucy,' he agreed.

Chapter Eight

Burns was standing with the CID team investigating Karen's death in the incident room when Lucy arrived just before noon. Two smaller desks had been pushed together in the centre of the room, around which were placed ten chairs. The two main walls were covered with corkboards onto which already a variety of crime scene pictures had been pinned, including ones depicting Karen's remains in situ. A timeline ran along the top of the noticeboard, marked from Thursday, when she had first gone missing, until Sunday night, when she had been found. A few markers had already been placed along its spectrum.

DS Tara Gallagher was standing at the coffee urn with a newly promoted DS whom Lucy had met before called Mickey Sinclair, a thin faced, handsome man. When they saw Lucy, Tara raised a polystyrene coffee cup interrogatively, to which Lucy nodded.

'Inspector Fleming's not joining us?' Burns asked, approaching her. Now, out of the forensics suit he'd been wearing the previous night, Lucy could see that Burns's hair – loose, sandy curls – was already thinning. His face was a little shapeless, as if a little extra weight had robbed him of his definition, his features soft, his cheeks fleshy.

But his eyes were still sharp and bright and Lucy realized with a little embarrassment that while she was studying him, he'd been doing the same with her. Instinctively, she put her hand up to cover her mouth.

'I've not seen him yet, sir,' Lucy said. Then added, 'I know he had some stuff to follow up this morning.'

'I see,' Burns said. 'In that case, we'll get started, shall we?' He turned to address the room. 'Grab your coffees, people, and take a seat.'

Tara brought Lucy over her cup. 'Milk and one,' she said. Lucy nodded, a little flattered that Tara knew how she took her drink.

Burns took his place at the top of the table and introduced Lucy to the team, then quickly introduced each of them in turn.

'Mickey, perhaps you'd start us off with the results of the PM?'

Tara nudged Lucy as Mickey stood up. 'Cause of death was the cut to the throat. Time of death was sometime on Sunday between eight in the morning and lunchtime, despite her body not being left on the train tracks until that evening.'

'Which means the killer held on to the body until dark before moving her,' a DC commented unnecessarily.

'The stomach contents included peanuts,' Mickey continued. 'But little else. She didn't seem to have eaten much. There were signs of sexual contact in the hours before death. Significant signs, the pathologist said. He'd taken samples for testing, along with toxicology samples for drugs and drink.'

'Was she raped then?'

'He wouldn't rule out consensual,' he said.

'Not that that means anything,' Burns commented. 'Anything else?'

'That's all he had to start with. The full report will be sent on when it's done.'

'What about SOCO, Tara?'

Unlike Mickey, Tara stayed in her seat, clearing her throat before addressing them. 'Blood smearing on her clothes suggested she'd been wrapped in plastic sheeting for the transport of her remains. And they pulled dog hairs from her boots. Black dog hairs.'

'DS Black, maybe you can update us on the work you'd done, to put it in context for the team.'

Lucy nodded. 'I'm afraid there's not a huge amount to tell, sir. She went missing last Thursday. She didn't come back to the unit from school but that wasn't entirely unusual.'

'She was in residential care?'

'Yes. Social Services contacted us and we started looking for her in the usual haunts: shopping centres, the Walls, places like that.'

'Had she run away before?'

'A number of times,' Lucy said, nodding. 'Initially we assumed it was more of the same. She usually came back the next day – often she'd spent the night with friends, boyfriends maybe.'

'Did she have a boyfriend?'

'Nobody serious. Not that we know of so far.'

'But she *was* sexually active?'

43

'She was fifteen, sir,' Lucy said.

Burns nodded, jotting down notes as Lucy spoke.

'So you put out the press appeal?'

'After she went missing, the social workers in the residential unit found her phone in her room which panicked them. They alerted us and we did the press release,' Lucy said. 'Then someone found out about the connection with her father yesterday and the papers ran with it.'

'Any idea who told them? Could it have been one of us?' He glanced around the room as he spoke. 'One of you' was actually what he meant, and Lucy knew it. PPU had been handling the case – herself and Tom Fleming essentially.

'I wouldn't think so, sir,' she replied. 'Derry's a small city. Everyone knows everyone else here. You'll find that once you're here a while.'

'Do you think she was targeted because of who she was?' Mickey asked.

'The father asked the same thing,' Lucy said. 'It seems unlikely. She wasn't using his name. He did suggest the family of the bank man he shot in the robbery might have cause for revenge, but I'm not convinced.'

'We'll follow up on it,' Burns commented. 'Was anything useful found on the phone?'

'Actually, I spoke with someone in ICS just before coming up here. She was befriended on Facebook by someone called Paul Bradley. He made first contact in September. About eight weeks ago they met and she seems to have managed to get an iPhone that she's since kept hidden from the residential unit. ICS are trying to track Bradley through his internet address.'

'Brilliant,' Burns said. 'I'll need the details of the officer in ICS. Is Bradley known to PPU?'

'Well, I ran him through the system based on the personal information on his Facebook page, but no luck,' Lucy said. 'It could be a cover name.'

'He could be a known offender then,' Burns said. 'We'd best speak to the usual suspects first.'

Burns flicked through his notes, words forming silently on his lips as he read through what he'd written. 'Was she using drugs?'

Lucy shook her head. 'Maybe a little – it wasn't something we ever investigated. It didn't seem relevant.'

Burns nodded. 'Everything can be relevant,' he said. 'Toxicology will show if she was using prior to her death. How long had she been self-harming?'

'It was first noticed when she was nine. She went into care about then after her mother was locked up to dry out for the first time. Karen had been looking after her for four years by that stage. The social workers asked Karen about when she'd started cutting herself, but she wouldn't tell them. Still, she continued with it until ... well until she died, I suppose.'

Burns nodded. 'Was she ever considered a suicide risk?'

'Not to my mind,' Lucy said. 'Or Social Services.'

'Despite the cutting?' Mickey asked incredulously.

'Self-harming, especially the type of cutting that Karen did on herself, is a way of coping with life, a way

45

of surviving. She did it to make life tolerable, not to end it.'

'Why?'

Lucy shrugged. 'How else could she deal with adolescence and babysitting her alcoholic forty-year-old mother?'

'Was there any history of alcohol abuse in the girl?'

'The usual,' Lucy said.

'How did you come to know her so well?' Burns asked.

'I didn't know her that well. I just met Karen at the residential unit a few times when I had to call up there about some of the other kids. We got on OK.'

'Why?'

Lucy considered the question. 'I just got her.'

Burns considered the response. 'OK then, so who was she? Describe Karen Hughes to us. Help us better understand her.'

Lucy shrugged. 'She was nice. She was caring, looking after her mother. She was patient, putting up with all the crap that she dealt with. She had a weird sense of humour. But she was troubled. She had ... she had very low self-esteem.'

'There's a reason the ACC wanted you in PPU, obviously,' Burns commented.

Lucy silently reflected that there was more than one reason her mother had pushed her into the PPU, but she did not speak.

'These hairs Forensics pulled from Karen's clothes. I don't suppose Social Services have a dog in the residential unit?' Burns said.

46

'No, sir.'

'What about known sex offenders? Have you followed up on those?'

'Inspector Fleming and I had already begun interviewing known sex offenders in the area as part of the search for Karen.'

'How many are there?'

'In the Foyle Command area alone we have sixty-six. We'd seen most.'

'Any black dog owners?' Burns asked, with a laugh.

'Actually one of the offenders we've yet to see has,' Lucy said.

'Maybe make him a priority for a visit. What's he called?'

'Eugene Kay. He prefers Gene.'

'Does he, now?' Burns asked, noting the name. 'If you and Tom could follow up on it and let me know your thoughts, I'd appreciate it. The ACC has already approved your working alongside us on this.'

Lucy stood to leave, then stopped. 'There's something about the timing of the trains last night,' she said. 'The previous train passed there at ten, so the body would have been—'

Burns raised a hand to stop her. 'We're already on top of that.'

'There's also the metal theft,' she added. 'There's every chance that whoever was cutting those cables may have seen who brought Karen down to the tracks. Considering the timing of the trains. The previous train ran—'

'We're on that too,' Burns commented, smiling. 'We're following it up.'

47

'A gang robbed the cemetery the night before, too,' Lucy said. 'They could be the same people.'

Burns looked at her. '*That* I didn't know,' he said. 'But it could be useful. Tara, maybe you'd contact the local scrapyards and see if anyone's been selling stuff they shouldn't. Mickey, I want you to contact the school and see what you can find out about the girl from there. Ian, check if the CCTV system in the city centre picked up any activity around St Columb's Park last night. OK?'

There were general murmurs of agreement as the team got up to leave. Lucy could sense Tara's annoyance as she shoved her seat under the table and left the room.

Before leaving, Lucy approached Burns. 'I'll update Inspector Fleming, sir,' she said.

Burns smiled. 'That's fine.'

Still she stood and did not leave.

Burns's smile faltered a little. 'Is there something you want to ask me?' he said, uncertainly.

'I was wondering about the state of the Alan Cunningham investigation, sir,' she said, finally.

'Remind me,' he said, his fingers interlinking, his joined hands resting on the notebook in front of him on the desk.

'He set fire to his partner's house in Foyle Springs last year. The parent, Catherine Quigg, and her daughter Mary were killed. The baby, Joe, survived.'

'I remember reviewing the file before I started here,' Burns said. 'My recollection is that it hit the three-month flag without progress and was relegated. This Cunningham character went over the border, is that right?'

48

Lucy nodded. 'To Donegal initially.'

'I've a feeling I read there was intelligence on the ground that he'd settled in Limerick, but we asked the Guards to follow it up and they got nothing. The inquiries here hit a dead end, too. There was a suggestion that Cunningham was being protected. His family were well known Republicans.'

'I see.'

'Why?'

'I knew the girl who died. She'd come to our attention in the days before her death. She called me on the night she died, but I didn't get the call until ... until after.'

'I see,' Burns repeated.

'I was just wondering if any progress had been made.'

'None, I'm afraid,' Burns said. 'Nor will there be any until Cunningham comes back over the border, or makes a public appearance in the south so that the Guards can get to him. But I'll double check for you. As I say, I just reviewed the more recent open files. I might have missed something.'

Somehow, Lucy doubted it.

Chapter Nine

Tara was waiting for her in the corridor outside the room when Lucy came out.

'Schmoozing with the boss?' she asked, a little petulantly.

'He's not *my* boss,' Lucy commented. 'I wanted to check up on something.'

Tara waved away the explanation. 'Sorry. It's bloody Mickey Sinclair. He's the blue-eyed boy since he got DS. He gets to run down leads in the school, and I'm struck tracing thieved metal. This whole bloody unit is all politics. You're lucky you ended up in PPU.'

Lucy grunted by way of offering sympathies for Tara's complaint. 'If you do find anything, I'd be interested in knowing,' she said. 'About the stolen metal.'

Tara frowned. 'Why?'

'Someone stole the metal railings off the grave of a friend.'

'Scumbags. I'll let you know what I hear. We've targeted a scrap merchant called Finn out in Ballyarnet. Apparently he'd been shipping metal with Smart dye on it from electric cabling. Whoever's stealing is selling through him. He's going to let us know when they bring the next load down to him to sell.' She considered a moment, then added, 'He's a fence.'

Lucy smiled at the joke. 'So you don't like Burns then?'

'He's OK. Hard to impress. Mind you, do you know why he got where he got?' she added, warming to her gossip.

Being based in the centre of town, Tara seemed to glean all the station gossip. Lucy, on the other hand, sharing a unit with Tom Fleming out at Maydown, heard nothing.

'Why?

'The ACC!'

'What?'

Tara nodded, smiling. 'Apparently. The two of them were spotted out having dinner in Eglinton.'

'Said who?'

'The community team was doing a drink-driving campaign, going around the local pubs. I know one of the fellas who spotted them.'

Lucy smiled, trying to remember the name of the man she'd met the one time she'd visited her mother's house. Peter? Paul? She'd obviously moved on.

'At least that explains his meteoric rise to the top,' Tara said. 'Eh?'

'Mmm,' Lucy agreed. Not for the first time, she felt awkward with Tara. By rights she should have told her about the ACC being her mother. But each time they discussed her, it was generally Tara being critical. To admit to the relationship would just make things awkward. Lucy knew though that whatever time the information became common knowledge, Tara's

51

seeming proximity to the grapevine would result in her being one of the first to know. How that would change their friendship remained to be seen.

'That's not all they saw,' Tara went on. 'Your man was spotted too.'

'*My* man?'

'Tom Fleming. He's back on the sauce. Not that I blame him, mind you, the shit you have to deal with. Being an alco seems to be a survival technique.'

Like self-harming, Lucy reflected.

After stopping to pick up lunch of a sandwich and a packet of crisps from the supermarket along the Strand Road, Lucy headed back to Maydown to see if Tom Fleming had arrived in. At first, his office looked empty. Then Lucy noticed his keys lying on the desk and heard, a moment later, the flushing of the toilet behind the kitchenette. Because of the nature of their work, theirs was one of the few blocks in the station to have access to their own kitchen where juice and biscuits were kept for interviewees.

Lucy headed across to the kitchenette, just as Fleming came out of the toilet. He looked as though he had just arrived indoors, his face flushed, his breathing quick and shallow.

'Afternoon,' she said.

Fleming grunted. 'I missed your calls.'

'We had a meeting with Superintendent Burns earlier,' Lucy explained.

'Was he asking for me?'

'I told him you had a few things to follow up.'

'I was at the dentist,' he explained. 'How did the meeting go? Anything useful?'

'They've found black dog hairs on Karen's clothes, apparently. He asked about known offenders with black dogs. I mentioned we'd yet to see Gene Kay and he suggested that we make him a priority.'

'Did he indeed? Giving orders to all divisions now? He's really being groomed for greatness, isn't he?'

Lucy thought again of what Tara had said about Burns and her mother. She also recalled the comments about Fleming himself, standing now, florid faced, his breath sweet with the Polo mints he was cracking between his teeth.

'He said we were to work alongside CID on Karen's case. The ACC approved it.'

Fleming allowed himself the briefest flicker of a smile. 'Of course she did.'

'Should we do it, then?'

'Have we a choice?' Fleming said. 'I'll get my coat.'

Chapter Ten

Kay lived in Gobnascale, in the Waterside. A staunchly Nationalist area, it abutted the equally hard-line Unionist area of Irish Street, the interface between the two marked by the point where the alternating red, white and blue paint on the kerbstones changed to green, white and orange ones. Kay's terrace house was the end one of four. The front garden was small, the scrap of land thick with grass, trodden down in narrow lines by his dog, presumably.

As they stood at the front door, Fleming nudged Lucy and nodded towards the end of the street. 'We're being watched,' he said.

Lucy followed his gaze to where a half-dozen youths stood at the corner, staring across at them. 'They'll hardly start anything,' Lucy commented. 'It's still early.'

They heard the dead bolt click and the door opened. Gene Kay was short, not much taller than Lucy herself, but stocky, broad-shouldered. His face was jowly, his hair and moustache white. He glanced past them at the group of boys.

'You may come in,' he said, without looking at either of his visitors, then turned and moved back inside the house.

Kay led them into the lounge. Two brown tweed armchairs faced a small TV jabbering away in the corner, tuned to a daytime chat show. In the other corner, a glass cabinet stood, its shelves empty of anything but dust. Behind the furthest armchair was a small drop leaf table with two wooden seats placed either side of it. A computer sat on the table, the screen black.

'What do you want then?' Kay wore jeans and a red sweater. He was barefooted. His hand shook as he pulled a hand-rolled cigarette from a tin on the mantelpiece and lit it. Flakes of flaming tobacco fluttered to the ground and he stepped on them with his bare foot.

'We'd like to ask you a few questions, Gene. As part of an ongoing inquiry,' Fleming began.

'Do I need a lawyer?' Kay said, sitting on the armchair in front of the table. On the wall behind him was a painting of a child, a single tear perfectly formed on his face, his doe eyes, huge and brown, stared down beneath a ragged blond fringe. He held a cap in his hand. Lucy had seen similar pictures before, remembered in fact a newspaper story that suggested they were cursed in some way.

'That's your right, Gene,' Lucy said. 'But at the moment, we're just hoping to eliminate you from our inquiries. Do you know this girl?'

She handed Kay a picture of Karen, which Social Services had provided, taken from her care plan. He studied the face, before handing the picture back.

'I think I saw her picture on TV earlier. Didn't catch her name. She's missing or something, is that right?'

'She's dead, Gene,' Fleming said. 'She was found last night.'

Kay nodded. 'Well, it had naught to do with me. I'm sorry for the wee girl.'

'Where were you yesterday morning, Gene?' Lucy asked.

Kay considered the question. 'I was at church at eleven,' he said. 'Then I went straight to my sister's for Sunday lunch. I took a taxi to church, so I left here just after half ten. I didn't come back until about six.'

'Did you go back out again last night?'

'I don't go out at night,' Kay said. 'That group of thugs out there hang around the streets drinking every night. It's not safe. Not that the police do anything about it.'

'You didn't have anyone here with you, who could confirm that you were at home?'

'What do you think?' Kay snapped. 'Of course I didn't.'

'What about last Thursday? Do you remember where you were on Thursday?'

'I was in bed sick most of last week,' Kay added. 'I've a prescription from the chemist's to prove it. I can get it if you want.'

Fleming nodded. 'That would be helpful. Nothing serious, I trust.'

Kay hoisted himself out of the armchair and padded out to the kitchen. He returned with a small bottle of cough mixture, dated the previous Thursday.

'Does your pharmacist deliver?'

'No. I had to go out with a dose to get it.'

56

Fleming glanced at the bottle. 'Of course, that doesn't prove you were in your bed sick.'

'Well I was,' Kay said. 'You people are torturing me, you know that? That gang out there, seeing you coming here. They'll be attacking me while I sleep.'

Lucy had to stop herself from commenting on the irony of such a comment. Kay had been arrested in Limavady after several years of abusing one of his neighbour's sons. He had first assaulted the child while babysitting for the couple when the wife went into labour. The abuse had continued for eight years. Kay had served less than half that in prison as punishment.

'Karen Hughes was murdered, Gene,' Lucy said. 'Black dog hairs were found on her clothing. You have a black dog, don't you?'

'Half the town has black dogs.'

'But not a record for sexual assault as well,' Lucy retorted.

Kay straightened himself, regarded Lucy coolly. 'You're a smart one, aren't you? I'd nothing to do with whoever was killed. I never killed no one. The only person I'll ever be hurting is myself someday if you people don't leave me in peace.'

'It would be really helpful if we could maybe get a strand of your dog's hair,' Lucy said. 'To compare with the strands we found.'

'Don't you need a warrant for something like that?' Kay asked.

'We could get one,' Lucy agreed.

'Although, making us go for a warrant suggests you're reluctant to help with our inquiries,' Fleming added. 'It might look like you have something to hide.'

'I don't want her hurt,' Kay said. 'I won't have anyone hurt Mollie.'

Lucy said nothing.

At Kay's mention of her name though, the dog itself appeared at the door of the kitchen, yawning lazily, its tongue lolling to one side. Mollie crossed to Lucy and sniffed at her legs, the dog's tail offering a desultory wag, then falling limp.

Lucy reached into her pockets and pulled on a glove. Bending down, she held out her hand. Mollie approached tentatively, sniffing at the latex of the glove before tasting it with a quick lather of her tongue. She moved closer to Lucy, allowing Lucy first to rub her hand across the dome of the animal's head, then to bury her hand among the thicker fur at the top of her spine. Lucy rubbed vigorously at the fur, as if petting the dog, then checked her hand. A few black strands of hair clung to the glove.

'Do you consent to our taking these for testing?' Lucy asked.

Kay nodded, once, curtly. He took a last drag from his cigarette then threw the butt into the hearth, before dropping down and calling the dog to him. As he kissed its snout, Mollie licked at the tobacco rich air of his breath.

'Thank you,' Lucy said. She pulled off the glove inside out to trap the hairs, then placed it in an evidence bag.

'We'll be in touch,' Fleming said. 'And of course, if you think of anything else, do let us know.'

Lucy opened the front door and stepped out. The group of youths had grown larger now and had moved directly across the road. They stood beneath the street lamp opposite, without words. One of the youths, at the centre of the group, regarded her coldly. He was tall, wearing a black T-shirt beneath a badly worn leather jacket. 'All right, love?' he called, winking at her, to the amusement of the rest who stood around him.

As she reached the car, Lucy recognized another of the youths, standing at the outer edge of the group. He wore a grey woollen hat pulled down low over his head, covering his scalp completely. He had thick black eyebrows, both of which had a stripe shaved down their centre. Lucy started to raise her hand, then thought better of it and stopped.

'Someone you know,' Fleming asked, when she closed the door.

'Gavin Duffy,' Lucy said. 'He's in the residential care unit. His father was Gary Duffy. He hung himself about a month ago. Gavin's grandparents asked he be moved closer to them.'

'Gary Duffy? The Louisa Gant guy?'

Lucy nodded. Louisa Gant had been a nine-year-old girl who vanished in 1998. The girl herself had never been found. Lucy and her father had moved out of Derry by that stage, though she recalled the case for the child had gone missing the day the Good Friday Agreement had been finally signed, her vanishing a coda to news reports filled with images of bleary-eyed politicians heralding the beginning of a new future for Northern Ireland and Blair's sound bite about the 'hand of history'. Lucy remembered sitting with her father, watching events unfolding. Then, at the end, Louisa Gant was mentioned.

Her remains had never been found, but, within a few days, the police investigation changed from missing persons to murder. The reason Lucy remembered it so clearly was because during one of the press conferences covered by the TV news on the case in subsequent weeks, it was her mother who read a statement about the investigation in her newly appointed role as Chief Superintendent. It was the first time Lucy had seen her in months.

Despite not recovering the child, police charged local man, Gary Duffy, with her murder in 1999. Following a tip-off from an informant, police had discovered one of the girl's chunky black shoes in Duffy's garage, the pirate motif decorating its strap distinctive. The shoe had been badged with the girl's blood. Though he claimed innocence, Duffy had been tried, found guilty and imprisoned. He had been released on parole only a few months previously. And had committed suicide soon after.

'The young lad's found himself some new friends already,' Fleming said.

'So it seems,' Lucy said, glancing out again at the group, her stare being held by Gavin's all the way to the corner of the street.

Chapter Eleven

Before finishing for the day, Lucy drove back to Gransha Hospital to see Karen's mother, Marian Hughes.

She'd met her once before when Karen had been taken to hospital eight months earlier after cutting her wrists too deeply. Lucy had been visiting Robbie on her evening off when the girl cut herself while having a bath. Lucy had helped dress her while waiting for an ambulance to take her to hospital.

Karen had apologized over and over for spoiling their evening. Her face had paled, her lips bloodless beneath her small teeth.

'What were you thinking?' Lucy had asked.

Karen had shrugged, her head tilted to one side.

'You could have killed yourself,' Lucy said. 'Or is that what you wanted to do?'

Karen shook her head, her hair falling across her face as she did so. Lucy pushed it back with one hand, her other helping Karen keep the pressure on the towel they had wrapped around the wound. The broken pieces of a safety razor lay on the floor, the blade she'd removed from it glinting darkly beneath the sink.

'I can usually control it,' Karen said. 'My hand slipped is all.'

Lucy knew girls from school who'd hurt themselves, understood only too well the impulses that drove them to it. So, she'd said nothing more, but simply put her arm around the girl, pulled her closer to her, stayed like that until the ambulance arrived.

Marian Hughes had turned up at the hospital later that evening. She'd already been drinking before she got there, her breath warm and ketonic in the closeness of the room in which Karen sat while her arm was stitched.

'Should someone not have been watching her?' the woman had asked.

'Karen was having a bath, Mrs Hughes,' Robbie explained.

The woman shook her head, muttering to herself, as she sat by the girl. 'Someday you'll do it for real,' she said to Karen; her first words to the girl since her arrival. 'Some day you'll actually manage it and give us all peace.'

Karen had stared at her arm, watching the doctor as he worked, never once lifting her head to look at the woman.

'Someone should have been watching her,' the woman repeated to the room, looking from face to face in hope that one of them would agree with her. The doctor coughed embarrassedly and kept working.

Marian Hughes looked considerably older now, the drinking having taken its toll. Her hair, brown though streaked with grey, was tied back from her face accentuating the sharpness of her features. The skin of her cheeks, taut against the bone, was waxy in appearance save for threads of burst veins. She sat in the chair next to her bed, wearing a hospital gown and pink slippers, while Lucy and a doctor spoke to her about Karen's death. She was sober now, but clearly the days of drying out seemed to have left her in a daze of sorts, for if she understood what Lucy had told her, Hughes showed little sign of it until Lucy stood to leave.

'So, did she kill herself or not?' she asked, looking up at her with vacant eyes.

'No, Marian,' Lucy said. 'Someone killed her.'

The woman nodded her head. 'That's what I thought.'

'Can you think of anyone who might have had reason to hurt your daughter, Marian?' Lucy asked.

The woman pursed her lips, her brow knotting briefly as she considered the question. Finally she shook her head.

'Were those Social Service people not watching her?' she asked.

'They were,' Lucy said. 'She'd been missing for a few days now.'

'Why wasn't I told?'

Lucy glanced at the doctor. 'You were here, Marian. You weren't really in a fit state to receive the news.'

'I should have been told,' Marian said. 'She never told me nothing.'

Lucy glanced again at the doctor who shook his head lightly. She laid her hand on Marian's arm. 'If you do think of anything, Marian, will you let someone know? They'll get word to me.'

63

As Lucy left the room, she heard the woman address the doctor who had remained with her. 'I told her that would happen. She was always cutting at herself. I warned her about that.'

Before leaving Gransha, Lucy walked across to the low block where her father was resident. She hadn't seen him in a few weeks and was shocked to see how frail he looked. He lay in the bed, his wrists strapped to the side bars. His pyjama jacket had pulled open revealing the curve of his chest, his hair white and tangled as it rose and fell with each breath. He smacked his lips as he slept, his eyelids not quite closed, his breath wheezing in his throat.

The skin below his left eye carried a yellowed bruise, while a small stitch bulged on his lip. The wooden chair next to his bed creaked as she sat, causing him to open his eyes.

'Who's that?' he asked.

'It's Lucy, Daddy.' She stood and leaned across him to kiss him on the forehead, his skin clammy beneath her lips, the air between them foul with the funk of his breath. 'What happened to your eye?'

The man shook his head, then lifted his right arm ineffectually pulling at the limits of the strap. 'I can't remember.'

Lucy nodded, sitting again next to him, her hand resting on his.

'I was thinking of the fountain. In Prehen,' he said suddenly.

'There was no fountain in Prehen, Daddy,' Lucy said softly.

His eyes flicked across to stare at her. 'On the lane. The cottage on the lane. You used to climb onto my shoulders so you could see it.'

'Jesus.' Lucy remembered now. A lane ran along the back of the housing estate, between it and the woodland. It had been the coach track from the big house at the top of the park, once owned by the Knox family. Legend had it that their daughter's lover had shot the girl as she passed in their coach driving along this lane in the seventeenth century. He'd intended to kill her father.

Near the bottom of the lane was a cottage, surrounded on all sides by a dense laurel hedge. The owners had a fountain in the middle of their garden. When Lucy was a child, she'd been unable to see above the hedge. Her father used to lift her, swinging her up onto his shoulders, holding her fast by the ankles as she craned up to see the fountain. That achieved, she would cling to him, resting her chin against the thickness of his hair.

For a second, she felt a rush of warmth towards him that was instantly dispelled by the memory of what her father had done. Had he, even then, already embarked on an affair with a teenaged girl? She pulled her hand quickly from his and sat back in the seat, recoiling at the thought of what she had learnt about him the previous year.

'I was thinking of the fountain,' he said. 'Is it still there?'

'I'm not sure,' Lucy managed, barely trusting herself to speak.

'Will you help me to see it? If I can't see over the hedge any more?'

'I need to go,' Lucy said, swallowing down the tears and the bile that burned at her throat. 'I'll see you before Christmas.'

Chapter Twelve

She joined a tailback on the roundabout at the end of the Foyle Bridge, just outside Gransha and could see, by the flashing blue lights on the Limavady Road, that a road traffic accident had happened that would see the road closed for a while. She considered driving across to offer help, but she'd had a long day and the last thing she wanted was to get caught up in something on her way home. Instead, she drove up the dual carriageway, into the heart of the Waterside, planning on cutting through Gobnascale and down the Old Strabane Road to Prehen along the back road bordering the old woodland.

She was just reaching the junction of Bann Drive with Irish Street when a youth thudded onto the bonnet of her car as he careened across the road in front of her. He righted himself quickly, glancing into the car, long enough for Lucy to see his face. Then he set off, eight other youths in pursuit.

Lucy grabbed her phone and speed-dialled the residential care unit as she pulled out onto the road, steering one-handed. It was Robbie who answered.

'Lucy, it's g—'

'Robbie, is Gavin there?' She spoke over him.

'What? No, he's out. What's wrong?'

'I think I've just seen him being chased by a gang. I'm going after him.' She cut the call immediately.

She could still see the gang running after him along Irish Street. Suddenly, Gavin, about twenty yards in front, sprinted across the road, weaving his way around cars coming in the other direction. The gang in pursuit split, some continuing on the same side of the road, others following him across to the opposite pavement. Lucy sped up, angry that being in her own car, she didn't have a siren that might help scare the gang away.

Up ahead, Gavin darted off the pavement, slipping through a gap in the wooden fencing to his right and into the car park area at the front of the River City Apostolic Church. The building itself was a basic single storey affair, with a set of steps to the front and little other external ornamentation that would mark it out as a place of worship. By the time Lucy pulled to a stop opposite it, the youths who had been pursuing Gavin had gathered in a scrum at the front steps of the building. Gavin was lying on the ground at the centre of it taking a beating from a dozen Nike shod feet.

Ignoring the oncoming cars, Lucy sprinted across the street, calling out to the gang to stop. Some pack instinct, though, seemed to compel them for none paid her any heed. She reached the outer edge of the scrum and pulled the youth nearest to her backwards, away from the melee. He spun, raised his fist and slashed at her, but she'd anticipated it and slipped to the side. Quickly, she gripped his flailing arm and twisted it sharply back, against the joint. The youth screeched, following the direction his arm was being tugged to alleviate the pain. Lucy tucked her leg behind his and pulled him off balance, onto the ground.

'Police,' she shouted. 'Disperse, now.'

One of the others had turned to see what had happened to his friend and swung a kick wildly in Lucy's direction. It glanced off her side. He lifted his boot a second time, aiming to stamp rather than kick. Lucy deflected the kick, bringing herself in close enough to him that she could grab his jacket and pull him away from Gavin.

'I'm the police,' she shouted at him.

The boy stared stupidly at her for a moment then helped his mate to his feet and ran.

Lucy turned to face the rest of the gang, but the numbers were winnowing out. Two boys continued to kick and stomp on Gavin, who had curled himself almost into a foetal ball by this stage, his hands up over his head, the blood marking his face black under the street lights. They took a final kick, then both turned and ran. One spat at Lucy as he did so.

'Fenian bitch,' he shouted.

Lucy followed them a step or two as they ran, then gave up. Several cars had stopped on Irish Street now, the occupants staring at her. One man was standing out of his car, a mobile phone raised, recording what had happened.

A second man was just getting out of his car. 'Are you all right?' he called, coming across to her. The mobile phone man continued to film even this.

Lucy grunted thanks for his help and they both went across to Gavin. The boy still lay on the ground, but had brought his hand down from his face. His head was closely shaven, just as Lucy had remembered it from when she had last seen him. In addition to assorted grazes and cuts, a bruise was forming on his cheek. His mouth was slick with blood when he looked up at her. She could tell that he was dazed and was trying to work out how he knew her.

'Gavin. It's Lucy. Robbie's ... friend. Can you hear me OK?'

He looked around him, staring wildly at the man who had come to help. 'Who's he?' he said, then tried to turn and lift himself up a little. Lucy and the other man gripped him around the trunk to help him up, earning only a shriek of pain from him as they did so.

'His ribs could be broken,' the man said. 'He seemed to be taking quite a beating.'

'What happened, Gavin?'

'I don't know. I never seen them before. I was just walking home and they chased me,' Gavin said. 'I never said nothing to them.'

'That wasn't the crowd I saw you with earlier?'

Gavin shook his head. 'Nah. The ones you saw me with are my friends. I don't know who *that* crowd were.'

'They maybe saw this,' the man said, pulling the lapels of Gavin's jacket back to reveal the blood-spattered green and white hoops of a Celtic football top. 'Not the right colours for this part of the town, son.'

'I can wear what I want,' Gavin snapped, then turned and spat a bloody globule of saliva onto the ground.

'This man is only trying to help, Gavin,' Lucy said.

'I don't need help,' the boy replied. 'I need to go, or your boyfriend will be looking for me. He'll probably phone the cops.'

'Maybe we should phone them,' the man muttered to Lucy.

'I am one,' she replied. 'I'll take him up to the hospital for a check-up, then get him home.'

'I'm not going to the hospital,' Gavin said, limping away from them. 'I'll walk home myself.'

'I'll drive you back at least, Gavin,' Lucy said.

The boy turned to look at her, then looked around him, as if to see who was watching. 'Me in a cop's car? Not a fucking chance.'

Chapter Thirteen

In the end, after walking almost half a mile towards the residential unit with Lucy trailing him slowly in her car, Gavin gave in and agreed to be taken to Casualty. Lucy called Robbie, who was nearing the end of his shift in the unit and was waiting for his replacement for the evening shift. He suggested that if Lucy could take Gavin to A & E, he would come across and relieve her as soon as he was done.

The waiting area in Casualty was busy, though it was early enough in the evening that the habitual drunken injured hadn't yet begun to seep in. A few obvious fracture injuries were waiting. A young man who had fallen through a pane-glass doorway was rushed through, the blood trailing behind him all the way in, despite his best efforts to stymie its flow from his arm.

Gavin sat sullenly next to Lucy, playing a game on his phone. He slouched low in the seat, his hood pulled up over his head.

Lucy glanced at the phone. 'Do you play Angry Birds?'

Gavin answered without looking at her. 'That's ancient,' he said.

'That's a nice phone. Is it new?'

His head twisted within the hood so she could only see his left eye, squinting suspiciously. 'I didn't steal it if that's what you think.'

'I didn't think anything,' Lucy said, though she was immediately reminded of the new phone Karen Hughes had been given.

'Anyway, it's not a phone. It's an iPod Touch. My granda bought it for me.'

'It's nice.'

Gavin grunted in response, then resumed playing.

'I was sorry about Karen.'

'It's shit,' Gavin muttered. 'She was nice. When I moved into care, like, she was good to me.'

'Between your dad's death and now Karen. I know she wasn't family or that, but, you know ... it must have been a difficult few weeks for you.'

'Me da was a useless bastard. No loss that he topped himself.'

Lucy said nothing, glancing across at the couple opposite who were watching them, perhaps attempting to work out how Lucy, in her late twenties, could have a son Gavin's age.

'He had issues,' Gavin offered suddenly, making speech marks in the air with his fingers. 'So the shrink told me.'

'The shrink?'

'They made me see one – a thingie. To talk about it.'

'How's that going?'

'It's a load of bollocks. She says that loads of men from the Troubles and that are killing themselves now. She says they have inter-somethinged their guilt and anger.'

73

'Internalized.'

'Aye, that's it.'

The fingers stopped sliding over the screen. 'What does that mean?' he asked quietly. 'I didn't want to ask her in case she thought I was stupid.'

'You're not stupid.'

'I didn't say I was. I said I didn't want to look it. There's a difference, you know.'

Lucy ignored the comment. 'It means when the Troubles were happening, people had places to direct their anger, to get rid of it. When it all ended, that anger didn't go away too. It was still there, except a lot of people couldn't get rid of it the way they used to.'

'Like in riots and that.'

'Aye. Or even just quietly supporting what was happening. Turning a blind eye to things. People can be complicit without doing anything.'

The boy didn't speak and she knew she had lost him, though he wouldn't admit such after the previous comment.

'Anyway, whatever. It means that, because they can't get rid of their anger – or guilt in your dad's case – the way they used to, they turn it inward, on themselves.'

'Like hurting themselves. Like Karen.'

Lucy was momentarily surprised that Karen had confided in Gavin about her self-harming. They'd not known one another long. Then again, they had been in the residential unit together, both let down by their families. The same boat.

'Yes,' Lucy said. 'Like Karen.'

Gavin nodded.

'Did Karen ever mention any boys to you? Anyone called Paul Bradley, maybe?' Lucy asked. If she'd confided her harming to Gavin during the period when they had been in the care unit together, she might have mentioned the new boyfriend, if that was what Bradley had been to her.

The boy considered the name then shook his head. 'I saw her once or twice with a fella. A bit older than her, short dark hair. That was it. She never mentioned him though. Never mentioned any names anyway. Is he a suspect?'

'She met someone on Facebook. We're not sure if the name's real or not. It's something we're following up,' Lucy said. 'Speaking of following, why *were* that crew following you tonight?'

'Maybe they had anger issues too.' Gavin chuckled darkly to himself, then resumed the game again.

By the time Robbie arrived, Gavin was already being assessed by the doctor on duty. He'd removed his top to reveal a series of vivid bruises forming along his back and ribcage, a mixture of reds and purples. There were other, yellowed bruises too, healing already from earlier beatings.

'It's just scars on top of scars,' the doctor said to them disgustedly after the assessment. 'He has bruised his ribs, so I'm going to get some X-rays done. He has taken a few blows to the head, too, but no concussion. Maybe keep an eye on him tonight. Wake him a few times during the night to make sure he's OK. We'll get him back from the X-rays as soon as we can.'

Robbie and Lucy went back out to the waiting area again and Robbie bought them two coffees from the vending machine humming in the corner. It was the first time they had been alone together since Lucy had broken off their relationship a month earlier after hearing from one of the kids in the residential unit that Robbie had been seen kissing one of the other social workers at a Hallowe'en party. Robbie had tried to explain to her that the kiss had gone no further than that. To Lucy's mind, a kiss was already too far. As she watched him approach, bearing two steaming polystyrene cups, she wondered, not for the first time, whether she had overreacted.

The first drunk had arrived and was declaiming to all those still waiting as to just why Christmas was so shite. He waited for fifteen minutes before announcing that he'd been kept too long, and so left. It was never clear to anyone else there what the nature of the injury that had brought him to A & E in the first place had been.

'Thanks for the coffee,' Lucy said, sipping at it.

They sat for a moment, drinking in silence.

'You don't need to stay if you have somewhere to go,' Robbie said.

'I know,' Lucy said.

Robbie nodded. 'So, any plans for Christmas?'

'Not yet. You?'

'I'll cover the day shift so that the workers with families can be at home with their own kids. Then in the evening I'll probably head home to Omagh. My parents still like us all to come home for Christmas. We all muck in and make dinner. It's always good fun. For an hour. Then you remember why you moved out.'

Lucy laughed lightly. 'I don't remember family Christmas',' she said. 'I've vague recollections of Santa and that, but the one I remember clearly was when I was eight, just after Mum left. Dad decided I was old enough to be told the truth after he read my Santa letter that year.'

'Why?'

'I'd asked him to bring my mother back.' Lucy glanced at Robbie, the expression of concern on his face, and smiled. 'That was the last time I wanted that, mind you.'

'Santa's a bastard that way,' Robbie said. "I always wanted Mousetrap, and he never brought that to me. That and a James Bond attaché case.'

Lucy laughed, then turned her attention to the polystyrene cup in her hands, tearing the rim and folding down the top of the cup.

Robbie nudged her and handed her a folded piece of paper.

'What's that?' she asked. She took it, unfolded the page and found an address written on it.

'You'd asked me where Mary Quigg's baby brother, Joe, ended up. Before we ... you know. Before.'

Lucy nodded. 'Thanks, Robbie,' she said, refolding the page slowly and slipping it into her back pocket.

'A token of my regret,' Robbie said. 'Over all that happened.'

'And mine,' Lucy added, though she suspected not referring to the same events as Robbie.

'Nothing broken,' Gavin said, interrupting them. They looked up to where he stood. 'No bones at least,' he added, looking from one of them to the other.

Tuesday 18 December

Chapter Fourteen

The following morning, Lucy drove into work via the Culmore Road. The note Robbie had given her sat open on the passenger seat. The address listed was in Petrie Way, a fairly affluent area of the city. Joe Quigg had been the only survivor of the fire that had killed Mary and her mother. With no family left, he would be placed with foster parents in the hope that someone might adopt him. Lucy had asked Robbie, while they had still been together, for details of the family with whom the baby had been placed. He'd refused then; it said something about the guilt he felt that he should give it to her now, she reflected.

The house in question was detached, two storeys, with a faux Tudor facade. A silver 4 X 4 was parked in the driveway, and, behind it, a smaller Ford. Lucy had intended to drive past, but when she reached the house, she found herself parking up on the kerb a little down the street from it, then twisting in her seat to better examine the place.

Just then, the front door opened and a man stepped out, dressed in a suit, clutching a plastic shopping bag which looked to contain his lunch. He was perhaps mid-thirties, Lucy thought. His wife appeared at the doorway, dressed in jeans and a white T-shirt. In her arms, she held an infant. Lucy felt her throat constrict as Joe lifted a small fist and reached out to the man, looking to be held. Joe had only been a baby the last time Lucy had seen him. He'd grown in a year. The man moved quickly towards him and embraced him, then turned away and climbed into the 4 X 4 while Joe cried and the woman shushed him, bouncing him lightly in her embrace.

As Lucy watched the woman and child retreat back inside their house, the husband passed her in his 4 X 4, staring in at her, as if realizing that she'd been watching his home.

Tom Fleming wasn't in his office when she arrived nor had he left a note to say where he was. However, the phone was ringing in the main office and Lucy went in and answered it.

'Can I speak to Tom Fleming, please?' a young, female, English voice asked.

'I'm afraid not,' Lucy said. 'He's not here.'

'Do you know where he is?'

'I'm afraid not,' Lucy repeated. 'Can I help?'

'This is Euro Security. Mr Fleming's burglar alarm has registered an intruder. Are you a key holder?'

'I'll check on it,' Lucy said, hanging up.

She was already on the dual carriageway towards Fleming's house in Kilfennan when she reflected that she should, perhaps, have asked someone to accompany her, in case there actually were intruders in the house. She comforted herself with the thought that, if Fleming himself had been there, he'd have used his panic button. She decided to get as far as his address. If it appeared that there was a need for backup, she'd call for it then.

As she pulled into the street, her stomach constricted. Fleming's car, still owned from his disqualification for drink driving, sat in the driveway, as she'd expected. The curtains in the windows of the house, however, were closed. She pulled up outside and went up the drive. The alarm continued to blare, the blue light on the box attached to the front of the house winking, as if against the morning breeze.

None of the windows or door to the front seemed disturbed, though all were curtained, including one across the front door. Lucy skirted the side of the house, climbing the low gate into the back yard. Again, the windows were shut and the back door locked. She peered in through the kitchen window, using her gloved hand to shield her eyes from the glared reflection on the glass.

The kitchen gave way onto the hallway to the immediate right of which climbed an open staircase. As Lucy squinted to see better, she thought she could make out something, at the far end of the hall, at the foot of the stairway. Shifting her position slightly for a better view, she caught clearer sight of it. Someone was lying at the foot of the stairs.

Taking out her phone, she called for an ambulance immediately. She hammered on the back door a number of times, leaning against the window and calling Fleming's name, but the body did not move.

Finally, she hunted through the overgrown flowerbeds bordering the garden until she found a rock. Using it, she smashed the pane of glass in the back door and, reaching in, grateful for the protection of her work gloves, she unbolted the door and ran into the kitchen.

Tom Fleming was lying face down in the hallway, the lower half of his body still stretched up the staircase from where he had fallen. A pool of vomit haloed his head, sticking to his hair and skin. Lucy pulled off her gloves and placed her hand against his cheek. His skin was pale and clammy, his breath rank with sickness and alcohol.

'Inspector Fleming,' she said, shaking him. 'Tom.'

He moaned, but did not rouse from his torpor. The ringing bell of the outer alarm had been replaced in here by an intense electronic tone that was pitched at such a level it made Lucy wince.

She slapped Fleming's face lightly, all the time calling his name. Eventually, unable to rouse him that way, she went into the kitchen, filled a kettle with cold water, brought it back to the hallway and poured it on his face.

The effect was instantaneous. He jerked awake, staring around him blindly. He caught sight of Lucy standing above him and seemed to struggle to focus on her or place her in the context of his own home. He smacked his lips together dryly and looked as if he might speak. Then he twisted and vomited again onto the carpet, his back arching with each retch.

Lucy heard the wailing siren of the ambulance cut through the white noise of the alarm.

'What's the code for the alarm?' she asked.

Fleming looked up at her, then turned to the floor once more as he dry-heaved. Finally he struggled to stand, seemingly not realizing that his feet were still on the stairs.

'The alarm, sir,' Lucy said. 'What's the code?'

'One, two, three, four,' he managed hoarsely.

So much for police officers being security conscious, Lucy thought.

Lucy had just managed to get the code entered and the alarm silenced when the blaring of the siren outside crescendoed, then stopped abruptly. She could see the flickering of the blue lights through the chink in the curtain over the front door. She pulled the curtain back, turned the key left in the lock and opened the door, flooding the stultifying atmosphere of the hallway both with light and fresh air.

'Is there an officer down?' the paramedic asked, stepping into the hallway and catching sight of Fleming at once.

'I thought he was injured when I looked in from outside,' Lucy explained. 'I don't think it's quite as serious as I thought.'

The paramedic approached him. 'Sir?' he said. 'Can you hear me?'

Fleming groaned and tried to shift himself again.

'Is he pissed?' the paramedic asked incredulously.

Lucy nodded, the gesture greeted by Fleming's grumbles of disagreement.

'I'm sorry,' she said. 'I thought it was ... you know. I looked in and saw him lying there.'

'We'll give him a quick check over,' the man said. 'He might have injured himself in the fall.' He shifted across to Fleming again. 'We're going to lift you, mate, all right?'

Fleming muttered something, but the man moved in and, gripping the drunk man under the armpits, hefted him to his feet.

'Sit there a moment and I'll get some help,' he said as he helped Fleming to sit on the bottom step of the staircase.

Fleming slumped on the step, then leant sideways, against the wall. His face was pale, his stubble grey against his skin, flecked with his vomit.

'Are you OK, Tom?' Lucy said, stepping past the pool on the floor and laying one hand on his shoulder.

He stared at her accusingly. 'What the hell did you call them for?' he said.

Chapter Fifteen

She was making coffee for them both in Fleming's kitchen when Tara Gallagher called. They'd had a hit on the metal thefts. Finn's scrap metal yard had called to say that a team was offloading cabling at that moment. Finn, keen to avoid charges of handling stolen goods, had said that if the police were quick enough, they might catch them in the act.

Finn's yard was on the outskirts of the city, past Ballyarnett, where Amelia Earhart had landed following her cross-Atlantic flight in 1932. The yard itself was a half-acre compound, enclosed on all sides by a metal palisade fence. A small portable unit from which the owner operated his business sat behind the front section of the fence, at the single gateway into the yard.

The PSNI teams had parked some distance away and were watching the gang as they moved to and fro, shifting metal from the rear of their white Transit van, which was parked on the roadway that bisected the yard.

To the left-hand side of the road, the skeletal remains of crushed cars sat atop each other, three high, six piles deep, against the palisade fence. The other half of the yard, to the right of the gang's van, was comprised of piles of scrap metal and skips, some already filled, as best Lucy could tell. She could see four men moving backwards and forwards, removing scrap from the back of the van and depositing it in different piles and skips, perhaps in an attempt to mix the stolen metal more thoroughly with the legitimate scrap.

Lucy approached Tara. 'What's the plan?'

Tara smiled. 'There's only the one roadway, with the entrance, next to the Portakabin,' she pointed out. 'We'll block it with the Land Rover and move in and arrest them. Simple.'

They climbed into the Land Rover, alongside the four Tactical Support Unit officers who had accompanied Tara and the driver down. They wore blue cargo pants and fleeces over their shirts. They all carried guns with them.

The Land Rover's doors slammed shut and the vehicle's engine roared into life as the driver accelerated it up the roadway towards where the van was parked. Leaning forward, Lucy could see through the reinforced windscreen over the driver's shoulder. The four gang members outside heard their approach and instantly dropped what they were doing. One's instinct was to run for the white van, possibly too shocked to realize that he was already blocked in by the police. The other three, however, scattered in different directions across the yard. One made for the area of scrap to the right, scrambling over the pile nearest to him, failing to find purchase on the metal, which slid away beneath his feet with each step he tried to take. The other two cut left towards the carcasses of the cars.

Lucy felt the Land Rover brake suddenly then one of the uniforms flung open the back doors and the four men jumped out and set off in pursuit of the gang members. Lucy and Tara followed, Tara heading straight for the man struggling through the piles of scrap, accompanied by a TSU officer.

The other three TSU men made for the piled cars, in pursuit of the two who had run, leaving Lucy to approach the white Transit van. She pulled her own gun from its holster and, holding it in front of her, both hands to steady it, banged on the side of the van three times in quick succession.

'PSNI,' she shouted. 'Show me your hands.'

Behind her, she heard the thud of the police Land Rover door as the driver got out to support her.

She could see the face of the man in the white van reflected in the side mirror as he tried to gauge the likelihood of his escape. Then, incrementally, she saw the side window begin to lower. Instinctively she pressed herself against the side of the van, gun ready.

'Show me your hands,' she shouted again. 'Now.'

The window cranked down faster now and, slowly, the man's two hands appeared through the gap.

With the PSNI driver approaching from the passenger side of the van, Lucy stepped up and pointed her gun into the van cabin. A single man, in his late teens at most, sat in the driver seat. His face was swarthy, a raw black beard on his chin. His eyes focused on the tip of Lucy's gun and did not waver. Then he heard the passenger door of the van open behind him and turned to face a second PSNI gun.

'Please,' he whimpered, turning to look at the other officer.

Lucy pulled the cable ties from her belt and quickly looped them around his hands, then pulled the plastic tight, cuffing him. Then she opened the door and gripping the man by his shirt front, pulled him out of his seat and onto the ground.

He lay on his face while she sat astride his back, frisking him quickly to check for any weapons. Satisfied that he had none, she twisted him round, onto his back. The PSNI driver had approached them now and stood above them.

'What's your name?' he asked.

'Marcus,' the man said, wide eyed.

As the officer cautioned the man, Lucy moved to the back of the van and climbed inside to see what the men had been shifting. Coils of copper wiring were stacked to one side of the van, while against the back wall wads of folded lead flashing were piled to the height of the seats in the cab beyond. To the left-hand side were various bits of scrap metal, among which Lucy spotted one section of the cast metal fencing she'd had placed on Mary Quigg's grave.

She climbed back down from the van, just as Tara approached with the second man in cuffs.

'Well?'

'It's the right team for the churches and graveyards anyway,' Lucy said. Over to her left, Lucy could see the other three uniforms tracking their way through the rows of piled cars, still searching for the two men who were presumably hiding inside some of the wrecks.

Lucy grabbed Marcus and, pulling him to his feet, brought him round to the rear of the van.

'Is this cabling from the train line?'

The boy nodded. 'It wasn't us,' he said.

'This wasn't you?'

'No. The girl. She was there when we arrived. We'd only cut a bit and we came round the bend and saw her. She was just lying there. She was dead already.'

The boy was clearly terrified, perhaps believing that the police suspected the gang of Karen's killing.

'So you say,' Lucy snapped.

'I swear,' the boy managed. 'We saw someone leaving when we arrived. An old guy, grey hair. He was getting into a car. It was red, I think. I didn't see what make. But it was small. Like a Fiesta or something.'

'What about the stuff from the graveyard?' she demanded. 'Did you take that?'

Marcus glanced at the officers standing around and nodded.

'We'd best leave this till we get to the station,' Tara cautioned.

Ignoring the comments, Lucy pointed to the fencing from Mary's grave. 'This was taken from a child's grave. Who stole it?'

The man shook his head. 'Not me. That was Shaun. In the red T-shirt. He did the graveyard while we did the church roof.'

He nodded towards the piled cars. Shaun was evidently one of the two men still hiding there.

As they glanced across towards where the man had indicated, they suddenly saw that one of the columns of cars, close to the fencing, was beginning to sway. Below it, in the small pathway between the carcasses, they could see the uniforms moving, searching for the two missing men.

'Jesus,' Tara shouted, as the uppermost car of the moving pile, a red Skoda missing a door and bonnet, seemed to teeter at the edge, then fell forwards, knocking into the adjacent pile in the next row. In a moment, in a domino effect, the piles of scrapped cars began tumbling one into the next, bits of the car bodies dropping into the gaps between the rows where the three uniforms were, trapping them beneath the debris.

With the uppermost car now fallen, Lucy could see Shaun, the man in the red T-shirt, his back pressed against the far fence, using his legs as leverage to the uppermost car in the next pile over, recreating the effect again. Then he turned and began scrambling up the metal fence, using the barbs at the top as a grip to pull himself up.

As Tara and the two uniforms ran towards the fallen cars to look for their colleagues, Lucy sprinted down the roadway out of the scrapyard, trying to keep an eye on Shaun's progress. As she reached the main gateway, she saw him swing over the top of the fence, as if to drop to the ground beyond.

Puffing furiously, she sprinted the circumference of the fence, aware now that at least one other TSU officer was following some distance behind her, realizing that she needed support.

As she neared the spot where Shaun had been climbing, she realized that he'd not made it down, as she'd expected. His trousers had become entangled in the barbs and he was caught at the top of the fence, tugging at the material, trying to tear himself free. Just as Lucy approached, she heard the rip of fabric and he fell onto the ground in front of her. He struggled to get to his feet, but Lucy covered the final few yards and fell onto him, pinning him back down.

He writhed beneath her, trying to buck her off his back as Lucy laid her full weight against him. Finally, the TSU officer arrived and, dropping beside her, laid his weight on Shaun's legs, effectively pinning him to the ground.

'You're under arrest for theft,' Lucy managed. 'Put your hands in front of you.'

Shaun tried to kick and shifted his weight, but he was overpowered. Finally, Lucy felt him slump, and he extended his two hands out in front of his head, his face pressed into the dirt of the ground where he'd fallen.

Lucy moved quickly, looping the cable ties around his outstretched hands, pinching them tight against the skin of his arm. His hands lay flat on the ground, the wrists bound together, his arms outstretched above his head.

The TSU man stood up, dusting himself as he did so, then turned quickly to look into the yard through the gaps in the fence to where one of his colleagues lay on the ground beneath the scrapped Skoda.

'Are you OK, Danny?' he called.

Lucy leaned down close to Shaun's ear. 'You stole from graves, is that right?' she said.

Shaun looked up at her, his face smeared with mud. 'No comment.' He smiled.

Rising, Lucy stepped on his hand with her steel-capped boot, pressing down until she heard the fingers' crack behind the screaming of the man and the shouts of the TSU officer as he tried to pull her away.

Chapter Sixteen

A fire tender was at the scene within minutes, with cutting equipment, lest it should be needed. They shifted the remains of the cars as carefully as possible in order to create sufficient space for the PSNI men trapped beneath to crawl out. In addition, it became apparent that in pushing over the cars, Shaun had trapped one of his own gang members beneath a badly rusted Scenic. He cried out periodically in rage as the officers worked first to rescue their own colleagues before coming to his aid.

The metal gang members were brought back to Strand Road station, where Tara, preening herself on having overseen the operation to arrest them, briefed Burns. Lucy was called into his office after he had spoken with Tara.

'I understand you questioned one of the suspects?' he said, without preamble.

Lucy nodded. 'I wanted to be sure we had the right people,' she said. 'I'm sorry. I should have waited.'

'You should indeed,' Burns said. 'You got a description apparently. What did he say?'

'As they arrived, they saw an older man, grey haired, getting into a red car in the parking bay. He drove off and they started harvesting the metal. As they moved down the line, they came across Karen's remains. He said they didn't touch the body. They scarpered when they found it.'

'You should have left it until he was brought back here.'

'We have a description now, at least, sir.'

'Though there's no guarantee that the man they saw had anything to do with Karen's disappearance.'

'It seems a little odd that a man would be in the park at that time of night for any legitimate reason.'

Burns accepted this with a curt nod. 'Regardless, we needed him to make a proper statement.'

'Sorry, sir,' Lucy said.

'I understand you also broke another suspect's fingers.'

'That was an accident. I didn't feel his hand beneath my boot until he cried out.'

'You were asking the first suspect you arrested about taking fences off a child's grave, apparently. I hope the two things aren't connected.'

'No sir,' Lucy said, thinking back, trying to remember who had heard her asking Marcus about Mary's grave. Then she remembered.

As she left Burns's office, Tara sat at her desk in the incident room, watching her. When she saw Lucy, she raised her hand meekly. Lucy nodded curtly and left without speaking.

* * *

After leaving Strand Road station, Lucy had headed back to Maydown. Fleming was in his office at least, though with the door closed. Lucy considered knocking to ask how he was feeling, but decided against.

She'd just made it into her own office when her phone rang.

'Dave Cooper here, Lucy. I think Bradley is about to go online.'

'Is this some sixth sense, ESP thing?'

Cooper laughed. 'No. He's online already. Just not as himself. Come across and I'll show you.'

Cooper's office was as cluttered as it had been the day previous. The large iMac sitting on the main desk displayed Karen Hughes's Facebook account profile.

'I checked out Bradley's account yesterday, tracing through all of the friends that he had, in case there were other girls there he was targeting,' Cooper explained. 'I have a feeling that a number of these friends are sock puppet accounts.'

Lucy shrugged. 'What's that mean?'

'I think Bradley created a whole load of accounts, all in different names, which he then befriended.'

'He made friends with himself? Why?'

'To make him seem more normal.'

Lucy raised a sceptical eyebrow.

'Look,' Cooper said. 'If he sent you a friend request, and he only had one or two other online mates, you'd think it a bit strange. If instead he has loads of friends, all your age, all with similar interests, he looks less suspicious.'

'How do you know they're sock puppets?'

'A lot of the accounts either aren't fully developed, or their content is repetitive, where the same message is being posted in fourteen or fifteen accounts almost in rotation. Look.'

He showed her Paul Bradley's page. He'd posted a status update the previous Saturday saying 'Saturday lie-in =)'.

'See this,' Cooper said. 'Watch.'

He opened a second Facebook profile, this time for someone called 'Liam Tyler'. 'Look.'

On the previous Saturday, 'Tyler' had posted the same status update. A girl named Annie Marsden had attached a comment with a smiley face of her own.

'You think "Tyler" is actually Paul Bradley?'

Cooper nodded. 'If Paul Bradley is even his real name. That could simply be another alias.'

'But one of his aliases has gone online?'

Cooper nodded. '"Simon Harris" went on about ten minutes ago. Watch.'

He pointed to a small pane in the lower half of the page, which listed online friends of Bradley's. A green circle marked the name 'Harris'. Suddenly the name vanished.

'We've lost him again?' Lucy asked.

'Wait,' Cooper said. 'If I'm right, you'll see one of these other names go live.'

Sure enough, a moment later, a green dot appeared next to the name 'Tom Gallagher'. Cooper pointed to the screen. 'That's another of them.'

'How many does he have in total?'

'I think about twenty,' Cooper said. 'We need him to log in as Paul Bradley though; I've got Facebook to agree to give us Bradley's ISP address when he next logs in. But we can't ask for that for all of these accounts too unless we can prove they're all the same person.'

'I'll update Burns anyway,' Lucy said, going out of the unit and phoning through to CID. As she was explaining to Burns what Cooper had told her, Cooper himself appeared, barely able to contain his excitement.

'They've been in touch. Bradley's just gone online. I've reverse-checked the ISP address they've given us. It's a restaurant in the Foyleside shopping centre.'

Chapter Seventeen

The Foyleside Centre was built in the early nineties, covering four floors and housing almost fifty different stores. Level four was little more than a central concourse with shops lining both sides. The two middle floors, however, were more open-plan, meaning that there were a variety of approaches and escape routes, should Bradley try to make a run for it. Fortunately for them, the Wi-Fi address they had been given belonged to the fast-food outlet on the uppermost floor.

The difficulty was that, although they had a picture of Bradley from his account page, there was no guarantee that the man in question would even look like his picture. They did, though, have the description from the metal theft gang, who'd seen a man with grey hair in the area where Karen's body had been found.

All of this was explained to the team by Burns who briefed them in the back of the Land Rover on their way to the Foyleside. The rear of the Land Rover was stuffy, the benches on each side lined with members of one of the two Tactical Support Units accompanying the investigating team. The proximity of the bodies, and the vague smell of sweat generated by the boiler-suit type uniforms the officers wore made it difficult for

Lucy to concentrate on what Burns was saying. She wanted to get out and get moving.

'Lucy and Tara go in together first. Get something to eat, scope the place out. We're probably looking for a man, on his own, using a phone. Grey-haired particularly. Obviously if you recognize anyone on the Offenders Register let us know immediately. We'll hold back on a full entrance until we have a target,' Burns said, before turning to Mickey and the DC sitting next to him. 'You two hang around outside; be ready in case anything goes down. We'll post one TS Unit outside the main entrance and a second at the bottom of the stairs to the fourth floor. If he makes a run for it within the centre, they can close in on him from top and bottom floors.'

'How come they get food and we have to window-shop?' Mickey complained.

'How many women only window-shop?' Burns asked. 'Besides, you've had a few too many dinners recently by the looks of you.'

The team erupted into laughter, the loudest of which belonged to Mickey himself, keen to ingratiate himself with the boss.

Lucy and Tara stepped out into the light mizzle of rain that seemed to hang perpetually over the city. Lucy glanced at the shoppers passing, arms laden with bags, looking forward to Christmas, blithely unaware that a possible child killer was sitting in their midst.

'What do you fancy?' Tara asked as they entered the Foyleside. 'I'll get the grub, you have a look around;

you've a better idea of some of the weirdos out there through the PPU anyway.'

Lucy grunted, already scanning the area as they entered the central concourse. If the Wi-Fi signal was strong enough, there would be no need for Bradley even to sit inside the restaurant.

'I'll have a cheeseburger and Diet Coke,' Lucy said. 'I'll grab a table near the door. That'll give us a good chance to look around.'

As it transpired, that would prove difficult. The centre was heaving with people, burdened down with shopping, presumably trying to complete Christmas shopping. They could already see a queue for the fast-food place stretching out through the main doors.

'We've another week to go and I'm sick of bloody carols already,' Tara said as a piped version of 'In the Bleak Midwinter' began playing over the centre's speakers.

There were two doors into the restaurant; the main one where the queue had formed and a second exit to the left, nearer the front entrance of the Foyleside itself.

'You take the main entrance and join the queue,' Lucy said, 'I'll take a look around the place, like I'm looking for seats.'

Lucy moved to the nearest door and pushed her way in. As she did, she phoned Cooper.

'Is he still online?' she asked quietly.

'He's switched accounts again,' Cooper said. 'I think he's currently "Steven Burke".'

Lucy ended the call and began weaving between the packed tables, looking for any single men. To her left was a harried family, four kids climbing on the seats while their father and mother tried to distribute their boxes of food. The youngest, a girl with tight curled hair, smiled up at Lucy who winked at her in return. Her three brothers, meanwhile, were fighting over who was getting the first strawberry milkshake.

Over to the right, a number of tables were filled with young girls, out shopping together, five of them crowded around one bag of chips and a drink. All had phones, probably sending texts to one another as they sat there, Lucy reflected. Then a little further ahead, she saw the actual recipients of their messages: a table of teenage boys, similarly clumped around food for one, watching across at the girls.

A man banged into Lucy, his tray held in front of him defensively.

'Sorry,' he managed. Lucy glanced at him, middle-aged, grey-haired, then checked his tray, three drinks, enough food for a family. Across to the right, at the window, she saw a man, mid-twenties, black hair, sitting alone. He had a phone in his hand, the crumpled wrapper of his burger lying on the table in front of him. As she moved towards him, she got a clear view of the table and saw a woman and child also sitting at it.

Suddenly, Tara's voice crackled through her earpiece. 'In the corner. The grey coat.'

Lucy glanced across to where Tara had indicated. A grey-haired man sat alone, staring intently across the restaurant. He had a coffee cup in front of him and the remains of a doughnut. He was holding his phone, raised off the table, glancing occasionally at the screen. He seemed to be holding it steady. Lucy followed the direction of the phone and realized it was pointing at the table of teenage girls.

The man looked up and, for a moment, caught Lucy's gaze. He recognized her at the same moment she recognized him.

'Gene Kay,' she said. 'It's Gene Kay.'

As she spoke, Kay got to his feet, pushed his way through the gathered queue and made for the exit.

'He's moving,' Tara said. 'Middle-aged, grey coat. Can we pick him up?'

'Mickey, pick him as he comes out,' Burns ordered.

Kay had started to move towards the main door, then seemed to realize that the two men moving towards it from the outside were coming for him. He cut quickly towards Lucy, pushing past a young man, knocking over his tray.

'Mr Kay, stop,' she shouted.

Lucy reached out to stop him as he approached, but he rushed her, pushing through, shouldering her off balance and knocking her to the ground, then bolted for the second exit, the doorway Lucy had just entered.

There he must have seen the Tactical Support officers coming in through the Foyleside entrance for he turned and ran back down the concourse towards the escalators leading to the lower floors. Lucy glanced across to see that Mickey and the DC had come into the restaurant after him through the other door and were now trying to get back out again, having become caught in the middle of a crowd of school children being herded in through the main doors by their teacher.

Lucy pushed through towards the exit Kay had taken and, once on the main concourse, turned to see his retreating back as he reached the top of the escalators. He hesitated, then took the stairs instead. At least the second TS Unit would pick him up, she thought. But, if Kay had seen them on the lower floor down there, why had he willingly gone down?

'Are the TSU in place on level three?' Lucy breathed into the earpiece.

'Can I get a location?' she heard Burns snap.

'Floor two, sir. We've been held up with three shoplifters coming out of Boots. We're on our way up.'

Lucy weaved through the crowd, travelling seemingly against the direction of foot flow, as the rest of the team finally appeared through the other door.

'Fucking pantomime trips,' Mickey spat, rounding the last of the school children.

They took the stairs, two at a time, and reached the third floor, which opened out in four directions from the bottom of the stairs.

'I'll take straight ahead,' Mickey said, taking control. 'You go left, Tommy; Tara go right; Lucy check the shops. TSU will catch up.' Then he set off before anyone could argue.

The first shop to her left was the book store, Eason. Lucy ran in then stood on tiptoe to better scan the shoppers. She couldn't see Kay and left, moving towards the next shop. The neighbouring units were all similarly clear. The last store was a larger department store, and Tommy had headed in there. She cut across and began checking the shops along the opposite wall. She was just coming out of a clothes shop when she spotted Kay, his coat off now and hanging over his arm, as he walked out of the O_2 shop. The central portion of level three had actually been cut away, allowing those on the level to look down to the one beneath. The shop from which Kay had come was on the opposite side of the gap from where she stood, meaning Lucy would need to move around it to get to Kay. He would undoubtedly see her approach. In fact, even now, he was glancing around, obviously looking to see where the police were.

'He's here,' Lucy said.

'TSU are on the level now. What's your location?' Burns snapped.

'He's outside the O_2 shop,' Lucy said, 'moving towards the lower escalator.'

Kay must have spotted the two uniforms coming up the escalator he was about to take for he turned suddenly. Then he saw Lucy too, stood, holding her gaze, the space between them the ten-foot opening in the floor, surrounded by guard rails, giving way to a drop of about twenty feet down to level two. At the centre of the space below, a small water feature twinkled beneath the fluorescent centre lights.

Kay glanced to his left, where the two TSU officers were approaching, then to his right, where a team from above was likewise fanning out as they approached him.

He stared across at Lucy, placing both his hands on the rail, as if to brace himself for a jump.

Lucy shook her head. *Don't*, she mouthed.

Kay paused a second, then lifted his leg and began clambering over the guard rail.

'He's going to jump,' Lucy shouted. Glancing down, she saw Mickey and Tommy arrive beneath them.

Instead, the man pulled his phone from his pocket and flung it to the floor below. Looking down, Lucy could only watch as it shattered off the side of the tiled water feature below and slid beneath the water to rest on a bed of winking good luck pennies.

Chapter Eighteen

Lucy and Tom Fleming were sent to Kay's house first to search for evidence that might connect him with Karen Hughes. There was no doubt that, like all abusers, Kay would have a collection of material somewhere in the house, most likely stored on his PC. The difficulty with abusers' collections, however, was that they were not always obviously related to the abuse that had been carried out. Any officer would pick up a box containing obscene photographs straight away; a box of seemingly innocuous souvenirs might not be noticed. Burns reasoned that Fleming and Lucy would have a better sense of what to look for than CID.

When they entered the living room, however, the first thing Lucy noticed was the space on the table where the computer had been.

'PC's gone,' she said to Fleming.

'We'll keep an eye out for it,' Fleming commented. 'You do the upstairs rooms, I'll do down here.'

There were three rooms upstairs. The first, a bathroom, was almost bare. The walls were blue, the paint bubbling and blistered in places behind the sink. A scum-ringed glass on the windowsill. Toothbrush, razor, a rolled tube of paste. A few bottles of cheap aftershave on the windowsill next to that, and a bottle of talc. There were no obvious hiding places. Lucy pulled the plastic front off the bath and peered underneath, illuminating the space with her torch beam, but there was nothing there.

The second room was a spare bedroom. The wardrobe was empty save for an old suit jacket, which, judging by the musty smell coming from it, had not been worn in some time. Lucy checked the room, under the bed, the dresser in the corner, but there was nothing of interest.

Finally, in Kay's own bedroom, she found what she'd been looking for: a box on the top shelf of his wardrobe. She quickly checked the rest of the room then, when she was sure there was nothing else of interest, she took the box down to the living room to catalogue with Fleming present.

Fleming came struggling in through the back door carrying a black rubbish bag.

'In the bin,' Fleming explained, dumping the bag on the ground. 'What did you find?'

Lucy laid the box on the table, opened it and began sifting through the contents. It contained mostly objects rather than pictures. Among them was a teddy bear, several pairs of ticket stubs, some to a local cinema, two pairs to the circus, though dated on different years, and a dried-out daffodil. At the bottom of the box were a handful of sea shells, a single glove, a doll. With each object, Lucy reflected on the child whom it represented to Kay. Trips to the circus and cinema suggested the family of the child had trusted him, known him well, had allowed him to inveigle his way into their home.

'A bit careless of him keeping these in the house,' Fleming said.

'They don't prove he did anything wrong,' Lucy muttered. 'He's probably hidden his other collection much more carefully.'

She knew that there would be another collection, the one which, despite her time in the police, she knew would still make her stomach twist with revulsion when she saw it. But, strangely, she found these collections – the objects – to be equally disturbing, reflecting as these did the innocence of the ones Kay had clearly been grooming. In the bottom corner, beneath the glove, she found a bar of hotel soap and pointed it out to Fleming, who groaned.

'Some of these stubs are years old,' Lucy commented.

Fleming shook his head. 'Anything you see there connect him to Karen Hughes?'

'No,' Lucy said. 'If anything, if all this stuff is connected to his victims, they're a little young in comparison with Karen. She was mid-teens, this stuff suggests that might have been too old for Kay.' She gestured towards the black bag. 'What was he dumping?'

Fleming lifted the black bag and emptied it. Pictures cut from newspapers and magazines spilled out onto the floor. One by one, they picked through them, examining each. While each image was of a child, none were of a sexual nature. The children pictured were predominantly pre-teen.

They worked through each image, but again, none related to Karen Hughes.

'He must have other stuff somewhere,' Fleming said. 'Presumably on his computer. He's stashed it somewhere after we called for the dog hairs.'

'Would he have destroyed it?' Lucy asked. 'Or hidden it in the garden?'

Fleming shook his head, his breath sweet as he exhaled. 'If Kay's been building these collections for years, his real one will be massive. He'll not just get rid of it. Someone's keeping it for him or he's hidden it somewhere. It's not out back. I searched the shed, checked the lawn for signs of recent disturbance. Nothing.'

They had just finished bagging the collections to be transferred back to the Strand Road when Fleming took a call from one of the district teams to say that another fifteen-year-old girl, called Sarah Finn, had been reported missing.

Chapter Nineteen

Sarah Finn's mother, Sinead, sat on the sofa in the living room of their family home in Fallowfield Gardens, in Gobnascale. She was in her mid-thirties, at most, dressed in a heavy white dressing gown over her pyjamas. She wore thick grey bed socks into which she had tucked the legs of her pink pyjama bottoms. Her legs were crossed, the foot of the upper leg jittering as she spoke.

'The school phoned just after lunch to say she's been off all day. I thought maybe she'd bunked off with friends.'

'Had she bunked off before?' Lucy asked.

Finn shrugged lightly. 'A few times, maybe.'

'And she's not been in touch since?'

The woman shook her head. 'I checked when I got in from the shops but she weren't in her room. She normally gets herself back in from school and that.'

'So when was the last time you saw her?'

The woman reached across to the pack of cigarettes on the table next to the sofa and withdrew one, shaking it free of the pack. She lit it, dragged deeply, then held it between the fingers of the hand resting on her knee. Lucy couldn't help but notice that her nails looked freshly painted. She glanced across to where the cigarette box sat and, sure enough, a bottle of nail polish stood behind them. If she'd been concerned by the news of her daughter's absence from school, it hadn't affected her cosmetics routine.

'Last night some time.'

'Last night?' Fleming asked, glancing at his watch. It was almost three. 'What time?'

'Before seven, maybe. She were going out with her friends.'

'You didn't see her come home last night?'

'I went to bed early.'

'And this morning? Was she home this morning?'

The woman shrugged. 'I don't know. She normally sorts herself out in the morning.'

'Was her bed made or unmade?' Lucy asked. 'Had she slept in it?'

Again a shrug. 'I don't know. It was made, I think. But she always makes it.'

'Has she ever run away before?' Lucy asked.

'Never.'

'So you last saw her before seven last night. Almost twenty hours ago,' Fleming said.

The woman laughed embarrassedly. 'It sounds bad when you say it like that. She went out to the local youth club. I went to bed early last night.'

'Did she?'

'Did she what?'

'Go to the club?'

'I don't know,' the woman said, blankly.

Fleming moved from the window, finally, and sat on the armchair against the opposite wall. 'You might be best to check,' he said.

Sinead Finn dragged again on her cigarette, then folded it into the ashtray balancing on the arm of the sofa. She rooted through the pocket of her gown until she produced a mobile phone.

While she rang Sarah's friend, Lucy glanced around the room. It was cramped, the three-piece suite on which she sat much too big for the room. An electric fire flickered on the hearth. Above it, on the mantelpiece, a small gold carriage clock squatted, the lower works spinning back and forth. It was framed on either side by two small pictures. One was of Sinead Finn herself and a man.

Lucy struggled out of the seat, went across to the mantelpiece and lifted the photograph. It looked fairly recent, judging by the appearance of Sinead Finn. The man was small, little taller than Sinead, his head shaved, though the shadow of stubble across his skull carried a reddish sheen. The buzz cut accentuated his ears, which seemed to protrude a little. His eyes were narrowed, his mouth frozen open in a laugh. He stood slightly behind Sinead, his right arm reaching around her neck and across her chest, the bicep flexed protectively in front of her, the hand lightly clasping her left breast.

Lucy put the photograph down and lifted the second. It was, presumably, Sarah Finn, for the person in the picture wore a school uniform. She sat in front of a bookcase, laden with red-spined leather volumes. Lucy guessed it was a screen backdrop used by the school photographer. Sarah was brown haired, her features soft, still carrying a little puppy fat on her face. She looked up at the camera from below her fringe, her mouth frozen in an embarrassed smile.

Lucy turned and handed the picture to Fleming, then returned to her own seat.

'Linda? Sinead Finn again. Was Sarah at the club with you last night?'

Lucy sat, clasped her hands between her knees. Instinctively she stretched them out towards the fire, then realized it was electric and returned them to between her legs. She could hear the raised murmur of the other speaker for a second as Sinead adjusted the phone against her ear, reaching for another smoke.

'Well she said she was going with you,' Sinead said.

Linda obviously took exception to this last comment for her voice became loud enough for them to hear.

'She said she was with you,' Sinead countered, raising her voice too, as if in so doing, she could convince Linda that she was mistaken and that Sarah had indeed been at the club.

Sinead snapped the phone shut and, lifting her lighter, lit the cigarette.

'She weren't there at all,' she explained, unnecessarily.

'Has Sarah a phone? Have you tried calling her?' Lucy asked.

'I'm not bloody thick,' the woman snapped. 'Of course I tried. There's no answer. I've left her a message to call me, but nothing yet.'

Fleming nodded. 'So you didn't notice that she hadn't come home last night?'

Sinead Finn stared at him a moment, teasing out the implied criticism of his question. 'Sometimes she's home late,' she explained. 'The friends she runs around with and that.'

Fleming rose from the seat a little sullenly, crossed to the window and turned his attention again to the road outside.

'Is this Sarah?' Lucy asked, lifting the picture from the arm of the chair where Fleming had left it.

Sinead smiled. 'That's her. She looks so pretty.'

Lucy nodded in agreement. 'She's lovely,' she said. 'Is it a recent picture?'

'A few months ago just. The start of the new term.'

'Can we hold on to this, to show people if we need to ask around?'

Sinead nodded. 'Seamy, my partner, was heading off early this morning, so we had a few drinks and an early night. That's how I didn't notice she was gone.' She folded her arms against her chest, staring at Fleming.

'Where's he gone?' Fleming asked, turning back to the woman again.

'Manchester. He's a lorry driver. He had to leave at five this morning to get the early ferry across.'

'This would be Mr Finn, would it?' Lucy asked, pointing to the picture on the mantelpiece.

'No,' Sinead said, with a confused laugh. 'That's Seamy.'

'What's his full name, Mrs Finn?'

'Sinead, Jesus,' the woman replied. 'Seamus Doherty.'

116

'Who does he work for?'

'H. M. Haulage. Harry Martin's his boss. He's H. M.'

'I see,' Lucy said, jotting down the name. 'Sarah wouldn't be with Mr Doherty, would she? Maybe went to keep him company?'

Sinead shook her head. 'No. They don't really get on. Sarah's dad left a few years back and it's still raw, like. You know?'

'How long have you been with Mr Doherty?'

'A year or two.'

'Does he live here?'

Finn nodded. 'When he's not working. He drives a lot.'

'Have you checked with him that Sarah's not with him at the moment?'

'His phone's switched off,' Sincad said. 'Besides, he'd have phoned to let me know if she was with him.'

'And what about Sarah's father? Would she be with him?'

'I doubt it,' Sinead said. 'He lives in Australia. He headed out for work and never came back.'

'How did Sarah take to you having Mr Doherty staying here?' Fleming asked.

'It's my house, isn't it?' Sinead said.

She lifted another cigarette, lit it off the butt of the smouldering one she held, then flicked the dead one into the fireplace. She folded her arms again, facing Lucy and Fleming, as if challenging them to disagree.

'Of course,' Fleming said. 'Look, before we start a full search for Sarah, DS Black is going to take a quick look through the house. Just to double-check that she's not here. Is that OK?'

She bristled a little, perhaps at the implication that she may not have looked for her own daughter. Before she could speak, though, Fleming raised a placatory hand.

'I'm sure you checked already, but sometimes we get called out to houses and the child in question is hiding somewhere inside. Sometimes they enjoy all the fuss and attention of people searching for them. It won't take long.'

'Please yourself,' Sinead Finn said. 'I've looked for her already.'

'I understand,' Fleming said, attempting a smile. Not quite managing it. 'A fresh pair of eyes and that. How about you sit and tell me a bit more about Sarah? Give us a sense of who she is.'

Chapter Twenty

Lucy went to the rear of the ground floor first and worked her way up. The back room was a small toilet, plain. A raft of coats hung on coat pegs screwed to the wall. She patted through the coats; just to be sure Sarah wasn't in there. The kitchen and dinette were next. There were precious few places where a fifteen-year-old girl could hide.

The kitchen itself was small, something accentuated by the amount of stuff cluttering the worktops. The remains of a Chinese takeaway from the previous evening congealed to two plates. The tinfoil trays remained, half filled, among the torn scraps of a brown paper bag. Two wine bottles sat next to them; one empty, the other perhaps a quarter full. Two glasses sat beside it. The sink was filled with older dishes again: a pan with spaghetti sauce hardened to the surface, a scattering of plates and cups beneath it, forming a pyramid of crockery that spilled over onto the draining board.

The next room was the sitting room where Fleming and Sinead Finn sat. Lucy could hear a snippet of the conversation as she passed the room and headed up the stairs to check the first floor.

The upper floor had two bedrooms and a bathroom. The bathroom was to her left. She took a quick look in; nothing out of the ordinary. A white T-shirt and a pair of boxer shorts lay discarded behind the door, nestled on top of a sodden bath towel.

Lucy stepped across to the glass above the sink which held toothbrushes and paste. Three brushes. Assorted pieces of make-up were scattered across the windowsill.

Moving back out to the landing, she glanced into the next room, knocking on the door as she did so. It was, presumably, Sinead Finn's bedroom. A double bed with the clothes spilling onto the floor. A pint glass of water sat on the bedside cabinet on one side, a crowded ashtray on the other. The face of the old-style alarm clock behind it was magnified through the glass. Lucy picked her way across and, lifting the clock, checked the alarm time: 4.30 a.m. As she replaced the clock on the cabinet, she noticed a number of small oval scorch marks blackening the cabinet surface.

Two built-in wardrobes faced the bed. Lucy checked the first. A smattering of shirts and jeans, all male. Two pairs of sneakers sat on the floor.

The dressing table between the wardrobes held more cosmetics and a large pine jewellery case, so full that the lid did not close properly. The second wardrobe contained Sinead Finn's clothes, crammed tightly together in the space; Lucy struggled to make room to check that Sarah was not hiding behind them.

Finally, Lucy dropped to the floor and checked under the bed. Another pair of trainers, a used condom folded on itself, a spoon, lying face down, the curve of its back blackened with soot. Quickly she got up again, wiped her hands on her trouser leg.

The room next door was clearly Sarah's. It was simply furnished. A single bed, white wooden frame. A desk and a wooden chair. A single standing wardrobe. A small cabinet beside the bed on which sat another alarm clock with a space on top for docking an iPod. Instinctively, Lucy checked the alarm time on this: 7.30 a.m. The alarm was turned off.

The bed was neatly made, the pink duvet something Lucy would have expected in the room of a child many years younger than Sarah Finn. Again, she glanced under the bed, but the space was empty.

She opened the wardrobe. Fewer clothes hung in this compared to Sinead's. But what was there was hung neatly, first tops, then jumpers, then jeans. No dresses or skirts, Lucy noticed. Mind you, she didn't wear either that often herself.

'Are you lost up there?'

Lucy looked out to see Sinead Finn mounting the final steps onto the landing.

'I'm almost done. Is there anything missing from her room? Anything obvious?'

The woman stepped into the bedroom and glanced around, mouthing quietly to herself as if counting off items on a list. 'She's an old rabbit sits on her bed,' she said finally. 'That's about all.'

'An old rabbit. A toy?'

The woman snorted lightly. 'Aye. An ole white thing her father gave her. She'd taken it down from the attic a few weeks ago and started sleeping with it.'

'Any reason why?' Fleming asked.

'Why what?'

'Why she started sleeping again with a childhood toy?'

The woman looked at him, then shrugged, pulling her dressing gown around her as she did. 'I dunno,' she said.

Chapter Twenty-one

Fleming stood at the door of the car, waiting for Lucy to unlock it. 'What's your feeling?'

'Hard to say,' Lucy commented. 'She could have run away if she's taken the rabbit toy with her.'

'Though we need to get to the bottom of what made her start sleeping with it.'

'Maybe she missed her dad,' Lucy offered.

'Maybe,' Fleming agreed, though he sounded unconvinced. Lucy was well aware what he was thinking; older children regressing to childhood toys in that manner could be an indicator of something more sinister.

'So, we know the mother started up with the new fella,' Lucy said. 'Maybe the girl was struggling with it a little.'

Fleming nodded. 'Follow up on the partner, Seamus Doherty. See if his work has a way of contacting him.'

'He has another place,' Lucy commented. 'The clothes in the wardrobe upstairs look like spares he keeps for when he stays over. He's living somewhere else.'

'Check again with Sinead Finn, see if she knows where else he might live.'

'And one of them is using heroin. I found works in their bedroom.'

'Of course you did,' Fleming said, shaking his head. 'That might explain why she didn't even notice if the wee girl hadn't come back last night. We'll do a sweep around of the local shops, see what people have to say. And try to find out whereabouts on the road to Manchester Mr Doherty is at the moment.'

They drove across to the small shopping area to the left of the local primary school. The block comprised a hairdresser's, post office, supermarket and chip shop. They decided Lucy might have best luck in the hairdresser's. Fleming volunteered to take the chippie.

As she approached the shops, she noticed a gang of teenagers standing on the corner of the block. She thought she recognized some of them as having been with Gavin Duffy when she saw him standing opposite Gene Kay's, but she couldn't be sure.

As she approached them, she realized that one of them was slightly older than the rest. The group fanned out behind him in a semicircle.

He raised his chin slightly at her approach and she recognized him as the one who had shouted and winked at her when she and Fleming had left Kay's house.

Lucy scanned the group behind him for Gavin but could not see him.

'I need some help,' she said.

The boy at the head of the gang smirked. 'Do you now?'

Lucy produced the picture of Sarah Finn and showed it to him. 'Do any of you know this girl? She's a local lass. She's missing.'

The youth shook his head.

'That's Sarah, Tony,' one of those behind him said, earning a scowl for the comment from the youth whom Lucy now took to be Tony.

'You do know her?'

Tony nodded. 'I know of her. She goes to the youth club times. That's all. We've not seen her in a while though.'

'We?'

Tony nodded towards those behind him. 'If they'd seen her, I'd have seen her.'

'Will you let someone know if you hear anything of her whereabouts?' Lucy asked. She pulled out her card, which Tony looked at but did not touch.

He nodded. 'We hear anything, we'll pass it on,' he said, then turned from her, indicating that, for him at least, their discussion was concluded.

As it turned out, Lucy was finished much sooner than she expected in the hairdresser's too. There were only two customers in there, neither of whom knew Sarah Finn. Like Tony and his gang, the girls working in the place knew her, but hadn't seen her in a few days. They did promise to keep an eye out for her. Similarly, the post office next door was quiet, with only two people in the queue ahead of Lucy.

The man behind the counter knew Sarah well, he said. She often came in on messages for her mum. She was a very sensible girl, he said. A little awkward, maybe. A little shy.

'Have you see her today?'

'No,' the man said. 'Not since yesterday afternoon. Why?'

'She's not come home,' Lucy said. 'Her mum's asked us to look out for her. If she comes in at all, can you give me a call?' Lucy handed the man the card Tony had refused to take through the gap at the bottom of the glass partition between them.

'Of course,' he said. 'You know the mother then?'

Lucy nodded. 'Mrs Finn contacted us about Sarah. She's very worried.'

'Mmm,' the man replied.

Lucy waited a beat to see if he would elaborate, but to no avail. 'What was Sarah in for yesterday?'

'She was taking money out for her mother,' he said. 'Her card account. She withdrew two hundred pounds from her child benefit account.'

'You've a good memory,' Lucy said. 'A police officer's best friend.'

'I remember that,' he said. 'Normally you wouldn't let a child withdraw that kind of money, but Sarah did a lot of that type of stuff for her mother.'

'I see,' Lucy said.

The man leaned closer to the glass. Lucy noticed his name tag resting against the partition. Ian Ross.

'Have you met the partner?'

'Seamus Doherty?'

Ross nodded. 'He's a strange one. Quiet. He's away a lot.'

Lucy nodded, leaning closer in the hope that Ross might elucidate, but the man simply nodded knowingly.

'Thank you, Mr Ross. That's very helpful.'

The man sank back to his stool. 'I'll call if I see Sarah,' he promised. 'I'll ask about too, with the customers.'

'That would be very helpful, Mr Ross,' Lucy said.

She headed back out to the car again, but there was no sign of Tom Fleming. The people in the corner shop must have been more talkative than he expected, she thought.

Ian Ross's comments had reminded her, however, that she was to follow up on Seamus Doherty.

She took out her phone and googled H. M. Haulage. The first result gave the contact details and a Google map of the office location in Coleraine.

A friendly sounding girl with a broad Ballymena accent answered the call almost immediately.

'Can I speak with Mr Martin, please?' Lucy asked, having introduced herself.

'With what is it in connection?' the girl asked.

'With a missing person inquiry,' Lucy replied tersely.

She was put on hold without further comment and for almost two minutes Lucy listened to an electronic version of 'Greensleeves'. Given the choice, she'd rather have listened to silence while she waited.

Finally she heard a click and Harry Martin introduced himself. His voice was deep, gruff, his accent a little closer to home, as best Lucy could tell.

'Yes, Inspector Black,' Martin said. 'You needed to speak to me.'

'It's Sergeant,' Lucy said. 'Thanks for your time. I'm trying to contact one of your drivers, Seamus Doherty.

His mobile phone is out of network apparently. I was wondering if you might have some kind of system where I could contact him in his lorry.'

'We do,' Martin said. 'But I'm not sure how much use it will be. Seamus isn't out today.'

'His partner told us he left at five this morning for a trip to Manchester.'

'Not for me, he didn't,' Martin said. 'We don't have any contracts in Manchester.'

Chapter Twenty-two

Fleming appeared out of the chip shop a few minutes later, carrying two small brown bags in his hand.

'Lunch,' he said, tossing one of them to Lucy.

'It's gone three, sir.'

'Dinner, then,' Fleming said.

'Bit early for chippie grub, sir,' she commented, opening the bag. A floury bap sandwiched sausage, bacon, egg and potato bread. 'Mind you, I did have an early start.'

Fleming had already started into his own, chewing happily, his cheeks dimpled with dollops of tomato ketchup.

'Seamus Doherty's not in Manchester,' Lucy said, opening her own bap and peeling the rind of fat off the bacon, before replacing the upper part of the bread and taking a tentative bite.

'Where is he then?' Fleming managed through a mouthful of food.

Lucy shrugged as she chewed. 'Not where he said he would be.'

'And not answering his phone. Get the details of his lorry and organize a Be On Look Out.'

Lucy nodded. 'I'll have to ask Mrs Finn.'

'What did the boss say about Doherty? Anything useful?'

Lucy shrugged. 'Not much. Just they don't have contracts in Manchester. He said if he was going there, it wasn't for his company.'

'So either he's driving for someone else, or he's been lying to Finn every time he's told her he's doing a Manchester run. Sound her out on that too.'

'Yes, sir,' Lucy said. 'I spoke to the fella in the post office too. Sarah withdrew £200 from her mother's child benefit account yesterday afternoon.'

Fleming slowed in his chewing. 'Check if the mother knew. If not, the wee girl's run away.'

Lucy nodded agreement.

'The shop was useless,' Fleming added. 'But the chippie proved more useful. And not just for these. The owner's daughter was working in the place. She's a friend of Sarah's.'

Lucy understood why Fleming had bought food now. It gave him an excuse to stand longer, encouraging the girl to talk while the food was prepared.

'Sarah wasn't at the youth club last night. She had to go out with her mother and Seamus Doherty for dinner. Because he was headed away for the week today.'

'A week to go to Manchester?'

Fleming raised his eyebrows as he popped the final mouthful of his bap into his mouth. 'So she lied to both her mother and her friends. Plus she got herself a new phone a few weeks back. The girl has given me the number. Compare with the one the mother has and see if she knew about the phone,' he added, handing her a torn corner of a brown paper bag on which the number was written.

Lucy's mobile phone rang. It was the desk sergeant in Maydown, confirming that a team of uniforms had been dispatched to Finn's house to begin house-to-house inquiries.

'Best head back and meet the team,' Lucy said.

They met the teams outside Sinead Finn's house. Fleming split the uniforms into pairs and divided up the local housing estates around Fallowfield Gardens into six blocks, one for each pair. One of the men had brought copies of the picture Lucy had sent into the station.

'Meet back here at 5.30,' Fleming said. 'And call either myself or DS Black if you find anything. I'm going to call down to the youth club just to double-check Sarah definitely wasn't there last night.'

As the pairs dispersed, Lucy called back in with Sinead Finn. The woman opened the door, then hobbled back into the living room. She still had on the white dressing gown she'd worn earlier.

Lucy closed the door and followed her in. 'Any word?' she asked Sinead Finn's retreating back.

'Nothing,' the woman said. 'I've called all her friends. And her mobile, too,' she added. 'Nothing. No one's seen her. Her friends said she wasn't with them last night.'

131

'Can I check what number you're calling her on? Only one of her friends said she got a new phone a while back.'

'Not that I knew of,' Finn answered, opening her phone and checking the listing, before reading out the number. It did not match the one Lucy had been given by Fleming.

'I need a second,' Lucy said, calling ICS. She recognized Dave Cooper's voice when he answered, felt a little surprised at the pleasure it brought her.

'We've a second missing person,' she explained after introducing herself. 'The girl has a new phone ...'

'Like Karen Hughes?' Cooper asked.

'Maybe,' Lucy began. 'If I gave you the number, could you try tracing it?'

'No problem. I'll be quick as I can.'

Lucy thanked him after reading the number off the scrap of paper, then hung up. 'I've a few more questions,' she said, addressing Sinead Finn. 'Has anything like this ever happened before?'

Finn shook her head as she lowered herself into her seat. She pulled a pouffe across and raised her feet onto it. Lucy noticed balls of cotton wool between each of her toes. Her nails were freshly painted, having progressed on from doing her fingers.

'Never. She stayed out late at times, but she's a good girl. I never have no bother with her.'

'She went to the post office for you yesterday, is that right?'

Sinead struggled to remember. 'She might have. She ran jobs for me all the time. I've problems with my legs, you see.'

'I see. Sarah withdrew money from a child benefit account using your card yesterday,' Lucy said.

'Did she?' Finn looked towards the ceiling, trying to remember. 'I didn't ask her to do that.'

'A significant amount, Mrs Finn. Two hundred pounds. You're sure that wasn't for you?'

'Two hundred pounds?' Finn snapped. 'The wee bitch.'

Lucy bowed her head. 'You didn't—?'

'The post office shouldn't have given it to her. It's my account.'

'Apparently she did this for you a lot,' Lucy said.

Sinead gave a non-committal grunt.

'She told her friends she was going out with you and your partner for dinner last night, too,' Lucy added.

'We weren't going for dinner. I told you already – we ate here.'

'I know,' Lucy said. 'I'm just trying to be certain we have all the facts.'

'Well, where the hell is she then?' Sinead Finn said, her eyes glistening, as if, for the first time, she had begun to realize the seriousness of her daughter's absence.

'Did she have a boyfriend or anything?'

'She was fifteen for Christ's sake!'

Lucy wasn't sure how she was meant to interpret that and rephrased the question. 'Was there anyone she might have run off with? Taking the money and that suggests she might have had plans to go somewhere.'

'She'd mentioned the odd boy or two at the youth club, but no one special. Not that I remember.'

Lucy nodded. 'What about Facebook or Twitter? Did she have any friends on there?'

Finn shrugged. 'I don't know.' She leaned forward and picked up her cigarettes. Her dressing gown sleeve drooped over her hand and she slid it quickly up her arm with her free hand. For a second, Lucy caught sight of a network of small red scars on her inner forearm, then the sleeve slipped down and covered it again. Finn followed her line of sight, sniffed loudly, then wiped her sleeve across her nose.

'Do you have a computer that Sarah used?'

Finn shook her head. 'No. She used the ones in school or the club for school work and that.'

Lucy nodded. 'Have you had any luck with contacting your partner? Mr Doherty?'

Sinead Finn shook her head. 'He's going to message. And I've texted him. Maybe he doesn't want to answer when he's driving.'

'Maybe,' Lucy repeated. 'Does he go to Manchester often?'

Finn shrugged. 'Every few weeks. Sometimes he has other runs to do too – Dublin, Cork or that. But he'd do Manchester once or twice a month.'

'Always for a week?'

Finn raised her left shoulder. 'I guess. Why? What's that to do with Sarah?'

'Probably nothing,' Lucy said.

By five it had already become clear that Sarah Finn was not in the immediate vicinity. All her friends had been contacted; none had seen her since the previous day. The youth club leader, Jackie Logue, confirmed she had been absent the previous evening, which was, by his account, quite unusual.

'It's a bit of a family here,' he had told Fleming. 'I think Sarah loved coming and seeing everyone. She didn't get involved so much, mind you. But she liked having people around her, even if she didn't chat too much.'

The neighbours had not seen her, though all concurred with the general consensus, which was that she was a quiet girl. Friendly, but shy.

Fleming ordered for the search to be widened. Press releases were drawn up and distributed to the local radio and news stations ahead of a press conference the following day if Sarah had not returned.

Hospitals and doctors' clinics were already being contacted by uniforms in the Strand Road, though as yet had yielded no results.

Lucy and Fleming had just met back at Finn's when Lucy's mobile rang. It was Cooper.

'Lucy. The phone number you gave is ringing out. But I've been able to trace its position from the GPS in it. It's along the Glenshane Road. It seems to be in a picnic area, just opposite the turn-in for the Old Foreglen Road.'

'I know it,' Lucy said. 'Thanks, Dave.'

'Lucy,' Cooper added grimly, 'the phone isn't moving.'

Chapter Twenty-three

The lay-by in question was a popular one with long-distance lorry drivers. A small burger van squatted at one end, the owner seated in front of a portable TV, the fryers behind him empty.

He stood up when he saw the police cars pull in, reaching for the bag of cut chips and pouring them into the fryer basket in the expectation of business.

Three teams poured out into the lay-by. Fleming directed them to different sections of the space. They moved off to work quietly, all expecting to find not just Sarah's phone, but possibly the child herself.

Beyond them, the mass of the Ness Woods loomed, the dying light already darkening between the trees. To the west, three huge wind turbines stood on the hill to their left, where a mist had already begun rolling down into the Ness valley. Behind them, the dying light of the sun, already passed below the horizon, scorched the top of the hill, the shape of the turbine arms standing above it, piercing the mist, itself like molten gold inside the sunset, the whole image like Golgotha ablaze.

'It's beautiful,' Fleming commented, standing beside her, watching the scene.

'It is,' Lucy agreed.

'Why is every nice place you see tainted with the shit of what happens there?' he asked.

'Inspector,' a voice shouted. They looked across to where one of the officers stood, having emptied out the contents of one of the litter bins spotted around the area. He held, in his gloved hand, a black iPhone.

Lucy reached the man first, already pulling on her own gloves. She pressed the home button and saw that there were twelve missed calls. She unlocked the screen. The main wallpaper image was of a small cat. Clicking on the photo icon, she scrolled through the assorted images. Sure enough, there was picture of Sinead Finn and, in one, reflected in a mirror due to the angle of the shot, Sarah Finn herself could be seen.

She moved back to the home screen. A red numeral 1 over the message icon showed she'd an unread message. Lucy opened it. The name Simon H appeared at the top of the screen. 'We still OK for 8?' the most recent message read. It had been sent at 2.30 p.m.

'Get it down to ICS straight away,' Fleming said. 'See if someone there can't get something from it.'

'Wait,' Lucy said. 'Let me check something.' She scrolled up to the top of the page and clicked on the contact details for Simon. The next page listed his name, picture, email and number. The email address was a Facebook one. The name on the account was 'Simon Harris'.

Lucy opened her own phone and called Cooper.

'We got the phone,' Lucy said, without introduction. 'But I need you to do me a favour. "Simon Harris" – the one on Facebook this morning. Can you get up his picture and send it to me?'

'Give me a minute,' Cooper said.

It took less than that for a text message with the picture attached, photographed from the screen of Cooper's computer, to beep on Lucy's phone. She opened the message and compared the image to the picture Sarah had assigned to Simon H. It was the same picture.

'Shit,' Lucy muttered. 'It's one of the sock-puppet accounts belonging to Paul Bradley.'

Fleming took the phone and scrolled through the messages again. 'He's asked her to meet him tonight five times today. If he's doing that ...'

'She's not with him,' Lucy concluded.

'And he doesn't know she's vanished,' Fleming said.

Lucy thought for a moment. 'He wants to meet her tonight,' she said. 'So why don't we arrange it?'

Chapter Twenty-four

'It's too dangerous,' Burns said, stooping to lean on the table at which the rest of the Hughes Inquiry team, along with Lucy and Fleming, sat. Lucy glanced at Fleming, who stifled a yawn, earning a dirty look from Burns. 'We're working on the theory that "Harris" doesn't know she's vanished. For all we know, he could have picked her up somewhere since that last message was sent.'

Lucy accepted the point with a nod. 'But if he doesn't realize that she's gone, we could set up a sting and catch him. If "Harris" *is* Paul Bradley, we'll have Karen's killer, too.'

'It's a big if,' Mickey commented.

'Not according to ICS,' Fleming countered. 'The scrap metal thieves reported seeing someone in a red car leaving the scene where Karen was left. So, we make contact with "Harris", arrange a pick-up point, then watch from a safe distance. If someone does turn up in a red car, we tail them and see what we get.'

'This is all based on the belief that Gene Kay is not Karen's killer,' Burns said. 'Kay who is still sitting in one of our holding cells.'

'Has he said anything to make you think he is guilty?' Fleming asked.

Burns shook his head. 'The phone was unusable, so we don't know whether he was on Facebook or not. He claims he was taking snaps of a group of girls sitting at the table opposite.'

'Can we not do him for that?'

The door opened suddenly and Lucy felt her stomach sink as she recognized the slim figure of her mother stride into the room.

'ACC Wilson,' Burns said, straightening. 'Good evening, ma'am.'

'Mark,' Wilson said. 'Good evening folks,' she added, glancing around the table. Her gaze lingered a moment on Lucy, or, at least, so it seemed to her. 'Any progress on the Hughes killing?'

Burns exhaled sharply. 'We've a bit of a breakthrough. But a second girl has gone missing in Gobnascale.'

'Sarah Finn,' Wilson said, nodding. 'Are they connected?'

'The PPU team managed to locate her phone in a lay-by near the Ness Woods. She appears to have been receiving text messages from a "Simon Harris", which ICS believes is one of the sock puppet accounts owned by Paul Bradley, our suspect in the Hughes case.'

'How far back do the messages go?'

'A few months,' Burns said. 'Classic grooming pattern. They seem to have arranged to meet with some regularity for the past eight weeks, one night a week.'

'So?'

'"Harris" has texted several times today asking the Finn girl to meet him tonight.'

'So he doesn't know she's gone missing?'

'Possibly,' Burns said.

'I think Sarah has left with her mother's partner,' Lucy said, then realized that the others at the table had turned to stare at her. 'Ma'am,' she added.

Wilson nodded again. 'By force or choice?'

'We don't know yet, ma'am,' Fleming said. 'DS Black is trying to locate the partner. He's told the girl's mother he's in Manchester with work, but the work says he's not.'

'So are you going to agree to meet with "Harris"?' Wilson asked. 'I assume that's the topic of discussion here.'

Burns nodded. 'It does run the risk of alerting the suspect to the fact we have his alias.'

'The debacle in the Foyleside today has probably already done so,' Wilson said. 'Very publicly. My feeling is that it's worth the risk. The worst that will happen is that he doesn't turn up. What time was the last message sent to Sarah's phone?'

'Two thirty, ma'am,' Burns said.

'Was that before or after we lifted Kay?'

'Around about the same time,' he admitted. 'But we've not been able to connect Kay to Karen Hughes's killing yet.'

'I think the decision's clear then,' Wilson said. 'I'll see you when you're finished, Mark. Maybe I could have a quick word with DS Black,' she added, standing up to leave.

'Of course, ma'am,' Burns said.

Lucy pushed back her chair to stand while Tara, sitting next to her, leaned closer to her. 'Good luck,' she whispered.

Wilson was standing in the corridor when Lucy left the room. She nodded across to Burns's office which lay empty and led Lucy in.

'So how are things, Lucy?'

'Fine, ma'am.'

Wilson nodded, as if this was the response she'd expected. 'How's the PPU treating you?'

Again. 'Fine.'

'Have you seen your father recently? How was he?'

Lucy was unsure what to say, aware that both of them knew of her father's troubled past. 'He's fine. Considering what he did.'

Wilson nodded lightly. 'Yet you still visit him?'

Lucy folded her arms. 'Someone has to. Or he'd be completely on his own.'

'I see,' Wilson replied.

'If you're that interested, he's getting worse actually.'

'I'm sorry to hear that,' Wilson said.

'Really?'

Wilson sighed. 'Must every exchange we have be adversarial, Lucy? It's getting a little tiring.'

Lucy shrugged, aware that any further comment would seem petulant. She waited for her mother to speak, studying her face. She'd cropped her hair again, in a manner that accentuated the sharpness of her features. Instinctively, Lucy touched the ends of her own hair, aware, again, that the gamine cut had actually made her look more like her mother. She was more concerned that the similarity between them might run deeper than simply how they looked.

'What did you want to see me about?' she asked, keen to dismiss that last thought.

'I understand you assaulted a suspect during the arrest of the metal theft gang this morning. Is that right?'

'I inadvertently stepped on his hand,' Lucy said, not quite meeting her mother's stare. 'It was an accident.'

'Nothing to do with the theft of railings off a grave then?'

'Who told you that?'

'Never mind. Did you assault a suspect for stealing railings off a grave? Yes or no?'

'Dad was asking about the fountain in the house down the lane the last time I saw him,' Lucy said, using a trick of her mother's, shifting the conversation from the professional to the personal without warning. 'That place is a prison.'

'Then he deserves it,' Wilson countered, unfazed by the attempted distraction. 'You've not answered my question.'

'It was an accident,' Lucy said.

'I hope so,' her mother said. Her expression softened a little and she sat in Burns's chair. 'Close the door and sit down.'

Lucy shut the door, but contrarily remained standing.

Her mother looked up at her, waiting for her to sit, then continued regardless. 'How is Tom Fleming? I understand there was an incident at his house this morning, too?'

'He seems fine. You'd be best to ask him about anything that happened at his house.'

'I will. I thought I'd ask you first, since you were the officer who called it in,' Wilson said. 'So what happened to him?'

'He overslept,' Lucy said. 'Didn't hear the alarm.'

Wilson shook her head. 'I see. Nothing's easy with you, Lucy, is it? How's the boyfriend then? Are you still doing a line?'

Lucy suppressed a cringe at the twee comment. 'Broken off,' she said.

'I'm sorry to hear that. What happened?'

'We had a difference of opinion.'

'About?'

'Monogamy,' Lucy said, refusing to explain any further.

'I see,' Wilson replied. 'That's a pity.'

'What about you?' Lucy countered, reflecting on the gossip Tara had shared about her mother and the new Chief Super. 'Still seeing Mark?' Her mother stared at her quizzically. 'The night I stayed with you, you said your partner's name was Mark.'

'Ah. Same name, different man.'

'Is it Chief Super Burns by any chance?'

Wilson took off her glasses. 'That's a dangerous rumour to be spreading,' she said.

'I'm not spreading anything. I just asked. You asked about my love life, I asked about yours. You don't have to explain yourself to me. God knows, that was never a consideration before.'

Wilson allowed herself a brief, brittle smile. 'It's always a pleasure catching up with you, Lucy,' she said.

Chapter Twenty-five

The team was dispersing by the time Lucy made it back into the room. A few of them glanced at her as she entered, and she guessed from their expression, half pitying and half elated, that they thought she'd been called out by the ACC to be chastised.

'If you don't want anyone to know she's your mother, maybe you oughtn't to talk to her in public as if she is,' Fleming commented when she moved across to him.

'I'll bear that in mind,' Lucy muttered brusquely.

Tara approached them a little diffidently, her papers clasped against her chest by her crossed arms. 'Everything all right?' she asked. 'With the ACC?'

'Fine,' Lucy said, still angry that Tara had told Burns about her questioning a suspect over the stolen railings.

It was clearly on Tara's mind too. 'Was it about this morning?'

Fleming glanced up at the two of them sharply. Lucy suspected he'd guessed at the real topic of the conversation.

'I stood on a suspect's fingers during an arrest,' Lucy explained quickly, not wishing her boss to think that she'd been discussing him with her mother.

'I didn't think Burns would say anything, you know?' Tara said, touching Lucy lightly on the arm with one outstretched hand.

'It's fine,' Lucy repeated. 'I know you need to impress the new Super,' she added dryly.

'It wasn't like that,' Tara said. 'We don't all get private audiences with the ACC, you know.'

The comment caught Lucy off guard. Did Tara know that Wilson was Lucy's mother? Maybe Fleming was right about her attitude to the woman.

'We're together on this tonight,' Fleming said quickly, providing a diversion for which Lucy felt most grateful. 'DI Burns has replied to the text message as Sarah, telling "Harris" that she'll meet him. "Harris"'s messages in the past suggested several times that they meet at the entrance to Glenaden Industrial Estate. Burns reckons that's their usual pickup spot. We're to be parked down at the Northern Bank opposite the hospital to pick up "Harris"'s tail if he goes that way.'

Lucy knew the spot. It wasn't far from the residential unit where Karen had been. It also afforded "Harris" a choice of directions to go. Along the Belt Road, he could go west back into Gobnascale, or east towards the hospital, with smaller roadways leading off into the Waterside or out towards Ardmore. There were potentially four different directions he could take. Added to that, they didn't have a great description of the car save for that it was red and small, like a Fiesta.

'We'd best grab something to eat,' Fleming said. 'Before we take up our positions.'

Tara joined them for food – burger and chips from the chippie across from the station – clearly in the hope that Lucy would eventually forgive her for having betrayed her to Burns. It meant that Lucy and Fleming were not alone again until they climbed into her car to head up to the spot to which they'd been assigned to wait for 'Harris'.

'So how was ACC Wilson?' Fleming asked for the second time as they pulled out onto the roadway past the thick metal gates which had rolled back to allow them exit.

'Fine,' Lucy said, reflecting that she really needed to find an alternative statement of non-comment. 'Good.'

'Anything wrong?'

'Nothing,' Lucy replied. Though Fleming knew that Wilson was her mother, he'd never asked before when she'd spoken to her. Lucy wasn't sure whether to tell him that her mother knew about the incident in his house, or whether to leave it lest he react badly.

'Personal stuff, or ... work related?'

'Personal stuff,' Lucy agreed.

'Not the suspect's hand then?'

'No,' Lucy said.

'I take it she knows about this morning then?' he said finally.

Lucy looked across at him. 'I'm sorry, Tom. I didn't say anything, I —'

Fleming held up his hand in placation. 'It was bound to get back to her. An ambulance being called for an officer. Especially one in the state I was in.'

'If I'd known, I wouldn't have called them,' Lucy said. 'I panicked.'

'It's done now,' Fleming said. 'You did what you thought was right. I'll give you a key the next time.'

'Will there be a next time?' Lucy ventured.

'Probably not,' Fleming said.

Lucy nodded, though she realized he couldn't see the movement, staring as he was out the side window now.

'Is everything all right?' Lucy asked. 'Is there anything I can do?'

He glanced across at her, as if evaluating the sincerity of the question.

'My ex-wife has moved away,' he said. 'She and her new husband. They've emigrated to Australia for a few years. Part of his job.'

'I'm sorry to hear that,' Lucy said. Fleming had mentioned his wife once before, when telling Lucy about his losing his licence. It was the only time he'd ever spoken about his family.

'Oh, I don't give a monkeys about her going,' he said, smiling sadly. 'She's taken our daughter with her.'

'I didn't know you had a daughter, Tom,' Lucy said.

'Megan,' Fleming said. 'She's fifteen.' He obviously read the expression on Lucy's face, for he added, 'I married late.'

'I didn't say a word.' Fleming had been a colleague of both Lucy's parents, which suggested he was in his fifties by now.

'Nor did you need to, Sergeant,' Fleming said with a brief laugh, stressing Lucy's rank.

'I'm sorry to hear that though.'

Fleming nodded, dragged his hand down his face, as if wiping sleep from his eyes.

'They won't be here for Christmas then?'

Fleming shook his head. 'No. The tickets are cheapest in November, because no one wants to travel then apparently. They had to leave last month or it would have cost them an extra three grand.'

'I'm sorry,' Lucy repeated.

'What about you, Lucy? Any plans for Christmas?'

Lucy shook her head. 'I'll visit my dad. Eat crap and watch TV.'

'We're doing a soup kitchen,' Fleming said. 'My church. We're doing Christmas dinner for the homeless and that. You'd be welcome to come along if you wanted some company.' Lucy had forgotten about Fleming's conversion. He'd mentioned to her before that he'd found God after he swore off drink. It appeared that the two were not mutually exclusive.

'Thank you, Tom. I might,' Lucy said, quietly thinking that the last thing she felt like at Christmas was company.

'Bear it in mind, Lucy,' he added. 'If you're stuck.'

Chapter Twenty-six

The car park at the Northern Bank was deserted, the area afforded some shade from the street lights lining the roadway by the overhanging branches of the fir trees bordering the garden to the rear of the building. Lucy and Fleming were parked off the eastern side of a crossroads, along any arm of which the car might approach. The cold had already begun to sharpen, the bonnet of the car sparkling with the first frost fall. Fleming turned up the heat, wrapped his coat around him and sat back in his seat.

'I *am* sorry about this morning,' Lucy said, finally.

'Forget it. I'd have done the same,' he admitted.

They sat in silence for a few moments, watching the clock's display flicker towards eight. Finally, Lucy clicked on the CD player but there was nothing in it, being an unmarked squad car and not her own.

Just then, the radio buzzed into life.

'Movement at the estate,' Burns said. 'We've a red car passing. Looks like two people inside. Can someone pick up their tail?'

A click responded in the affirmative, then Lucy heard Tara's voice. 'They're turning in towards the Waterside. We have them, sir,' she said.

A moment later, Tara spoke again. 'They've turned in at Next, sir. An elderly man and woman.'

'Get their names,' Burns said. 'The guy at the park had grey hair apparently.'

'This one has *no* hair, sir. He's bald.'

Fleming snorted quietly.

'Get the car details, at least. We'll follow up on that.'

'Another vehicle.' Mickey's voice crackled through the speaker. 'Red Corsa. Old model. Approaching from Ardmore.'

This meant the car was coming up the southern approach to the crossroads, running just behind the bank where Lucy sat. Mickey's team was placed in the car park of a pub halfway up that roadway.

'He's indicating to turn left.' Towards Glenaden. 'Should we follow?'

'Hold your place,' Burns said. 'If he sees the girl's not there, he may head back the way he came and you can pick him up then.'

Lucy found herself craning to try to see past the tree line, which was obscuring her view of the entrance to the industrial park a few hundred yards further along the western arm of the crossroads.

'It's slowing,' Burns said. 'He's approaching the entrance. He's moved off again, towards Gobnascale. Someone get ready to pick him up.'

'He's turning,' another voice cut in. 'I think he's heading back for a second look.'

Lucy, unable to wait, opened the door of the car and stepped out, then moved across to the pavement, past the tree line, where she could better see what was happening. In the distance she could see the lights of the car as it completed a U-turn and came back towards the industrial estate. Towards her.

'If he cuts back down towards Ardmore, pick him up Mickey. PPU, be ready to assist.'

Fleming leaned out of the door. 'Get in. We're to pick up with the Ardmore team.'

Lucy watched the car speeding up as it drove away from the estate. 'He's not turning in,' she muttered, slipping as she turned to get back into the car. Sure enough, a second later, Mickey's voice. 'He's passed our turn-off,' he said. 'He's on his way towards the bank.'

'PPU, pick up; Mickey assist.'

Lucy started the engine and pulled out to the entrance of the car park, just as the red car pulled up at the junction next to where they sat. The driver, an older man, jowly, looked both ways to see if the path was clear. For a second, he caught Lucy's eye, held her stare, then he pulled out quickly into the traffic, without waiting for a gap, causing an ambulance, coming out of the entrance to the hospital on the other side of the junction, to have to swerve to avoid him.

'He's running,' Lucy said, pulling out herself into the middle of the traffic in pursuit, the blur of wailing horns in her wake.

Fleming, meanwhile, lifted the radio. 'Red Corsa. NHZ 4635. Can we get details on the owner?'

The car in question accelerated towards the roundabout at the hospital. A left turn would take him

153

back towards where Tara's team would be approaching. Straight ahead would take him into the Waterside. Turning right would take him onto the dual carriageway, which would lead, eventually, to the Foyle Bridge. Without indicating, it was this path that he chose.

Lucy floored the accelerator, pulling onto the oncoming lane to get past a car struggling towards the roundabout, the L driver inside gripping the wheel with both hands as she stared out at them.

'He's on the Crescent Link,' Lucy reported. 'In pursuit.'

The Corsa swerved in and out of the traffic, which was moving its way slowly towards the Tesco store a mile or so further along the carriageway. Lucy followed suit, trying to keep visual contact.

'The car belongs to Peter Carlin,' Burns said. 'The address we have for him is 144 Foreglen Road. Where is he?'

Carlin was, at that moment, cutting across the two lanes of a roundabout at a shopping complex, shearing off the bumper of a car in front of him. For a moment, the drag of the impact seemed to slow him, then he accelerated again, the bumper bouncing in the roadway, effectively blocking one of the lanes, while the car to which it had been attached blocked the other.

'Go the other way,' Fleming shouted.

Lucy pulled onto the roundabout, cutting right, following the lane clockwise as the oncoming traffic pulled to a stop.

'Police,' Fleming shouted as he wound down the window. 'Move.' He leaned forward and flicked on the blue lights and siren. The cars slowly inched forward, allowing just enough room for Lucy to squeeze through and complete the circuit back onto the correct lane again. Carlin had made some distance on them now, though Lucy could see the blinking of his brake lights on the curve of the road in the distance as she slowed to avoid colliding with someone.

'He's heading towards the Foyle Bridge,' Lucy shouted. Again, the roundabout here would offer him a number of choices: left towards the Waterside, straight through onto the bridge and into the city, or right, out towards Strathfoyle and Maydown, where the PPU was based.

As Lucy passed a car on the inside, beneath the overhang of trees bordering one side of the carriageway, she felt the car shift slightly on the roadway. Ahead of them, Carlin pulled across onto the outer lane.

'He's not going into the Waterside,' Fleming said, pointing at the car. 'City or Strathfoyle, then.'

Lucy slowed as they approached the roundabout, its centre island so heavily planted with trees they could not see which direction Carlin had taken. A few seconds later, they saw the red Corsa appear around the other side of the curve and cut down right, towards Maydown. Lucy glanced in the mirror, saw the flickering blue of the other police cars appear behind her, then she accelerated again, pulling onto the roundabout.

She took the curve at speed, the car again sliding a little in the angle, leaving her having to overcompensate as she straightened up again to continue on the carriageway the Corsa had taken. This road was quieter at least, so it was easier to spot the Corsa ahead.

'We've teams coming up from Maydown,' Burns said. 'They'll get him along the road.'

Sure enough, a moment later, Lucy could see the strobing blue lights ahead. So too could Carlin, for all of a sudden he swerved to the left off the carriageway, pulling down Judge's Road, alongside the rugby club.

Fleming relayed this information through the radio.

'Keep on him,' Burns shouted.

'Really? I was planning on letting him go now,' Lucy muttered to herself.

Lucy followed Carlin, taking the turn sharply then having to correct her position quickly as the road curved again. To their left now, the dark mass of Enagh Lough, reflecting the clear sky above, was visible past the boughs of the massive trees lining the road's edge. Ahead, the red tail lights of Carlin's car disappeared around another bend.

Lucy slowed a little, taking the corner more gently than the last. As she did so, she and Fleming caught sight of the red Corsa, which was now careening along the straight stretch of road. Suddenly, the car swerved and mounted the narrow pavement bordering the roadway before breaking through the tree line at the edge of the road. It seemed to sit suspended for a second then fell forwards into the lough.

'Jesus,' Lucy screamed, slamming on her brakes, the car sliding towards the gap in the trees now.

As her car screeched to a halt, Lucy undid her seat belt and jumped out, Fleming following her.

Carlin's car was already beginning to sink. She could see Carlin winding at the window, trying to open it in order to escape the vehicle.

Without thinking, Lucy peeled off her coat and launched herself into the water. The cold winded her, causing her muscles to spasm. She breathed through it, her teeth gritted. She'd swum every morning for years while she'd been working as a fitness instructor before joining the police.

She pounded against the water, aware as she neared the car that it was slipping deeper into the water. Carlin had the window down now, and was fumbling with his seat belt, the cold presumably making it hard for his numbed fingers to release the clasp.

She neared the vehicle, reaching in and gripping Carlin's jumper, while she held on to the roof of the car. Too much of the vehicle was submerged now for her to try pulling open the door against the weight of water pressing against it. Dragging Carlin out through the window was the best option.

'Get out,' she shouted, as the front of the car dipped under completely, the boot rising slightly in the water.

'Peter, get out,' she repeated, pulling at his jumper.

The water was past his chest now, his chin breaking the surface as he tried to look down at the seat belt.

He looked at Lucy, his eyes wide, his mouth open. 'I can't free the belt.'

'Keep trying,' Lucy shouted. She let go of him and tried pulling at the door, but knew already that the water pressure would make it impossible to open.

Carlin was screaming now as he tried to pull at the seat belt The water filled his mouth, causing him to spit it out again, angling his head back to try to keep his mouth clear of the surface. But already the level was rising.

'I'm sorry,' he cried. 'The girls. I'm sorry for them all. But I didn't do the killing. I didn't kill anybody. Jesus, forgive me.'

'Any of who?' Lucy shouted. 'How many girls?'

Carlin had stopped fumbling with the seat belt now and had begun winding up the window as the car slipped further below the surface. He turned to look at Lucy as the glass slid up between them, catching her hand, trapping it between the glass and the rubber of the frame. His face was drawn with terror as he opened his mouth.

The car dipped further, the water lapping the roof now, as Lucy pulled to free her hand from the window.

Beside her, a figure appeared, his baton raised. Mickey beat at the glass until it shattered, freeing Lucy's hand. Then he gripped her around the chest from behind as he pulled her away from the bubbles that surfaced as the car finally slipped below the water, even as she fought to get back to Carlin.

Chapter Twenty-seven

Burns, Fleming and the ACC were in discussion in the CID suite when Lucy arrived back in the incident room. She'd been brought straight back to the station, dismissing suggestions she attend A & E and instead opting for a hot shower in the station's locker room and changing into a spare uniform someone had managed to find, her own clothes still soaked through from the lough. Tara, along with a few other members of the team, sat in the main incident room, sharing tea and sandwiches.

'Are you all right?' Tara asked when Lucy came in. 'Do you want tea?' she added, not waiting for a response to the first question.

'Please,' Lucy said. 'I'm grand,' she added.

'You're nuts jumping in after him,' Tara said.

'Nearly cost you and Mickey both your lives,' someone commented.

Lucy glanced around; it was Mickey's partner, the DC from Foyleside. She sensed from his tone that only one of those outcomes caused him concern. She was acutely aware all of a sudden that she was not one of them, not CID.

'It was instinct,' Lucy offered by way of explanation.

'Your instinct should be to stay alive,' he countered.

The door of Burns's office opened and he peered out. 'You're back,' he said, nodding at Lucy. 'All OK?'

'Fine,' she said, taking the tea which Tara was offering her.

'Bring it in here for a quick chat if you're feeling up to it,' Burns said.

Tara raised her eyebrows quickly at Lucy then moved away towards her seat again.

Burns held open the door for Lucy and, as she passed him, she caught the faint scent of his aftershave. When she entered his room, she saw her mother sitting behind his desk, while he and Fleming had clearly been sitting on the opposite side. There was only one spare seat.

'You sit,' Burns said. 'I'm good standing.'

Lucy thanked him and sat down, sipping from her tea. Tara had added extra sugar to it, its sweetness too sharp.

'DI Fleming has filled us in on what happened up to Carlin going in the water,' her mother began without preamble. 'Maybe you'd help fill in the rest of it for us.'

Lucy nodded, took a second mouthful of tea, then set the cup on the edge of the desk. She glanced at Fleming who smiled briefly.

'After I saw the car going in, I went in after it. It all happened very quickly. At first Carlin was trying to get out. His seat belt must have been stuck or something, because he'd wound down the window, but seemed to be fumbling with the belt. I tried dragging him out, but the belt prevented it. When he realized he was going down, he said he was sorry.'

'Sorry?'

Lucy nodded. '"I'm sorry for them all," he said. "But I didn't do the killing."'

'You're sure of that?' Wilson asked.

Lucy nodded, glancing at both Burns and Fleming, neither of whom had spoken. 'He said "them all" and that he hadn't killed them.'

'"Them" plural,' Burns commented. 'We know of Karen Hughes. Who is the rest of "them"?'

'And how many?' Fleming added.

Lucy watched Wilson. Her face, always sharp, had thinned. When she removed her glasses, two red ridges marked the sides of the bridge of her nose. She was still attractive, Lucy conceded, but she was beginning to show her age. Either that, or her position as ACC was beginning to tell on her.

'And, of course, if Carlin didn't kill "them", then who did?' she added.

'What's happening at the site?' Fleming asked.

'The car's being removed from the lough,' Wilson said. 'But it'll be morning before it's out. The underwater team has recovered Carlin's body and any obvious belongings. We've sent a team out to start searching the house on the Foreglen Road to see what they can find.'

'That's on the way to the Ness Woods, where the Finn girl's phone was found, isn't it?' Burns said.

'Yes. Though we have to work on the assumption that, if Carlin was trying to make contact with her, then he probably isn't the one who took her.'

'Nor was Kay,' Fleming said. 'Unless he took her in the middle of the night, disposed of her, and then went for coffee to photograph groups of girls.'

'Have we anything connecting Kay to Karen Hughes?' Wilson asked.

Burns shook his head.

'So, in fact, he might have nothing to do with Karen Hughes at all. His being in the centre might have been sheer coincidence.'

'I don't believe in coincidences,' said Burns defensively.

'Why not?' Wilson snapped. 'They happen all the time. Cut Kay loose then, pending a file on the images he's admitted to taking. If we can ever recover them,' Wilson added.

'What about Carlin?' Lucy asked. 'Does he have a record?'

Fleming shook his head. 'All low-level stuff. He was questioned about flashing at a school girl in the bus depot a few years back.'

'What happened?'

'He was warned off. Told to stay clear of the depot. He was occasionally visiting the community mental health team. He was deemed a vulnerable person.'

'Not that that necessarily makes him a predator,' Wilson said.

Fleming nodded in agreement.

'We'll see what the searches of the car and house throw up,' Wilson decided. 'As for the events of this evening, the Ombudsman will have to investigate Carlin's death. You'll need to make statements about the events. Best get it out of the way tonight, while it's fresh in your mind. I've already contacted their office to get someone down here to take initial statements.'

Lucy nodded. It was standard practice that the Ombudsman would investigate the death of an individual who'd had immediate prior contact with the police.

'If it turns out that Carlin was abducting and killing young girls, no one's going to mourn his death,' Burns said.

'Least of all Eoghan Harkin,' Lucy reflected. He'd asked for half an hour with the person who'd killed Karen. If Carlin had told the truth, that person was still walking free.

Wednesday 19 December

Chapter Twenty-eight

It was pitch black in her room when the phone woke her at 6.30 the next morning. She'd only been asleep for two hours, yet had dreamed again of Mary Quigg and the fire. It meant that it took her a moment to realize she was awake when, upon answering, she was told that Gene Kay's house was burning down. And that he was still inside it.

When Lucy arrived, a number of Land Rovers lined the roadway leading to the junction of the Trench Road. At first, Lucy couldn't understand what was preventing them moving closer to where Kay lived. Then, as she got out of her own car, she noticed the flaming carcass of a car, angled across the junction, illuminating the pre-dawn scene. Behind it, their features covered with scarves, their figures seeming to ripple and shimmer in the heated air that rose from the burning vehicle, Lucy spotted a crowd of a hundred or more youths, already dressed for battle. Occasional bottles and stones arched over the burning car, breaking through the thick plumes of black smoke and skittering impotently along the tarmac of the roadway. Only once did one explode with a hollow thud against the side of a Land Rover, the sound being greeted with cheers by those beyond the smoke. Despite the attempts to provoke a response from the PSNI officers, Lucy knew why her colleagues were holding back. Any heavy-handed attempt by the PSNI to break through the line of youths would be immediately politicized and could undo years of painstakingly developed cooperation between the residents in the area and the community policing teams.

'The fire service can't get in near it,' Fleming told Lucy after he spotted her among the gathered officers. 'They've gone up the other way and are coming down the Trench Road from the upper end. We're going to try to push through here when they arrive. Hopefully, the kids will be so focused on what's happened at this end as we come at them, they'll miss the fire crews coming from behind.'

'Any word on Kay?'

Fleming shook his head. 'A case of bad timing. He was released before midnight. The first word of the fire came from a neighbour about half an hour ago. The crew who did it probably didn't even realize that he was back in the house.'

As they spoke, Lucy noticed teams of officers, in Tactical Support gear, moving quickly into formation behind the Land Rovers. They heard the heavy clunk of the doors on the vehicles closing and the familiar roar of the engines as they came to life. The kids on the other side of the burning car must have heard it too, their ears well tuned through experience to the sounds of a gathering force. Lucy could make out, through the smoke, as they fixed their scarves around their lower faces, some passing round bottles and stones. She noticed a few of them huddling together, their backs turned to the officers, then saw the blooming of light between them as they ignited the first of the petrol bombs.

There was a thud as the first Land Rover pulled off the kerb, where it had been parked, and, revving its engine, it began moving towards the car, inching its way forward. It was clearly hoping to push the vehicle to one side, thereby allowing those vehicles and officers behind enough space to move towards the gathered crowd.

'The plan is to push the kids back down the Old Strabane Road and free up the junction so we can get to Kay. Tactical Support will hold them in bay once we get them shifted,' Fleming explained.

Stones began clattering against the armoured sides of the Land Rover now, a bottle shattering against the reinforced windscreen. Then the first of the petrol bombs was thrown. It had been sloppily packed, and the flaming rag became dislodged as it turned in the air, a horsetail of flame in its wake as its contents spilled, so that, by the time it hit, the flames it produced on the Land Rover's bonnet spluttered and quickly died.

The Land Rover pushed forward, its front grille now making contact with the burning car. The driver had approached at an angle so that, as he moved, the car shifted down to the right, into the junction.

Lucy glanced up to the left. She could see the flickering blue of the Fire Service vehicle lights intensify as it seemed to bounce off the gable walls of the houses beyond.

A sharp pop, followed by a cheer, brought her attention back to the scene in front of her. A petrol bomb had broken across the windscreen of the first Land Rover, leaving it ablaze. The driver turned on his wipers, scattering the fluid in flaming drops, to right and left.

She heard a faint whistle, then the body of officers moving silently behind the vehicles suddenly split, scattering in all directions. A moment later, a firework exploded on the tarmac where they had stood, in a ball of magnesium white. Another cheer from the crowd.

At a signal, several of the support vehicles drove around the front one and cut sharply towards the assembled kids, forcing them backwards, herding them down towards the Old Strabane Road, away from Kay's house, effectively hemming the crowd of youngsters in.

'Let's go,' Fleming said.

He and Lucy moved up quickly through the gap towards Kay's house. The Fire Service had already reached the street and was pumping water into the house. Another crowd had gathered here; spectators this time, watching with macabre fascination as, one by one, the windows at the front of Kay's house exploded with the pressure of heat ballooning from within. Some, though, were clearly neighbours driven from their own homes due to their proximity to the fire.

On the front of the house, sprayed in paint, blood red in the blue wash of light thrown off the fire tenders, were the words 'Paedos out!'

Kay's black dog, its fur soaked by the overspill from the flumes of water splashing against the window frames as the fire crew aimed their hoses, whimpered as it gingerly approached the front door of the house, then hastily withdrew before trying to approach again.

'The poor wee dog,' Lucy heard someone near her say as she passed. 'Someone should lift it.'

It was almost eight thirty before the blaze had been controlled to the point that the first fire crew struggled in through the remnants of the front door, the charred remains hanging off the still bright brass hinges.

The crowd had thickened now, including younger children stopping on their way to school gawping at the scene, necks craned to see past their parents who stood, in groups, commenting on the events, some in condemnation, many in quiet agreement with what had happened. Only the man who owned the house next to Kay's was receiving any sympathy from those around him.

After the first of the fire crew re-emerged from the remnants of Kay's house Lucy and Fleming moved across to where the men spoke with their District Commander, a man who Lucy had met once before outside the charred remains of Mary Quigg's home. If the man recognized her, he didn't show it. She, on the other hand, would never forget him.

'Well?' Fleming asked.

The man shook his head. 'One dead inside,' he said. 'Looks like a male.'

'That would be right,' Lucy said. 'Any sign of how it started?'

The man nodded towards the front of the house. 'Judging by the damage done to the door, it started there. I'd hazard we'll find it was petrol through the letterbox. The fire seems to have been most intense at the front of the house. We'll need to do a proper investigation once the whole place is clear, obviously, so this is just an educated guess.'

'But definitely started deliberately?' Fleming asked again.

The Commander nodded. 'Looks like you can add another murder case to your workload.' He pointed to the writing on the wall before adding, 'You'll not have far to look for motive, though, judging by the graffiti.'

As she was making her way back to her car, Lucy noticed a heavy-bodied man, his hair thick and white, standing speaking with two of the officers on duty at the cordon, which had been set up near the junction to keep the rioters contained. He moved away as she approached.

'Concerned resident?' Lucy asked one of the officers.

'Community leader,' he replied. 'That's Jackie Logue.'

Lucy shrugged. She'd heard the name recently, but couldn't place it.

'He runs the community up here. He's been talking to the kids since we pushed them back. Most of the wee shits have buggered off home thanks to him.'

172

'Ah,' Lucy said, remembering now that he was the one with whom Fleming had spoken about Sarah Finn in the youth club.

'Oh, Jackie's a legend up here. Voice of moderation. He's the reason why we can usually come in and out of here without what happened this morning happening.'

'So what was different this time?'

The uniform shrugged as he stepped away to speak to the driver of a car that had approached the tape, clearly hoping to be allowed access.

Chapter Twenty-nine

After nine, Lucy and Fleming returned to Sarah Finn's house. The mood in the house seemed to have changed from the previous day. Sinead Finn sat at the edge of the seat now, her knee jiggling up and down, one hand clutching her dressing gown shut, the other holding her cigarette.

'Was that pervert involved? The one they burned out down the road?' she asked, after Fleming had updated her on the previous day's events.

Fleming glanced at Lucy before answering. 'We don't believe so, Mrs Finn. No.'

'Well, where is she?' she asked, her hand extended, palm up, the cigarette clenched between her fingers. 'What are you doing to find her?'

'We believe she may be with your partner, Mr Doherty,' Lucy said. 'We've followed up with his work and they tell us that he isn't in Manchester.'

'What do you mean? Where is he then?'

'We hoped you might be able to help us,' Fleming said. 'Have you had any luck contacting him?'

The woman shook her head. 'I'd have said if I had, wouldn't I?'

'I noticed yesterday, when I was looking for Sarah,

that Mr Doherty doesn't keep many clothes here,' Lucy began. 'Does he have somewhere else he stays when he's not here with you?'

'He's at work when he's not here with me.'

'Not according to his employer. Can you give us the dates of his most recent trips?'

'Did he take my Sarah?' she asked, one eye weeping against the smoke that twisted in the air off her cigarette.

Lucy sat, while Fleming moved across to the window again, glancing out. Lucy suspected he was a little on edge following the riot; two officers split from the rest of their team were easy targets.

'We know Sarah went to the post office and withdrew £200. We know she lied to both you and her friends about where she was going the previous night. Both of those things would suggest that she was planning on going somewhere. Then your partner ups and leaves in the middle of the night, saying he's going to Manchester, but we know he's not. The lack of his possessions here suggests he has somewhere else where he stays. Either he has taken her, or else his leaving is purely coincidental.'

'Experience suggests that generally these things aren't coincidence,' Fleming commented. 'You must have some idea where else Mr Doherty might be. Where is he from? We have no records for him.'

'He grew up in Donegal, I think,' Finn said. 'I think he said he had a house in Foyle Springs, but I'm nearly sure he sold it.'

'Do you know his date of birth, Mrs Finn? We have over four hundred Seamus Dohertys on the system.'

Finn angled her head in thought, then finally shook it. 'He never told me.'

'Even his age,' Fleming said. 'That would be a start.'

Finn shrugged. 'In his forties, maybe.'

As they left Finn's house, Lucy phoned through to H. M. Haulage again. The secretary who answered told her that she couldn't speak to Mr Martin as he had meetings all morning.

'This is part of a child abduction investigation,' Lucy explained.

'Mr Martin was very clear that he wasn't to be disturbed,' the girl explained, stuttering slightly. Lucy guessed she was young, afraid to annoy the boss, not confident enough to use her common sense.

'I spoke with Mr Martin yesterday about one of your employees, Seamus Doherty. We're having trouble locating an address for Mr Doherty and we really need to find him. Would you have an address for him?'

'I really think you need to speak to Mr Martin,' the girl said. 'I'm not sure I can give that information out. How do I know you're a police officer?'

'You can call my station if you want,' Lucy offered. 'Look, tell you what, how about you give me his driving licence number? If I'm not police, there's nothing much I can do with that, is there?'

'Wait a moment,' the girl said, and 'Greensleeves' clicked into action. After a dozen renditions, the girl's voice cracked on the line.

'There's no one else here,' she explained. 'I'm not sure if ...'

'Look, it's fine,' Lucy said. 'All I need is the number.'

She glanced at Fleming who rolled his eyes exasperatedly.

'We have GB5786345 on record if that's any good.'

'That's perfect,' Lucy said, repeating it while Fleming copied it down. 'Thank you.'

Within minutes, they had called the number through to the station and been contacted to be told that Doherty's last recorded address was in Norburgh Park. They were also told that he had a record for assault following a bar brawl in Belfast in the late eighties. Beyond that, and a few speeding tickets in the mid-nineties, Doherty had stayed off the system.

They pulled up outside the house twenty minutes later. Initially, they believed the place to be empty. Lucy banged on the door several times while Fleming skirted the perimeter of the house.

'All the ground floor curtains are drawn,' he observed as he joined her at the front step.

'One window up the stairs is the same,' Lucy said, nodding up.

'So someone's probably home.'

Lucy nodded. 'I've knocked a few times.'

'Maybe he can't hear very well,' Fleming commented, hammering his fist against the door three times, so sharply it rattled in the frame.

'I think the people in the next street overheard that,' she said.

'And success,' Fleming added, nodding to where a figure could be seen moving down the hallway towards the door.

They heard the click of the dead bolt being drawn back, then the door opened slightly. The man who peered out through the opening allowed by the security chain between door and frame had black hair. He pulled a blanket around his shoulders as he hunched over, clasping the gathered corners at his throat.

'Yes?' he asked, nasally, before sniffing audibly.

'Mr Doherty?'

'Yes?'

'Seamus Doherty?'

The man shook his head. 'No. Ian,' he said, straightening slightly. 'What's wrong?'

'You're not Seamus Doherty,' Lucy stated, though the young man misread the tone and responded.

'No, I'm not. Why?'

'We're sorry to have bothered you,' Fleming said. 'We're looking for Seamus Doherty. We were given this address as his last known residence.'

'You've the wrong Doherty,' the man said, standing taller now, his voice noticeably clearer.

'Do you know the other Mr Doherty?' Lucy asked.

'I bought the house last year,' he replied. 'I know the last owner was called Doherty. There's some of his post lying in here. I gathered it up in case he ever called to collect it, but he never did. Junk mostly, I imagine.'

'Can we see it?'

The man glanced backwards, hesitating, then finally closed the door, undid the security chain and allowed them in.

As Lucy followed him down the hallway towards the kitchen, she caught a glimpse of a second figure, female, turning quickly from the top of the stairs. She too had been wrapped in a blanket.

'Your cold's improved,' Fleming commented, glancing around the kitchen as the man padded across to a black unit in the corner and began flicking through the piles of paper shoved into it.

'I've thrown a sickie to be honest,' the man said. 'I thought you were someone from my work.'

The creaking from the room upstairs as the man's partner climbed back into bed made it fairly obvious why he'd thrown a sickie. He blushed slightly as he handed them a pile of white and brown envelopes.

As he did so, Fleming's phone rang. He glanced at the screen and, excusing himself, moved into the hall. Lucy heard him begin the conversation with 'Yes, ma'am.'

'Can you remember who sold you the house?' Lucy asked as she glanced at the envelopes. The name on the address labels was Mr S. Doherty. 'Was it an estate agent?'

'It might have been,' he commented at last. 'O'Day, or something like that.'

'If you could try to remember, maybe you'd give me a ring,' Lucy added, handing the man her card with the PPU number on it.

Fleming reappeared in the doorway. 'We're wanted back in the station, DS Black,' he said. 'Thanks for your help, Mr Doherty.'

'Bad news?' Lucy asked, as they made their way back to the car.

'When your mother phones it's always bad news. They've been in Kay's house. They found his collection.'

Chapter Thirty

The CID team was gathered in the incident room in the Strand Road when Lucy and Fleming arrived. A black bin bag lay on the table, on top of which sat a large metal security file box with a lock to the front. It had already been opened and some of the contents removed.

The vast bulk of the images already arranged on the table were Category 9 or 10. The young people pictured in the ones Lucy saw as she glanced across the collection were girls, all teenagers. They were engaged in a variety of activities, the men in all cases unidentifiable due to the angles at which the images had been taken.

'I take it they survived the fire because of the metal box,' Fleming said, as he leaned over, scanning the images.

'They survived the fire because they were in the shed,' a voice said. Lucy turned to where her mother had entered the room. 'I'd like to see you for a moment, Inspector Fleming.'

Fleming glanced at Lucy and raised his eyebrows. She guessed why her mother wanted to speak to Fleming. The box was so big, Lucy wondered how he could have missed it when he'd claimed he'd searched Kay's shed. She suspected her mother would want to know the same thing.

She worked with the rest of the CID team, sorting through the images, attempting as best they could to organize them into piles, each one assigned to a different girl.

Within minutes, Lucy had found a picture of Karen Hughes. Shortly after, someone handed her an image that, they believed, was of Sarah Finn. Lucy studied the picture, blanking out the background, the position in which the youth was pictured, focusing only on the girl's face. She was pretty certain that it was indeed an image of Sarah. A second was handed to her; this time, it was a closer shot of the girl and there was no doubting her identity. Yet, while she was facing the camera, her eyes were downcast, as if unable to meet the stare of the one photographing her, his hand just visible under her chin as he tried to raise her head to take the picture.

'DS Black. The ACC wants to see you,' Burns called.

Lucy put the picture down, nodding to confirm that it was Sarah Finn, then moved gratefully away from the images and in to her mother.

'Sit down,' her mother said as Lucy entered Burns's office. 'Everything OK?'

'The collection out there. It's a little … disturbing.'

'We're lucky we got it finally. We can catalogue Kay's lists of abuse.'

'It's a little late,' Lucy said. 'Considering the bastard died.'

'I agree,' her mother replied. 'In fact that's what I wanted to ask you. We found the collection in the shed. Who searched there the day you were at the house?'

Lucy held her mother's stare. 'I don't remember. It could have been either of us.'

'Was it you?'

'I don't recall.'

The ACC nodded. 'DI Fleming has already confirmed that he was the one who checked.'

'Then why did you ask me?'

Wilson ignored the question. 'He's also already accepted that he missed it.'

'We all make mistakes.'

'Indeed. Though had we found this yesterday, Kay would be in a cell and facing justice. Instead we have to deal with what he did, the fallout from his being torched alive in his house, and a second Ombudsman inquiry in so many days.'

Lucy's phone began to ring. She pulled it out and saw Robbie's name on the caller ID. Apologizing, she switched it to silent and put it away again.

'I'd like to know again what happened yesterday morning in DI Fleming's house.'

'I'm not sure that's relevant to what we're talking about,' Lucy said quickly.

Her mother retorted, 'I decide what's relevant, Lucy. And I think it's completely fucking relevant that Tom Fleming was so insensible with drink yesterday morning that you called an ambulance for him. So drunk he didn't even hear his own burglar alarm going off. Yet he then comes into work and misses one of the biggest paedophile collections we've managed to find in years. Gene Kay is dead today because Tom Fleming was drunk yesterday.'

'That's a little unfair,' Lucy countered.

'It's very unfair,' Wilson agreed. 'On you, and me, and the rest of the teams working these cases.'

Lucy looked down at her hands folded in her lap. 'Looking at the images out there, I'd say Kay got what he deserved.'

'That's not our call to make,' Wilson snapped.

Lucy shrugged.

'Inspector Fleming will be suspended pending an investigation,' her mother said.

Lucy glanced up sharply. '*That's* not fair. He needs help.'

'You're not the only one who cares for Tom Fleming, Lucy.'

'You've a funny way of showing it.'

'I remember the *first* time he went through all this,' her mother snapped. 'I saw what it did to him. He needs time to go and get himself sorted out. That's what he'll get. Do you think sitting out there looking at that filth is going to help him dry out? It's no wonder he drinks.'

'Yet you put me in the PPU when I asked to go to CID,' Lucy retorted. 'So it's OK for me to look at them, is it?'

'Don't make everything about yourself, Lucy.'

Lucy swallowed her immediate response, not trusting that her mother wouldn't have her punished for insubordination. 'So what do I do while he's off?'

'The Finn case dovetails with the Hughes murder,' the ACC said. 'Continue to work the case and report to Chief Superintendent Burns.'

Lucy stood, saying nothing.

'I admire your loyalty, Lucy. In this case, though, Tom needs more than loyalty.'

'I wouldn't expect you to understand,' Lucy replied. 'After all, loyalty was never one of your strong suits, was it?'

Chapter Thirty-one

Burns was waiting when Lucy came out of the office.

'You've heard about Inspector Fleming, I assume,' he said.

Lucy nodded.

'Look, I'm sure you know what you're doing. I'd appreciate your help with following up on Carlin. Was he known to PPU?'

Before I drove him into a lough, Lucy thought, bitterly. 'I'd not come across him before last night, sir,' she said. 'Inspector Fleming is the obvious person to ask though.'

'We already have,' Burns said. 'He'd not heard the name before either.'

Lucy folded her arms across her chest, then, being suddenly aware of the defensiveness of the gesture, unfolded them, before finally clasping her hands behind her back.

'We know he was being supported by the Community Mental Health team. I'd like you to speak to his care worker there and see what you can find out. To fill in the background, you know.'

'What about the house, sir? Has anyone found anything there yet?'

'Forensics are doing a full sweep. It'll take a while before we get any results.'

The Community Mental Health team worked out of Rossdowney House in the Waterside. Lucy knew most of those who worked there, not least because many of the children in the residential unit had been referred to them at one time or another. When she arrived, she was told that she'd best speak with the unit psychiatrist, Noleen Fagan.

'Good to see you, Lucy. Long time,' Fagan said as she brought Lucy into her office. 'Grab a seat.'

The room was small, the walls lined with bookcases, the desk – a modern beech affair – overloaded with green and red files, many of them bulging to the point that elastic bands wrapped around them had been knotted together.

'How're things?' Lucy asked. 'I've not seen you in a while.'

'The Trust took all the older kids' cases off us,' Fagan said. 'A few years back, they widened the remit of the children's team to take up to eighteen. We're adult only now.'

Lucy nodded. 'That must make things easier.'

'No change ever makes things easier,' Fagan laughed. 'You must know that. How's the PPU treating you?'

Lucy thought of the images she had been examining half an hour earlier. 'The same as always,' she said. 'I've been dispatched to find out about Peter Carlin.'

Fagan nodded. 'I heard this morning. He drove into Enagh Lough, is that right?'

'By accident. We were pursuing him and he lost control, I think.'

'You think?'

'His car swerved. The road was a little slippy ...'

'But?'

'He was on a straight stretch.'

'You think he drove off deliberately?'

Lucy shrugged. She'd not mentioned it to anyone; there seemed little point. Still, she had wondered how he could have lost control on a straight road.

'Why were you chasing him? What had he done?'

'We think he was grooming teenagers online. Someone online who had created a range of sock puppet accounts groomed Karen Hughes, the girl found dead on the railway tracks. That same person arranged to meet another girl last night at eight o' clock. Carlin turned up at the meeting, then did a runner when he spotted us.'

Fagan listened, threading the pen in her hand from between one finger to the next as she did so. 'How many accounts?'

'We don't know for sure. Certainly more than a dozen.'

'Are you sure it was Peter Carlin who arranged all this?'

'It looks that way. We think he was working with Gene Kay.'

'The fire in Gobnascale? I heard that this morning, too.'

'They unearthed a collection of images in his house. Including some of both Karen and the girl Carlin had arranged to meet.'

'That might make more sense,' Fagan commented. 'Carlin had paedophiliac proclivities, certainly. But Peter Carlin couldn't have arranged a dozen fake identities, let alone have been able to manipulate a child through a process of grooming. Carlin had a fairly extreme dependent personality disorder.'

'A personality disorder? Would that not predispose him to something like this?'

Fagan shook her head. 'Carlin was intellectually limited, to put it mildly. More importantly, though, he displayed almost all the defining features of dependency: extreme passivity, tolerating abusive relationships in order to feel wanted; not trusting his own judgement on anything. He was pathologically indecisive, unless someone told him what to do. He'd come in here some days with two pairs of socks and ask me which I thought he should wear for the day. He'd never be able to start something off his own bat. He'd need to be told what to do, to the letter.'

'And he'd follow the direction because ...?'

'Because he had a need to be accepted. If Carlin was involved in what you're saying – and I've no reason to doubt you – then someone was telling him what to do. Someone powerful in his eyes, someone whom he trusted and whose approbation he needed. If anything, Peter Carlin would have been just another puppet.'

'Could it have been Gene Kay?'

'Maybe. I spoke with him a few times to do a psychiatric evaluation after his release from prison a few years back. He wasn't the most charismatic or trusting. He didn't strike me as the type to work with others. They'd make an unlikely pairing. That said, stranger things have happened.'

'So it's possible that Kay controlled Carlin?'

'It's possible,' Fagan conceded. 'Anything is possible. But I'd be fairly certain that the idea of Carlin grooming someone is a non-starter. Though if he did deliberately drive his car off the road, it would have been because someone told him to. There was no one in the car with him?'

Lucy shook her head.

'He wasn't on the phone with anyone? Perhaps he'd tried to contact someone if he was being pursued. He'd have needed someone to tell him to run.'

'And if they told him to drive his car into a lake?'

'If he admired them enough – was controlled enough by them – he'd do it.'

'Jesus,' Lucy said, standing. 'I almost feel sorry for him now. Almost,' she added.

Fagan smiled lightly. 'I was sorry to hear about Karen Hughes. I worked with her over the self-harming before she was transferred to the children's team. She was a lovely girl,' Fagan added, standing to see her out.

Lucy nodded, not trusting herself to speak. 'She was,' she managed finally.

After leaving the block, she phoned through to the Incident Room to speak with Burns. She wondered if she should mention her doubts about whether Carlin going off the road was an accident. If he'd been on the phone, it would have been recovered when the car was pulled out of the lough. Unless he had been told to toss it out the window. It might explain why he'd had the driver's window down when he hit the water, despite the cold of the night. If that was the case, it would never be found.

'The team are out,' the officer who answered the call told her. 'They've gone to the Carlin house. Forensics have found a body. A young girl.'

'Is it Sarah Finn?' Lucy asked quickly, hoping that it would not be and yet aware that, even if it wasn't, it would still be someone's daughter. Another lost girl.

Lucy saw again, unbidden, in her mind, the image of Sarah Finn she had seen earlier, the girl's gaze not meeting that of the camera, her eyes downcast; a child already broken.

'I don't know,' he replied.

Chapter Thirty-two

The Foreglen, along which Carlin's house was situated, was one of the main routes out of the city, heading first to Dungiven, then on over the Glenshane Pass and down towards Belfast. It was the same route along which Sarah Finn's phone had been found.

Carlin's house was a two-storey block affair, the yellowed paint weathered, blistering and crumbling off the walls. To the rear were a number of dilapidated farm buildings, dominated over by a rusted barn, the roof jousts visible through the wide gaps worn through the corrugated metal front sections. A wooden door slanted off its hinges, exposing the insides.

Lucy parked up behind a marked car whose lights still soundlessly flashed. Its driver was on the phone and waved a single gloved hand salute out at her as she passed.

Lucy looked around for someone from CID. Despite her best efforts, the whole way from Derry, she'd been unable to contact anyone who might be able to tell her for certain that the dead body that had been found was Sarah Finn. There was a uniformed officer standing at the main door of the house while Forensics officers moved in and out wordlessly.

Despite the activity, Lucy was struck by how quiet the scene was. Those who passed did so without speech, their heads lowered, as if in show of respect to the one dead. It was always so when the crime involved children.

'Is the Chief Super about?' she asked the uniform, flashing her warrant card.

'He's at the scene.'

'Is it inside?' Lucy asked, nodding past the man towards the hallway of the house beyond.

The uniform shook his head. 'There's a pond up at the top of the next field across. They found a pit there where he'd been dumping stuff for years. She was in there.'

'Is it Sarah Finn?'

The uniform shook his head. 'I've no idea, Sergeant; I've not been up.'

Lucy thanked him, then cut round the side of the house in the direction the man had suggested. To the rear of the house, standing on bricks, was the wheel-less chassis of a car, the frame exposed and, like the barn, brown with rust. Lucy glanced over her shoulder, observing the back of the house. She could barely make out any movement in the rooms, the film of dirt on the windows being so thick.

The uniform had told her that the site was in the second field across. The first through which she trudged was water-logged, her boots sinking into the ground, the beer brown water pooling around her feet with each step she took. Eventually, she worked out to walk the circumference, the earth being a little firmer near the hedge bordering the field. The sky above was clear, the sun low, the shadows of the trees stretching across the grass towards her.

She glanced around, attempting to gauge the distance to Carlin's nearest neighbour, but there were none immediately visible.

She reached the top of the first field and, cutting across to the left through a gap in the hedging, saw in the distance a crime scene tape already tied between two trees. Beyond it, a team of people in forensic suits were moving about. Using the edge of the field again, she was halfway across when she met Tara coming in the opposite direction.

'Is it Sarah Finn?' Lucy asked as she drew near.

'I don't know,' Tara said. 'I don't think so. Apparently it looks like it's been there for some time. Years, like.' Without stopping, Tara trudged past. 'I've to get food in,' she offered.

Lucy felt immediate relief at the news, then felt instantly guilty at having done so. That the dead girl was not Sarah Finn did not mean that there was not still a dead girl.

When she reached the crime tape, she saw Burns and Mickey standing to one side, watching the Forensics team working. She understood now Tara's shortness; Mickey seemed to be constantly at Burns's side, while Tara herself was being dispatched on minor tasks. Lucy reflected that at least with Fleming she had never felt under-appreciated.

Lucy flashed her card again at the officer standing at the scene tape and ducked under. 'You'll need one of these,' the officer said, handing her a face mask.

'You're back,' Burns said, unnecessarily, from behind his own mask as she approached him.

'It's not Sarah Finn?' Lucy answered.

'Seems not,' he said. 'This one is old. Could have been in there ten years, they think. They've found all kinds of stuff. The place was full of asbestos. You'll need your mask.'

Lucy quickly pulled it on, pulling the straps taut against her scalp.

The pit, beyond where they stood, was about twenty feet wide, though she could not from this angle tell its depth. A few of the CSIs, dressed in industrial protection gear, were already removing the asbestos, sealed in plastic, shifting it to one side to allow the officers access to what lay beneath.

'They found a black dog in the house,' Burns said. 'We're checking the hairs against those found on Karen.'

Lucy nodded.

'They've found all kinds of stuff in the house,' Burns continued. 'Traces of fluids all over the place.'

'Blood?'

'And the rest,' Burns added. 'It looks like Carlin was doing all kinds of things to all kinds of people in there. An orgy site, one of the SOCOs said.'

'I spoke with Noleen Fagan,' Lucy said. 'Carlin's psychiatrist in the Mental Health team. She reckons it's unlikely he would be our groomer.'

'How had he not come to our attention before?' Mickey asked. 'Surely he should have been flagged up.'

'He had dependent personality disorder,' Lucy said. 'It doesn't mean he's likely to be a criminal. In fact, Fagan reckoned he probably wouldn't have been capable of grooming anyone.'

'Is she sure?' Burns asked. 'The evidence is pretty compelling at this stage.'

'He needed to be told what to do, by people whose approval he sought. He may even have been told to drive off the road the other night.'

'What?' Burns asked, exasperated.

'He looked like he swerved off the road deliberately,' Lucy said. 'Fagan suggested he might have been instructed to do so by someone. Maybe someone he was speaking to on the phone.'

Mickey scoffed. 'Or maybe he was on his phone and lost control. Nothing complicated about it.'

Lucy ignored him, addressing Burns. 'Fagan reckons he'd be more a puppet than a manipulator.'

'More puppets,' Burns said. 'This bloody case is built on puppets.'

Lucy shrugged and relayed the rest of what Fagan had said.

'Then he must have been in cahoots with Kay. He does the arranging, Carlin does the dirty work. Then they used this place as their spot for carrying out the abuse,' Mickey said.

'I thought that too. However, Fagan reckoned Kay wouldn't have been the type to work with others.'

Burns considered the comment, though Lucy could already sense without conviction.

'We'll wait to see what Forensics pull from the two houses. If we can connect one with the other, we're sorted.'

One of the suited men approached them, a camera held in his hand.

'This is what we've got, sir,' he said, handing Burns the camera. 'It's the best I can get for you at the moment, until we get all the asbestos moved. She's down near the bottom.'

Burns held one hand over the viewing screen at the back of the camera as he flicked through the images the man had taken. Mickey craned his head to see too. Lucy waited until he was done, then asked to see the images. Since she had started in the PPU, over a year earlier, four children in the area under the age of eighteen had gone missing who had never been found. That was low; she knew that there had been twenty-two missing across the North in a previous year alone. If this child had been in the ground for ten years, based on those figures, it could be any one of forty or fifty children in the Foyle district area who had been reported missing within that time period. That was assuming that the child had been reported missing in the Foyle district to start with.

Burns scanned through the images for a few moments, then handed the camera to Lucy. 'See if anything stands out.'

The body was small, clearly a child, though the legs carried a good length. 'What height is she?'

'We think about five foot,' the SOCO said. 'She's measuring four foot ten, so allowing for some curvature and that.'

She wore a T-shirt, yellowed and grubby with dirt, but originally white, Lucy guessed. She wore baggy jeans. Her hair seemed blonde. Her face, though wizened, was not decayed as Lucy had expected.

'He buried her in quicklime, we think,' the man said. 'It helped preserve her.'

Lucy nodded. Contrary to popular belief, quicklime didn't accelerate decomposition. Indeed, it was quite the reverse. She could understand why Carlin might have used it. If the farm on which he lived had been functioning at one stage, he'd have had to cover any of the animals that had died and been buried to kill the smell of the bodies.

'I can follow up on the clothes,' Lucy said. 'See if it matches any Missing Persons investigations.'

'And the shoe,' the SOCO said. 'I've a close-up of it further on.'

Lucy scrolled through the images. One of the last was indeed close up on the girl's shoe. She wore a chunky black shoe, whose sole was almost three inches thick. At the strap, Lucy could make out an off-white skull and crossbones motif.

'Just the one shoe?'

'So far,' the man replied.

'I'll run both through the older cases.'

'Do that,' Burns said. 'What about the Finn girl? Any luck tracing the stepfather?'

'He's not ...' Lucy began, then decided better of it. 'The last address we had for him was sold a while back. He didn't leave a forwarding address, but I'm going to try the estate agent who handled the sale to see if we can track him down through them.'

'What about the phone we found yesterday? Have ICS found anything on it?'

'I'm not sure, sir. I've not had time to check.'

'Get a press release out this evening asking for the stepfather to do the right thing and hand himself in. Then organize for the mother to do an appeal tomorrow morning for the news.' He held out his hand, looking for the camera to be returned. 'You need to stay on top of it, Lucy. Let me know if the techies find anything.'

Lucy demurred from pointing out that she and Fleming had been following it up when Burns had had them called back to the station to see the collection found in Kay's shed. For the foreseeable future, he would be her superior and she saw little value in unnecessarily antagonizing him. Instead she handed him back the camera with a simple, 'Yes, sir,' then ducked back under the tape and began picking her way back to the farmhouse.

'Sergeant?' the uniform called after her.

Lucy turned expectantly.

'Your face mask? I need it back,' the man said, smiling.

Lucy handed him the mask, then stopped, glancing back up to where Burns stood. Something struck her about the clothes of the child. Not the clothes. The shoe. She remembered again the shoe found in Gary

Duffy's garage, which had provided the evidence that led to his imprisonment. The distinctive skull and crossbones motif.

'Sir,' she called, moving past the uniform. 'Sir!'

Burns turned towards her.

'It's the shoes. I think I know who the girl is.'

Mickey glanced at her, his face sharp.

'I think she's Louisa Gant.'

Burns angled his head slightly. 'We'll check it up. Thank you, Sergeant,' he added, turning from her again.

Chapter Thirty-three

After pulling up in front of the PPU block, Lucy thought better of it and drove across to the ICS block. She buzzed at the door and waited, studying her reflection in the foiled glass of the door, fixing a stray hair behind her ear.

Cooper opened the door. He wore a black shirt, open at the collar, and jeans.

'Lucy, come in,' he said, holding the door open so that she could pass.

'I've been sent to find out if you got anything on the phone we recovered yesterday.'

'Not even a good morning?' Cooper smiled, leading her towards his workroom.

'Sorry,' Lucy said. 'It's not been good. More a fairly shitty one, to be honest. But good morning,' she said, then glanced at her watch. 'In fact, good afternoon. I didn't realize the time.'

'You've not had lunch then,' Cooper said. 'I'll make tea. Milk? Sugar?'

'Both,' Lucy said, sitting down heavily on the stool by the workbench where she stood.

'So what's happened?' Cooper asked.

'My boss has been suspended,' Lucy said. 'Both suspects in our case have died so far, we've not found the one girl we lost and I think we've found a girl that went missing years ago and whose killer is also dead.'

'That is fairly shitty,' Cooper agreed.

'Actually, it's probably business as usual, if I'm honest,' Lucy conceded. 'I just feel bad for Tom Fleming.'

Cooper carried across two mugs of pale liquid and handed one to Lucy.

'When you asked about milk and sugar, I assumed I'd not need to specify I wanted actual tea in my tea too,' she said, peering doubtfully at the mug.

'The bag's in there,' Cooper said. 'You can stir yourself.'

He pulled a Twix out of his coat pocket, opened the packet and handed Lucy one of the two fingers.

'I couldn't work out if you liked it weak or strong,' he added. 'You strike me as strong.'

Lucy pulled the bag up with her spoon and squeezed out the tea. 'So, any luck with the phone?' she asked, before lifting the finger of Twix and taking a bite.

'The same as with Karen Hughes,' Cooper said. 'Almost an identical pattern. "Harris" started contact with her on Facebook. She befriended him the same as Karen, they batted some comments back and forwards. She mentioned her favourite band was Florence and the Machine. Then when she changed her profile picture from a puppy to a shot she took of her garden, he posted a comment "Dog Days are Over".'

'One of her songs,' Lucy said, nodding.

'I had to google it,' Cooper admitted. 'Sarah got the joke though. She agreed to meet him not long after.'

'How long ago was this?'

'Ten weeks ago,' he said. 'Their first contact was on 9 October. Their first meeting was in early November. They seemed to meet up for drinks or coffee a few times, then he suggested they go to a party. It quietened down a bit after that, then they seemed to make contact more frequently, another party, now she's vanished.'

'Can you find out who "Harris" is? Assuming it's not his real name.'

'I thought "Harris" was lying in a morgue with two lungs full of Enagh Lough.'

'Regardless,' Lucy said. 'Has there been any activity on the accounts since?'

Cooper shook his head. 'Not a peep. Certainly none of the identities that I'd traced.'

Lucy supped at her tea, washing down the last of the chocolate, the taste cloying at her throat.

'Thanks for that,' she said.

'The first contact with Sarah Finn was on 9 October, right?' Cooper said. 'The first contact with Karen Hughes was on 18 September. We know that Bradley or "Harris" or whatever his name is selected these girls for a reason, groomed them online to meet them in the real world. Assuming that something made Bradley target these specific girls online, then he must have encountered them in some way in the real world prior to that first online contact. It might be worth looking at where the girls were or who they met in the days prior to the two first contacts. If you find something the two had in common, you'll not have far to look for Bradley, I'd have thought.'

Lucy felt her phone vibrate in her pocket and, pulling it out, saw Robbie's name on the caller ID. She realized that he had left her a message earlier which she hadn't listened to yet. She hesitated answering, feeling absurdly guilty, then excused herself and, moving out of the office, answered the call.

'Hey, Lucy,' Robbie said when he answered. 'I've been trying you and Tom all morning.'

'We've been busy,' Lucy said quickly, despite the fact there had been nothing accusatory in his comment.

'Sorry,' he said. 'It's about Gavin. He skipped out in the middle of the night. He didn't arrive back here until just after seven this morning. I got him out to school. He signed out of school at eleven to attend a Mass for his father with his grandparents. He's not come back to the school yet and I can't get in contact with the grandparents.'

Lucy exhaled deeply.

'I'm sorry to land this on you,' Robbie said. 'You know the protocol, though.' If a child in care didn't return to the residential unit when expected, Social Services were required to inform the PPU.

'It's no problem,' Lucy said. 'Why didn't you contact us last night when he went out?'

'I didn't know,' Robbie replied sheepishly. 'I fell asleep on the sofa in the common room. He'd already gone to bed and I'd the place locked up for the evening. I got up to wake him this morning and saw he was gone. I was about to call when he arrived at the front door.'

If Gavin had been missing during the night there was every chance that he, and his new gang of friends, had been part of the recreational rioting that Lucy had witnessed in Gobnascale earlier. 'I'll get onto it as soon as I can,' Lucy said. Despite her caseload, she would have to follow up on it, especially without Fleming to handle it.

'There's something else,' Robbie said. 'I stuck on a washing load after he went to school. When I gathered up his clothes, they were stinking of petrol. Especially the sleeves of his hoodie.'

'He was probably part of the crew rioting at the top of the hill this morning,' Lucy said. 'I spotted him with them the other day.'

'Great!' Robbie said, sarcastically. 'He's only here a matter of weeks and he's already found himself a gang.'

It was as she was hanging up that Lucy realized that if Gavin had been back at the unit just after seven the riot had not even started by that stage. In fact, the only petrol they knew of as having been used at that stage was the stuff that had been poured through Gene Kay's letterbox before being set alight.

Chapter Thirty-four

Gavin Duffy's grandparents' house was in Holymount Park, in Gobnascale. Lucy rang at the door and waited, but no one answered. She peered in the windows, smearing away the misting of rainwater that had gathered there, a result of the fine miasma which had swept up over the city from along the Foyle Valley. She angled her head to see through the cracks in the blinds, but the place seemed empty, the darkened outline of a small Christmas tree visible in the corner. Lucy considered that the couple would hardly feel like celebrating Christmas, having lost their son only a month earlier.

She was turning to leave when a couple came shuffling up the street under a black umbrella towards the house. The woman looked to be in her sixties, brown hair streaked with grey, her eyes rheumy. The man seemed older, balding with a grey moustache. He blinked at Lucy from behind rain-streaked glasses.

'Yes?'

'I'm looking for the Duffys,' she explained.

'That's us,' the woman answered, smiling uncertainly.

'I'm Detective Sergeant Black of the Public Protection Unit. I'm looking for your grandson, Gavin. He's not turned up at school. They've been trying to contact you.'

'We were at Mass, over in the chapel.'

They pointed towards the outline of the Immaculate Conception Church, across the road from the estate where they lived. 'We went to the cemetery afterwards.'

'It's our son's Month's Mind,' the man said. He shuffled past, pulling out his keys, and opened the door. 'You may come in, so,' he added.

The house was compact, three rooms downstairs – a living room, kitchen and cloakroom. The living room was cosy, the small fire smouldering in the grate surprisingly warming. The old man grunted as he bent and flicked on a switch at the wall, bringing the thin Christmas tree in the corner alight, throwing kaleidoscopic shadows on the wall.

'You'll have tea,' Mr Duffy said, a statement not a question.

'I was sorry to hear about your son,' Lucy said, a little insincerely, to the woman, who sat next to the fire now. She twisted slightly to address the husband who stood in the adjacent room, filling the kettle. 'It must be very hard. Especially at this time of the year.'

'We wouldn't have been celebrating it at all were it not for Gavin being here.'

Lucy heard a grunt of derision from the kitchen. 'When he's here. He was to be at the Mass this morning. His own father's Month's Mind.'

'It's a Mass for when—' the woman began.

'I know,' said Lucy. Catholic families celebrated Mass one month after the death of a loved one in their memory. Lucy had attended a number herself over the years.

'Oh,' Mrs Duffy replied, understanding the implication. 'He'd wanted Gavin to come. The wee boy didn't know his father at all.'

'Only his bitch of a mother,' her husband said, passing Lucy a cup of black tea and handing a second cup to his wife.

'Don't say that,' his wife commented, though without conviction.

The man reappeared a moment later with a small tray, a cloth doily on it, on top of which sat a milk jug, a sugar bowl and a plate of biscuits. Lucy took milk and sugar, declined the Bourbon creams, then regretted having done so having managed only a single finger of a Twix bar since breakfast.

'She ran off the first time Gary went inside. Then she remarried. Do you know what the new one did to the wee boy?'

Lucy had heard when he'd first been transferred in. His stepfather, in order to teach him a lesson for accidentally breaking the wing mirror of his car with his bike, had beaten him with the flex of a games console. His PE teacher had noticed the shape of the bruises the following day when Gavin was changing for football, his T-shirt riding too high up his trunk as he pulled his shirt over his head. The doctor who examined him said there were injuries consistent with punches around the boy's ribcage, in addition to repeated bruising from an electric flex.

The officers who had questioned his mother and stepfather, separately, said that the mother had accused the boy of injuring himself because he didn't like her husband. It was only after she read the extent of the injuries that she admitted what had happened. She claimed that the boy was uncontrollable, and that she could no longer look after him. At the age of twelve, Gavin had entered residential care and there remained, until his grandparents had asked to have him brought nearer their home after his father's death.

'What's he done then?' Mr Duffy asked.

'Nothing that I know of,' Lucy said. 'He's just not in school.'

'We hardly see him,' the man commented.

'We need to give him space,' his wife countered. 'It's been difficult for him.'

'He should have been there this morning,' the man repeated, earning a roll of her eyes from his wife.

'He wasn't at the Mass?' Lucy asked.

The woman shook her head. 'He's like his father. Wayward. Gary was the same. Even after he got out. He was so angry all the time when he was younger. Then they lifted him for that wee girl's killing – all the people who'd been his friends would have nothing to do with him. They wouldn't let him onto their wing in the prison. For his own safety. Then he became withdrawn, wouldn't talk about anything. We couldn't get through to him. We asked him to say where the wee girl's body was, to admit if he'd done it.'

'Did he?' Lucy asked, having debated whether to mention the body that had been found on Carlin's farm. There was no point. She'd still not heard whether she was right in believing it to be Louisa Gant.

The woman shook her head. 'He said he was innocent of it.'

'But you didn't believe him?'

The woman's eyes filled. 'That's a terrible thing for a mother to say. That she didn't believe her own son. But he was a bad boy. From he was a teenager, it was like something was broken inside him.'

'He'd his mother's heart broken before he ever went inside. Then, when he did, they all abandoned him. All the ones he ran with. He'd no one left in the end. Nowhere to go.'

'He even moved back here; we made him, to be near us,' Mrs Duffy added.

'For all the difference it made in the end,' her husband muttered.

'He went down to the river,' Mrs Duffy said. 'To spare us finding him. His father always brought him up his breakfast in the morning. He didn't want him to see him ... you know.'

They sat in silence, watching the flames curl round the briquette the woman had thrown on the fire when they'd arrived in.

'I'm sorry,' Lucy repeated again.

'We thought having Gavin around would help,' Mr Duffy said. 'But he's out with that crew more often than not.'

'The street gang?'

'Local lads is all,' Mrs Duffy said, quickly. 'He'll be out running around somewhere.'

Lucy drained her tea then placed the cup back on the tray. 'I'd best take a drive around and see if I can find him. Would they be anywhere in particular?

'I'd try the back of the shops,' the man said. 'That's where they normally be.'

The couple saw her to the door, where Lucy thanked them for the tea and offered her condolences once more.

'Gavin's very lucky he has you,' she said. 'He showed me the iPod you got him. You're very good to him.'

'What's an iPod?' Mr Duffy said, his face creased in bewilderment.

Chapter Thirty-five

Lucy drove across to the parking bays outside the shops where she and Fleming had gone looking for Sarah Finn. She jumped out of the car, the air heavy with the smell of hot grease from the local chip shop reminding her she should eat. She had no time, for now, she decided.

Lucy had considered whether it might be best to call for backup, but if there was a gang of fellas standing, bored, in the rain, a Land Rover-load of PSNI officers pulling up would be the perfect entertainment to keep them occupied after the events at Kay's house. She thought she would try to get Gavin's attention and take him away quietly, rather than having to take a heavy-handed approach.

As she opened the boot to take out her coat, she caught a glimpse of a red car parked at the outer edge of the bays. A stocky man, wearing a brown overcoat and a black beanie hat sat in the driver's seat while, at the open door, two younger boys, in their late teens at most, leaned in. She recognized one of the boys as Tony, the leader of the gang with whom she had spoken about Sarah Finn. For a moment, Lucy thought they were robbing him, until the three of them started laughing. The man seemed to sense her watching, for he stared across at her. It took her a moment to place him as Jackie Logue, the community worker who'd helped calm the riot during Kay's burning.

After pulling her hood up enough to cover her face, she slammed the boot shut and headed across to the shops. Aware that she was still being watched, she instead went into the shop to buy a bar of chocolate, rather than heading directly around the back.

Two women served in the shop; one looked to be in her early twenties. She was loading the display in front of the tills with bags of crisps, while the older woman behind the counter chatted to a customer.

It was the younger girl that Lucy approached first.

'Can I have a packet of those?' she asked, only realizing after she'd done so that they were Worcester sauce flavour. 'I'm looking for my nephew. I'm told he hangs around with a crowd of boys around here.'

The girl looked up at her, blinking against the strip lights above Lucy's head. 'What's he called? I'll know if he's been in.'

'Gavin,' Lucy said, aware that the conversation at the counter had stopped.

'He's round the back, I think,' the girl said.

'They're not doing any harm,' a voice said.

Lucy turned. Both the woman behind the counter, and the older man to whom she had been talking, were now looking at her.

'They're all right out there. The back's covered over, so they stand in there out of the rain. Besides, Jackie keeps tabs on them.'

'Jackie?' Lucy asked. 'Jackie Logue?'

'Gavin's your nephew, is he?' the woman said.

'Gavin who?' the old man asked in response.

'Gary Duffy's boy,' she replied, as if Lucy wasn't there.

'The Duffys only had the one,' the man commented.

'That's right,' agreed his co-conspirator. 'You're no aunt. Police, is it?'

'His grandparents are wondering where he is,' Lucy lied. 'I'll take a Bounty too.'

'He's doing no harm out there. Leave him alone.'

Lucy said nothing further about the boys, thanking the woman and leaving, pulling her hood up again.

The area to the side of the shops was covered by sheets of corrugated metal, providing a smoking area along the entirety of the row, presumably for the staff of the various shop units who were being forced to smoke outside in the wake of the ban on smoking indoors. A group of around twenty youths were congregated there, a mixture of boys and girls, in half shadow, their faces faintly illuminated by the green emergency exit lights above the rear doors of each unit.

Four plastic dumpsters sat to one side, and it was against one of these that Gavin was standing, a cigarette in his hand, talking to a boy and girl of about the same age as him.

One of the kids shouted, 'Five oh,' quickly killing the conversation. They all turned to look where Lucy stood. She knew there was no way they could have made her out as a police officer so quickly, so guessed the Five-O reference covered all adults. It was hard not to find it more than a little absurd that the kids who used the designation probably had no idea where it came from. Unless they'd caught the remake or *The Wire*, she reflected.

The gathered kids stared from one to the other, as if trying to work out who Lucy was looking for, before turning defiantly towards her again. Gavin was standing with his arm around a thin girl, mid-teens, perhaps, her face, sharp featured, accentuated by the glow of the lights above them. He waited a moment, then pushed himself away from the dumpster and moved towards Lucy, drawing on his cigarette as he did so. The blackness around his eye shone beneath the green exit lights.

'Is something wrong?'

Lucy turned to see Jackie Logue standing a few feet from her, Tony behind him.

'It's fine, thank you,' Lucy said, turning towards the gathered group again. 'Come on, Gavin.'

'Are you a relative?' Logue asked.

'I know Gavin,' Lucy commented. 'Thanks for your concern.'

'These kids have nowhere else to go, Officer,' the man said.

'Apart from school?' Lucy countered.

'We're too old for school now,' Tony muttered, earning a glance of rebuke from Logue.

'They're not doing any harm here, as you were told,' Logue himself said, turning his attention again to Lucy.

So the woman from the shop had gone out and told him Lucy was police. She could also hear the kids passing along word that she was a cop.

'What do you want?' Gavin said, standing a few feet from her, defiantly refusing to take the final steps towards her.

'Robbie's looking for you. Let's go.'

Logue moved a step closer. 'That's not very helpful. You don't have to go if you don't want to, Gavin.'

'Yes, he does,' Lucy said, turning to the man. 'Mr Logue, is it?'

Logue raised his chin slightly but did not answer.

'Gavin is still young enough that he should be in school.'

'He told me he was allowed off to go to Mass for his father.'

'He didn't turn up at that either. His grandparents are worried about him.'

'I am standing here, you know,' Gavin snapped. 'Stop talking about me like I'm not here.'

'Let's go, Gavin,' Lucy said.

Gavin hesitated, as if considering returning to his friends. Lucy shook her head lightly. If he didn't come with her now, it would be worse when a response team arrived for him.

'Later,' Gavin said, turning to the other kids. He winked at the girl with whom he'd been standing. 'See you, Jackie,' he added to the stocky man.

'Mr Logue,' Lucy said, as she passed the man, walking behind Gavin to stop him changing his mind and turning back.

Gavin barely spoke the whole way back to the residential unit, even when Lucy asked how he felt after the beating he had taken.

He shrugged his shoulders. 'It was nothing,' he said.

'Your grandparents seem very nice,' Lucy said. 'They seem really keen to have you in their family.'

Again, the boy shrugged.

'They didn't give you the iPod though,' she added. 'Did they?'

The boy twisted and glared at her. 'Are you checking up on me?'

'I want to make sure you're OK,' Lucy said. 'Everyone just wants to help.'

'You can help by not coming for me in front of my friends again. OK?' With that he got out of the car and slammed the door, storming past Robbie where he stood at the unit entrance waiting for him.

Chapter Thirty-six

The night had already thickened across the city by the time Lucy made it back to Maydown again. She'd called in with Sinead Finn after leaving Gavin at the unit, but there was still no word from either the girl or Seamus Doherty. The woman had agreed to do an appeal the following morning, wondering what she should wear.

'Anything,' Lucy had replied.

The Tactical Support Units had been doing further checks in the area, but it seemed likely that, by this stage, the girl had either been taken by Doherty, or had used his leaving as an opportunity to get away herself, having taken the money from her mother's post office account the day before.

Lucy went up to her office and began typing up the press release for the late evening news. She mentioned both Doherty and Sarah Finn as being missing and encouraged either to contact home or the police as soon as possible. She also included a description of both Sarah Finn and Seamus Doherty and added that they could be travelling together or separately.

She called Communications to tell them the release was on its way and to book a press conference for the morning in the Strand Road should Sarah Finn not be located before then. She'd just emailed it through when she heard a thud from the office below. She went out to the top of the stairs and, looking down, shouted, 'Hello.'

A moment later, Tom Fleming's face appeared from the gloom of the corridor below. 'I didn't know you were in,' he said. 'I've called to collect some stuff.'

Lucy came down to him. 'I'm sorry about the whole ... thing,' she offered.

Fleming accepted the comment with a light nod. 'It's fine,' he said. 'I could maybe be doing with a breather from all this.'

Lucy nodded, unconvinced. 'What are you planning on doing?'

'Dry out,' he said, without humour. 'Then, I'm not sure. Bits and pieces.'

Lucy nodded again. She forced her hands into her pockets, wondering why she was struggling to find something to say to this man with whom she had worked for over a year.

'I hear they found Louisa Gant,' Fleming added.

'Is it confirmed?' Lucy asked, trying to hide her annoyance that Burns hadn't come back to her to tell her she'd been right.

'It's on the news so it must be,' Fleming said. 'On Carlin's farm.'

Lucy nodded. 'I was there,' she said. 'We can include Gary Duffy in our list of suspects then,' she added. 'Along with Kay and Carlin.'

Fleming nodded. 'All dead.'

'And I suspect all incapable of having actually groomed either Karen Hughes or Sarah Finn.'

Fleming shook his head. 'I'll not miss any of this for the next few weeks,' he said. 'All this grimness and ... and nastiness. All these broken families.'

Lucy nodded. 'I can imagine.'

'No, you can't,' Fleming said, smiling sadly. 'Give it another few years. I've had a lifetime of this. Abused kids and abusive parents. Broken families, dead children. It changes you, you know?'

Lucy nodded again but did not speak.

'All this shit and filth,' Fleming continued. 'When did you last deal with a normal family? Apart from your own?'

'My own family are the least normal I know,' Lucy retorted, laughing.

Fleming smiled again, briefly. 'I began checking up on estate agents this afternoon,' he said. 'Before my suspension sunk in. I've not found who handled the sale of Seamus Doherty's house yet, but I can give you a list of all who didn't. You'll need to check the remaining local ones tomorrow.'

'I know,' Lucy said. 'The Chief Super has already told me I need to stay on top of things.'

Fleming snorted derisively. 'Clark in Forensics also came back to us this morning to say that the dog hairs we took from Kay's house didn't match those found on Karen Hughes's body. Apparently they're checking some mongrel they found wandering around Carlin's now.'

'So Kay might not have been involved at all.'

'Apart from the collection of pictures featuring Karen found in his shed. Eventually.'

'There weren't there the first day we searched it, were they?'

Fleming swallowed dryly. 'I honestly don't know,' he managed after a pause. 'I didn't see them when I checked, but I wasn't in the best of shape. We both know that.'

'It seems odd. All of the evidence suggests Kay, but nothing sticks. He was in the restaurant in the shopping centre where we know the groomer was, but we couldn't find anything on his phone to prove he was the one sending the messages. The dog hairs now are a non-starter. And the collection appears after he dies.'

'Have they found anything connecting him to Carlin's farm yet?'

Lucy shook her head. 'The first I'll hear about it will be on the news. I spoke with Carlin's shrink. She reckoned that he wouldn't have had it in him to groom anyone. That he was easily led.'

'Could Kay not have led him?'

'She said it was possible, but, in her opinion, it was unlikely.'

Fleming shrugged. 'They're both dead now anyway, so we'll maybe never know for sure.'

'Burns wants Sarah Finn's mother to speak at a press thing tomorrow. Make an appeal for the girl to contact her.'

'If you have luck with some of the estate agents and find Doherty with the girl, you might not need her to.'

Lucy nodded. 'And now Louisa Gant is thrown into the mix.'

Fleming straightened up. 'Well, any help you need with that one, your mother's the place to start. She led the original investigation.'

Chapter Thirty-seven

It was nearing nine by the time Lucy left Fleming in the car park, having locked up the Unit with his help. They embraced quickly, awkwardly, as she wished him good luck.

Once she was on the road, though, she did not feel like going home to the silence. When her father had been there, while it had been difficult on account of his condition, she had, at least, been so occupied with looking after him that she had little time to think. Now though the silence of the house was oppressive.

Instead of driving home, she cut across the Foyle Bridge at the roundabout, and drove across onto the Culmore Road and up into Petrie Way. She parked up on the pavement, a few houses down from where Joe Quigg now lived and, turning the engine off, sat in the darkness, watching the house. Through the uncurtained windows, she could see the couple who had fostered him moving about. At one stage, the mother came into view, Joe hoisted on her hip, her arm cradling his rump, his arms wrapped around her neck.

Lucy recalled Catherine Quigg, his actual mother. The last time she'd seen her alive had been when Lucy had had to break down the woman's bedroom door and try to get her to sober up and get dressed for her children.

Her mobile rang, and Lucy recognized the number as being the CID suite in the Strand Road.

'Black? Burns here. I was expecting you to call in with an update.'

'Sorry, sir,' Lucy said. 'I'm out on a call. I've the press release sent out and we've followed up on most of the local estate agents. We've not located who handled the sale of Doherty's house yet, but I should get it finished in the morning.'

'I've rescheduled the press conference for eleven,' Burns said. 'Karen Hughes's funeral is in the morning. Maybe some of the people who knew her might know Sarah Finn too, so I want bodies at the funeral to chat to the younger girls there. Discreetly, obviously.'

'Yes, sir,' Lucy said. 'I'd planned on going anyway.'

'Fine. We've been following up on Carlin,' he said. 'The black dog hairs that were found on Hughes appear to match a black collie Carlin had around the farm.'

'So we know she was in contact with *him* at least, if not Kay,' Lucy commented.

'Indeed,' Burns agreed. 'We've also spoken to the metal theft crew and shown them Carlin's image. Two of them have confirmed he was the figure they saw at the railway tracks.'

Lucy considered the comment. It had been dark, under tree cover. Their identification of him would be shaky at best if it went to court. Not that it would be going to court. Not now.

'Plus we managed to pull CCTV footage from along the Limavady Road that picked up Carlin's car on the way to St Columb's Park around the time Hughes was dumped.'

'Any clear pictures of the driver?'

'Certainly the figure driving looks like Carlin.'

Lucy said nothing, her breath fuzzing against the receiver.

'It'll never see court, but we got him, Lucy. And you were instrumental in that.'

'Thank you, sir,' she said.

'We've ID'd the remains found at the farm, too, as Louisa Gant.'

'I heard, sir. On the news.'

'Well, it looks like Carlin and Kay were in on things together. One of them must have been "Bradley" or "Harris" or whatever he was calling himself. Gary Duffy must have been part of their little group at one stage. Once we can establish that the case is closed. We're looking for the connections now.'

'I'd thought of contacting the schools of the two girls to see if there were any events or visitors common to both in the week or two before "Bradley's" first contact with them. That might help us find the connection between Kay and Carlin and we can work back,' Lucy added.

'Of course, what would be really useful would be to find Sarah Finn,' he stated. 'That's your priority.'

'Of course, sir,' she said.

'There is something else, Lucy. I checked up on the Cunningham case, as you asked.'

Lucy straightened. 'Yes?'

'Intelligence on the ground in Limerick is saying Cunningham is either home or planning on coming home soon. His mother is dying by all accounts. Maybe keep your ear to the ground. If we get a credible lead we'll get a team organized to see if we can't pick him up for the Quigg killings.'

'Thank you, sir,' Lucy said.

'We'll see what we can do.'

'Yes, sir.'

Lucy ended the call and looked up. Joe Quigg's foster father was standing at the end of his drive, a parcel in one hand, the boot of the car yawning open, his face turned towards her.

She started the engine and drove away quickly, avoiding his gaze as she passed.

Chapter Thirty-eight

'Keep an ear to the ground' Burns had said.

Lucy reflected on the comment as she drove. She'd been doing just that from the moment Cunningham had vanished, keeping her ear to the ground. But no one was talking. While none of those who knew Cunningham necessarily agreed with what he had done, nevertheless they had not been prepared to help the police to find him. She'd called at homes of his family and friends, asked local informers and petty criminals who might have known him, had called round the various divisions both of An Garda and PSNI where he was rumoured to be hiding, asking if they'd seen him. No one would help.

Lucy knew then that if Cunningham was back in Derry, there was only one other place for her to look. She didn't even need to check the system for Cunningham's home address. Like Joe Quigg's new family home, she had spent more than one evening sitting parked outside it on the off chance she might catch a glimpse of the man himself. She had not yet satisfactorily considered what exactly she would do with him when she found him.

* * *

The house was the middle one of three in a row of terraced houses. It comprised of two storeys, the front windows in each room curtained, lights visible through the thinness of the fabric. The door was heavy mahogany, with a single frosted glass pane set in the wood.

Lucy pulled up opposite the house and turned off the engine, leaving the key in the ignition to allow her to run the heater. She questioned whether she should call at the house, but knew that not only would she be refused entry, but it would alert Cunningham himself to her presence. Instead, she would sit in her car to watch and wait. Being in her own unmarked vehicle, she would not be recognized as a PSNI officer.

As she sat, a middle-aged couple shuffled past, barely glancing at her, then crossed over and moved up the Cunninghams' driveway. Lucy leaned forward to get a better view of the house. She saw the door opening, recognized the man answering it as Peter Cunningham, the younger brother of Alan. Peter was a low-level dealer who'd been in and out for drugs offences. Strangely, despite the claims by dissident Republicans that they were targeting all known drug dealers in the area, Peter had continued his trade unaffected by the shootings which had claimed a number of his peers. In fact, if anything, he had benefited from their punishments, their hasty retreat from the scene leaving a vacuum that he had quickly filled. The popular view in the Drugs Squad, she'd heard, was that Peter was paying off the right people.

The older couple stepped into the house, the man proffering a hand to Peter, and, for a moment, Lucy wondered whether the mother had already died and that her wake had started. She felt shame at the hope this thought engendered, for it meant Alan Cunningham would almost certainly come home. However, the two men began to laugh and she guessed not.

Lucy lowered herself back in her seat and fiddled with the radio presets until she found a station playing Villagers, singing about a new found land. Then she leaned back, resting her eyes for a few moments.

She jumped when she heard the sharp tapping at the window. Glancing across, she realized there was a child, perhaps little more than ten, standing by the passenger side door of her car. He tapped on the glass a second time.

Lucy tried to stretch across to open the door, but her seat belt restricted her. Instead she reached down and depressed the electric window button. The glass slid down and the boy stepped gingerly closer to the car, his chin almost resting on the lower edge of the window frame.

'Do you have a ciggie?' he asked.

'I don't smoke, I'm afraid,' Lucy said. 'Nor should you. It's not good for you.'

'My teacher says that, too.'

'Your teacher's right,' Lucy said. 'What's your name?'

'Why?' the boy asked, angling his head.

Lucy shrugged. 'Just being friendly.'

The boy raised his chin a little. 'I'm not meant to talk to strangers.'

'That's very true,' Lucy said. 'Did your teacher tell you that too?'

'Nah,' the boy said, spitting on the ground next to the car. 'Your lot did.' He smiled quickly then ran.

Lucy felt a sudden rush of cold air as the driver's side door next to her was wrenched open. She turned just as Peter Cunningham's punch connected with her, the movement meaning the punch glanced off her forehead rather than connecting with her temple as he had intended.

He leaned into the car, reaching for her. She felt his hands grapple with her, tugging at her jumper, trying to pull her out of the car. Her seat belt, still connected, prevented him from doing so.

She began to fumble with the keys in the ignition, trying to control her feet sufficiently to press the right pedals to shift the car into gear.

Cunningham continued to pull at her. 'Bitch,' he shouted. 'My mother's dying.' He gave a final tug, then, realizing the futility of it, leaned in and tried landing more punches instead. The first caught Lucy on the mouth, the second catching her below the eye as her head shifted sideways with the earlier impact.

'Bitch,' he spat again. Frustrated by the ineffectual nature of his blows, he moved backwards and, lifting his leg, attempted to stomp in at her, holding on to the door of the car to give himself sufficient leverage to do so.

Lucy finally felt the gear stick shunt into place, heard the engine rev as the ignition caught. She didn't even try to close the door, didn't check to see if anyone was coming. Instead the car jerked forward into the road. Cunningham, still using the door for balance, shifted suddenly sideways, falling backwards onto his rump. Lucy sped forward a few hundred yards, then slowed just long enough to pull the door shut and engage the central locking. She could taste blood in her mouth, like old pennies, could feel the building heat as the skin around her eye began to swell and tighten.

Rounding the corner at the end of the street, she saw the young boy who had stopped at her car standing with a group of kids. They watched her as she passed, each raising their middle finger in a silent salute.

Thursday 20 December

Chapter Thirty-nine

The following morning, the cut above her lip had sealed and thickened, swelling the skin of her upper lip into what appeared a parody of a pout. Though her eye had not swollen it was encircled by a bruise, which was sore to the touch when she tried applying foundation to it to cover it up. There was little she could do to conceal the injury to her mouth.

The first thing she did when she arrived in her office was to contact the two schools that Karen and Sarah had attended. Knowing the dates of first contact by 'Bradley'/'Harris', Lucy asked both if they could think of any events that had happened in the school, particularly involving outside visitors, during the week or two prior to that first contact.

The first contact between Karen Hughes and 'Paul Bradley' was made on 18 September. Lucy called Karen's school and spoke to the secretary.

'I'm looking specifically at the week running up to the eighteenth,' Lucy explained. 'Was Karen involved in anything that week? We need to know if she encountered anybody new, maybe through a club or something?'

'Give me a moment, please.'

Lucy listened to an electronic version of 'Ode to Joy' three times before the voice came back on the line. 'We had geography field trips on the Monday, a theatre company visit on the Wednesday, the school photographer on the Thursday and a Young Enterprise day on the Friday.'

'Can I get details of each of the events, please?' Lucy asked. 'Especially where outside visitors were involved.'

'I'll send them through.'

Sarah Finn's school was a little less organized. The secretary to whom she spoke, who appeared to be dealing with two phone calls at the same time, promised her she would fax through anything she found.

Before Karen Hughes's funeral, Lucy called on the remaining estate agents that Fleming had mentioned to her to check if any of them had been responsible for the sale of Seamus Doherty's house and might have a forwarding address for him. She got lucky on the second visit.

The man with whom she spoke, who introduced himself only as Richard, was from a different era. He was a heavy man, white haired, ruddy faced, wearing a three-piece tweed suit, the waistcoat straining at the buttons when he sat.

'I can't interest you in a place while you're here?' he asked, smiling as he lowered himself into his seat.

'Maybe later,' Lucy said.

'Now's the time to buy while prices are rock bottom. Someone with a bit of cash could make some canny purchases.'

'The "bit of cash" part is the problem.' Lucy smiled.

'For all of us,' Richard agreed, though his appearance suggested that the downturn in the market had not had quite the same impact on him as it had on everyone else.

'So, Seamus Doherty. He had a house in Foyle Springs.'

Robert nodded. 'I remember it well. It was one of the last things we sold to be honest. People can't get mortgages you see. We've had stuff on the books for a few years now.'

'Would you have a forwarding address for Mr Doherty? We're looking for him in connection with a missing persons case,' she added. It would be public knowledge after the press conference anyway, she reasoned.

'I see,' Richard said. 'Let me check.'

He turned his attention to the PC on the desk in front of him, his chin almost touching his chest.

Lucy glanced around the office. A secretary sat at the front desk, busily tapping at the keyboard of the computer in front of her. From this angle, Lucy could see that, in fact, she was surfing the net.

'Nothing, I'm afraid,' Richard said. 'I can give you the name of the solicitor who handled the deal for him, but I've no address recorded for him.' He grimaced, as if imparting this news caused him physical pain.

'That's fine,' Lucy said, trying to hide her disappointment. 'Thanks anyway.'

She stood to leave, but Richard remained in his seat, staring at the screen in front of him.

'Wait a bit,' he said. 'Now I think about it, I did price his parents' house for him too.'

'What?'

'After he sold his own house, he asked me to value his parents' house. I think his mother had died a few months earlier and he couldn't decide what to do with the house. He asked me to give him a valuation for it.'

'Did he sell it?'

'No. I don't think he thought the money he'd have got was worth it. The house was in a bit of a state from what I remember. It needed new windows, central heating, roof fixed, the whole bit. In the good days he'd have managed ninety plus for it, I thought, but with the crash, he'd have been lucky to have passed thirty-five.'

'Do you remember where the house was?'

Richard shook his head. 'I'm trying to think. It was past Dungiven. Up on the Glenshane. There was a circle of trees round it. I remember that. Bleak, like.'

'Would you have the address?'

'I should have somewhere. I have a diary I keep valuation stuff in, in case someone comes back to you. I'll need to dig out the old ones and take a check through it. It was a few weeks after we finalized sale of the one in the city, so it should be easy enough found.'

'Could you check now?' Lucy said, a little more impatiently than she intended.

Richard shook his head again, the skin beneath his chin wobbling with the effort. 'I've my old diaries in my office at home. I can take a run out and get it for you. I'll call you as soon as I find it.'

'Is home close?' Lucy asked. 'I could run you there.' She glanced at her watch. Karen Hughes's funeral was in three quarters of an hour.

'Ballybofey,' Richard said. 'I'll head up myself in a bit. I've a light morning anyway.'

Lucy knew that the journey there would take the guts of an hour. 'I have a funeral at ten,' she said. 'Would you be able to call me with the address when you find it.'

Richard nodded.

'The missing person case we're investigating?' Lucy added. 'The missing person in question is a child.'

The comment had the desired effect.

'I'll go now, then, so,' Richard said, pushing back his seat and standing.

Chapter Forty

A guard of honour, comprising a group of Karen's classmates, lined the pathway up to the church. Lucy passed along them, nodding at one or two as she did so. At the top of the walkway, Karen Hughes's mother, Marian, stood, supported by two older men, both bearing a strong familial resemblance to her. They held an arm each, as if the woman was physically unable to remain upright unaided. Her face was slick with tears as she nodded her head in acknowledgement of the condolences offered to her by two passing mourners.

Lucy approached her, her hand extended. 'Ms Hughes,' she said. 'I'm sorry for your loss.'

The woman stared at her, trying to place her perhaps, and Lucy could see in the glaze of her eyes that she had obviously taken something to help her make it through the morning.

'Thank you,' she said, having failed to recognize her. 'These are my brothers.'

Lucy smiled grimly as she took the hand of each, one after the other, and offered her sympathies on their loss. She reflected that, in the entire time she had known Karen, she had not once seen or heard of either man.

Across from where they stood, she caught a glimpse of Robbie and moved over to him. They hugged briefly, Lucy breaking away from the embrace first.

'What the hell happened to your face?' Robbie asked, holding her at arm's length as he examined her injuries.

Lucy moved out of his grasp. 'Nothing. They look worse than they are.'

'They look pretty bad. Who hurt you?'

'How are you?' she asked in reply.

'OK,' Robbie commented, reluctant to allow the subject to be changed. 'Considering.'

Lucy nodded.

'You?'

'OK,' she returned. 'Considering.'

It was Robbie's turn to nod. 'Apart from someone having beaten you up,' he added, a little bitterly.

'I wasn't beaten up,' Lucy remarked. 'How's Gavin?'

Robbie hesitated, clearly aware that Lucy didn't want to discuss her injuries further, but reluctant to let the topic drop. Finally he said, 'Not so good. He's inside already. He's hurting.'

'For Karen or his dad?' Lucy asked.

'Both,' Robbie said.

At that moment, a blue, unmarked car pulled up at the foot of the pathway and Eoghan Harkin stepped out, before the car drove away again. So close to his release, he would be allowed to attend the funeral unaccompanied. Still, Lucy could tell by the bulge around his ankle that he was wearing a tracing bracelet, just in case he had thoughts of not returning to finish

241

the final days of his sentence. Having made it this far, it seemed unlikely he would risk his early release for the sake of a matter of days.

As he approached her, Lucy could see he recognized her from the night she had broken the news of Karen's death. He barely glanced in his wife's direction, save for a curt nod to the two brothers, never raising his head enough to make eye contact with either. No love lost there, Lucy guessed.

'Inspector,' he said, as he drew level with Lucy.

'Sergeant,' she corrected him. 'I'm sorry again for your loss, Mr Harkin.'

The man acknowledged the comment with a slight raising of his chin. 'How are you doing?' he added, addressing Robbie.

'I'm sorry for your loss, Mr Harkin,' Robbie echoed.

'This is Robbie McManus,' Lucy explained. 'Karen's key social worker.'

'Thanks for all you did for her,' Harkin said. Lucy could see that Robbie was looking for any hidden meaning in the comment. 'What happened to you?' This time, he was addressing Lucy herself. He lifted one nicotine-yellowed finger and rubbed at the side of his mouth.

'Nothing,' Lucy said, then, realizing the response did not satisfactorily explain the injuries she bore, 'I had an incident with a suspect,' she lied.

'I thought maybe it was that Cunningham boy. I heard on the jungle drums that he hit a copper a few smacks last night for staking out his house.'

Lucy reddened enough for Harkin to know he'd hit a nerve. He smiled wryly. Lucy turned her head slightly, keen to avoid Robbie's gaze.

'Had Cunningham anything to do with Karen?' Harkin said quietly.

Lucy shook her head. 'His brother killed a child and her mother a while back, then did a runner. I'd heard he might be back in Derry. You didn't happen to hear anything about that did you? On your jungle drums?'

Harkin shook his head. 'Alan? He's a horrible wee bastard. That would be his form all right, killing women and kids.'

'It's a pity no one else shares your assessment. I can't get anything concrete on his whereabouts. No one will talk.'

'Somebody must be protecting him then. Someone with a bit of clout in the community,' Harkin reasoned. 'By the way, I heard you were there when the guy that killed Karen got it.'

'Gene Kay or Peter Carlin?'

'I was told Carlin,' Harkin said. 'Who's Kay?'

'He may have been involved too,' Lucy nodded. 'Did you know Peter Carlin?'

Harkin shook his head. 'Not until I heard about it inside. One of the guards told me.'

'But you knew Gary Duffy?'

'The guy who killed the Gant girl?'

Lucy nodded. 'They appear to have been working together.'

'I remember Duffy all right from years back,' Harkin commented. 'He was bad news. A real hawk. Jackie Logue is the one who could tell you about him. Jackie took over from Duffy after he went inside. Except Jackie wasn't as hard line.'

'Did he and Duffy know each other?'

Harkin shrugged. 'I'm not too sure. I never heard of this guy Carlin before all this though.'

Lucy gazed down towards the roadway, long enough to see Chief Superintendent Burns arrive. He made straight for Karen's mother, his hand outstretched.

'Did he suffer?' Harkin hissed suddenly. 'Carlin?'

Lucy glanced at him. 'He drowned. Make of that what you will.'

Harkin snorted derisively. 'It's a pity you let him die. If you'd kept him for me, I'd have made sure the world became a much lonelier place for Alan Cunningham as a thank you.'

'You know where Cunningham is?' Lucy said, quickly turning to face him.

Harkin shrugged. 'Not necessarily. But, as I said, someone with clout in the community could do all kinds of things. I'd have made sure he wasn't protected no more. You'd have had to find him yourself, of course.'

Lucy felt her breath catch in her chest, felt herself unsteady on her feet.

''Course, it's a moot point now, isn't it?' Harkin added, then moved on into the church, where his daughter lay.

'You went after Cunningham,' Robbie said suddenly, gripping Lucy by the arm. 'Jesus Christ, Lucy! You're going to get yourself killed, you know that?'

Lucy pulled her arm away. 'What should I do? Forget about her?'

'You don't need to forget her, but ...'

'But what?' Lucy demanded.

'But you need to let it go, Lucy.'

'I don't let things go,' she snapped.

Robbie swallowed dryly. 'You let me go,' he muttered.

Lucy was caught by surprise by the tenderness in his voice. The regret. She struggled to respond.

'Is that why you wanted the child's address? To reopen your wounds?'

'I wanted to make sure he's OK.'

'You know, he'll not even remember what happened, Lucy. Nor should you want him to. You're the only one still carrying that with you.'

Lucy nodded. 'That suits me fine. Someone has to give a shit.'

'People do give a shit,' Robbie whispered urgently, as the people around them began moving inside the church for the funeral service. 'We just don't forget to live, too. I'm sorry I ever gave you that address.'

Lucy felt a vibration in her pocket. 'Don't worry about it,' she said, pulling out her phone. 'I'll not tell anyone where I got it from.'

'That's not what I'm worried about,' Robbie managed, before she stepped away from him, putting the mobile to her ear. It was the estate agent.

'DS Black? Richard O'Dowd here. I've got that address for you.'

Lucy made her apologies to no one in particular and ran to her car.

Chapter Forty-one

The Glenshane Pass, cutting through the Sperrin mountain range, was named after the eighteenth-century highwayman, Shane Crosagh O'Maolain, who had operated there before being caught and hanged with his brothers in the Diamond in Derry. His name, Crosagh, referred to the pockmarks on his face which were a feature of his family. Ironically, the name applied equally well to the topography of area where he had lived, the thick bogland of which undulated along the valley.

The house that O'Dowd had valued was situated on the outer edge of the Glenshane Forest, just under ten miles beyond Dungiven. The Pass itself was heavy with traffic heading from Derry towards Belfast. The mountain area around it, though, was sparsely inhabited. The land was primarily peatland, the grass and scrub being grazed upon by a few hardy sheep, yellowed and wiry. The soil beneath, however, was black, meaning the run-off water from it was like stout as it cascaded down the rock face bordering the roadway on one side. To the other, Lucy could look down over the valley of the Pass beneath, where the River Roe began to gather strength as it cut down through the mountains.

Lucy had entered the address of the property in Google Maps, but it had not been recognized. Instead, she had taken a series of directions over the phone from O'Dowd. She had passed the entrance way to the abandoned quarry, which had carved into the sides of the mountain, its rusting equipment seeming to breathe dust with each gust of wind carrying up the valley. Further along the road, she passed the Ponderosa bar, a sign outside proclaiming it the highest public house in the country.

Finally, as the road began to flatten after the climb from Dungiven, she saw the roadway to her right that O'Dowd had said she should take. She pulled off the main Glenshane Road onto this narrower one and drove parallel to the main flow of traffic for a few hundred yards, before the road cut sharply to the right and took her down, into the valley, towards the dark mass of the forest.

O'Dowd had warned her to look out for a further turning, this time onto a laneway. In fact, she had already passed it by the time she registered its presence and had to reverse several hundred yards in order to take the turn.

The laneway was narrow, the hedging on both sides scratching against the doors of her car as she progressed along it. Up the centre of the lane, the tarmac had risen in a central ridge from which thick tussocks of grass had grown.

After a few minutes on the laneway, Lucy finally saw the house that O'Dowd had visited, standing enshadowed by a circle of trees surrounding it. While the building was not as ramshackle as Lucy had expected, it was, without doubt, in need of repair.

Still, as she pulled into the driveway, she noticed the two-tone effect of the roof slates where the newer red ones stood out against the moss-thick russet ones with which the roof had originally been tiled. There was no doubt that someone had been at the house more recently than O'Dowd's valuation visit. That didn't necessarily mean that Doherty hadn't managed to sell it to someone else, without O'Dowd's help, since then.

She drew up outside the house and, reaching across, unlocked the glove compartment and removed her service gun. Fitting it inside her coat pocket, she got out, leaving the car unlocked lest she needed to make a quick getaway. She realized that she should have brought support but, with Fleming suspended, there were few alternatives. Besides, there was no guarantee that the house was even occupied.

She moved across to the door, passing the main window that carried a single thick crack running across the width of its pane. The glass itself was coated with dust so she was unable to see anything in the gloom beyond.

She tapped on the door twice and, stepping back, regarded the front of the house. Despite her first impressions, she could see curtains hanging down the sides of the window of the small room to the left. She thought she saw something shift quickly from her sight and, moving across, she leaned against the window, using her glove to smear away the dust and allow her a view inside. She tensed as she now saw a small fire burning in the hearth. She stepped back and, glancing up, realized she had missed the thin skeins of smoke drifting against the cloud grey sky above the chimney of the house.

She heard a click and the front door opened. She shifted quickly back to come face to face with Seamus Doherty. He stared at her, clearly waiting for her to speak.

'Mr Doherty?'

'Yes?'

'My name is Detective Sergeant Lucy Black. I'm with the Public Protection Unit. Can I come in?'

She motioned as if to step into the house, but Doherty held his ground, moving more fully into the doorway to block the entrance.

'Why? Is something wrong?'

'I'm looking for Sarah Finn, the daughter of your partner. I'd like to search your property. Please let me in.'

Doherty licked dryly at his lip, glancing past Lucy, clearly trying to gauge whether she was on her own. His eyes flitted across her face, his thoughts racing.

Lucy moved her hand towards her pocket, feeling for the weight of the gun she had placed there. Doherty saw the motion and, in an instant, had slammed the door on her.

'Shit,' Lucy snapped, pulling her gun free of her coat pocket and, raising her boot, kicking at the door. Its state belied its sturdiness, for though it rattled in its frame, it did not move.

Lucy stepped back, allowing herself more room, and kicked a second time, harder. She heard the crack as the wood around the catch splintered. A third kick and the door swung open. She moved into the room quickly, her back against the wall, her gun held in front of her.

'Mr Doherty. My colleagues are on their way. Please surrender yourself.' She moved into the room proper, scanning for hiding places. A bookcase against one wall, a heavy unit in the centre of the floor, on which sat two cereal bowls. A threadbare sofa pulled forward to meet it.

'Sarah?' Lucy shouted. 'Sarah Finn?'

To the rear of the house, she heard a crash, as if a piece of furniture had been knocked over. Lucy moved quickly, still scanning the room, trying to keep her back to the areas she knew to be clear of potential hiding spots.

The room she was in opened out into the kitchen, where a chair lay on the floor. To her right was a hallway opening onto three further rooms. She moved up the darkened corridor, swinging quickly into the first room to the left. A bedroom, the bed unmade, a tangle of clothes on the floor. Jeans, a jumper, men's boots. A paperback book steepled on the bedside unit. The bed was old, cast iron, high legged enough to offer Lucy an unrestricted view through to the far wall.

Satisfied, she turned to the second room, just a little further up the hallway, on the opposite side. A bathroom. Untidy. The toilet seat down.

The last room was to her right again. Lucy pushed open the door with her foot, then moved quickly in. A second bedroom, bigger than the first, the lower half of the walls panelled in dark wood. The bed was made here. A bag sat on a chair in the corner. On the bed, its head resting against the pillow, sat a tattered child's toy, a white rabbit with one ear hanging loose over the eye, the stuffing showing at the stitching.

'Sarah?' Lucy shouted. 'I'm with the police. Don't be afraid.'

Lucy was turning to leave the room when she noticed a smaller door seemingly cut into the wood panelling in the corner opposite where the chair sat. She moved across and banged it with her foot. Gripping the small handle, she twisted it and pulled the door open. Beyond lay a set of wooden steps leading downwards, beneath the house.

'Sarah?' Lucy shouted.

She went down the steps towards the darkened room below. As she moved beneath the upper floor level, she realised that there was some natural light leaking into the cellar from a small window high up on the back walls.

Lucy moved down, surveying the area beneath as the objects scattered about began to take form in the gloom. She realized that at one end of the space, under the window, stood a heavy wooden table. Above it, hanging from small hooks in the wall, hung a set of meat cleavers.

Gasping, Lucy moved quickly across. The knives were clean, one or two badged with spots of rust.

'Jesus,' she muttered.

Suddenly she heard a movement behind her and turned. At first she thought Doherty was running at her, but as she raised her gun to shoot, she saw him grab at the handrail of the steps as if to pull himself up the steps again, as if to escape from where he had been hiding in the cellar.

'Stop,' Lucy shouted. 'I *will* shoot you.'

Doherty paused, his foot on the bottom step, then slowly raised his hands.

'On the floor,' Lucy shouted. 'Now! Face down.'

'You've got it wrong,' Doherty began.

'Shut up,' Lucy snapped, pushing him onto the floor, kneeling on his back as she pulled two plastic cable ties from her coat pocket and tightened them around Doherty's wrists.

Just then, something in the periphery of her vision moved and she saw a figure rush down the steps towards her. Sarah Finn.

She stood to embrace the girl she had rescued. Instead, Finn lashed out at her with her fists, battering at Lucy as she struggled to contain the child.

'Leave him alone,' the girl screamed. 'Don't hurt him.'

Chapter Forty-two

A response team soon arrived from Dungiven station after Lucy had phoned through for support. They had brought with them a local doctor who examined Sarah Finn in the large bedroom in which she had been sleeping. The girl had wept uncontrollably as Doherty had been led away to be taken into Dungiven where he would be held for questioning. Sinead Finn had been called and was being brought to her daughter by Chief Superintendent Burns himself. A forensics team was on the way from Derry as was a social worker, after Lucy had called Robbie. Sarah would not be allowed back with her mother until she had been assessed by Social Services.

Lucy, meanwhile, sat in front of the fire, warming herself. The girl's reaction was not unusual, she reasoned. Often, vulnerable children became attached to those who had exploited them, believing the abuse they had suffered to be a form of love. But Lucy found the use of the two bedrooms unusual. They clearly had been sleeping in different rooms. Doherty had told her she had got it wrong. Only when the doctor had finished, would Lucy be able to ask the girl herself directly.

* * *

253

The interview room into which they were led in Dungiven was old-fashioned, the ceilings high, the pipework of the heating system running along the base of the walls, the pipes painted the same puce shade as the walls. They could hear water gurgling through the pipes while they spoke, as the heating system shuddered into life.

Sarah Finn sat in the seat opposite Lucy. Ideally, Lucy would have preferred there to be no desk between them lest it create an adversarial atmosphere that she did not want.

Finn looked a little different from the school picture that Lucy had been using in the search for the girl. The brown hair of the image was actually sandy in reality. Perhaps as a result of the past few days, the puppy fat she had carried in the image had gone from her face, even if the top she wore seemed swollen a little around the softness of her stomach.

Robbie sat down, but not before pulling his chair around so that he was positioned midway between Lucy and the girl. Sarah wiped at the tears that had gathered around her eyes as she waited for Lucy to begin. She'd met her mother, Sinead, half an hour previous; their conversation had been little more than muffled cries from the girl and promises from the mother that she'd never let her go again.

Sinead Finn had protested when she was told that she could not be present when her daughter would be interviewed. Lucy explained to her that the girl was more likely to tell them the full truth without the

254

mother's presence distracting her. Especially when her statement might implicate Finn's own partner.

The man himself, having been already taken to another interview room in the station, had not said a word following his protestation to Lucy that she had got it wrong.

'It's good to finally meet you, Sarah,' Lucy began. 'I'm DS Lucy Black. I work for the Public Protection Unit. I deal with cases involving vulnerable people and especially young people.'

Finn swallowed nervously and nodded, though Lucy had not asked a question.

'This is Robbie. He's a social worker who will be sitting in on the interview. Obviously, you can tell us anything at all that you want. Nothing you can tell us will shock us or make us think any less of you. I can't promise that what you tell us will be confidential; we might need to use some of the things you say, if we decide to prosecute someone because of your abduction.'

The girl muttered something, her head lowered, her fingers playing with a strip of laminate peeling off the edge of the table.

'Sorry?' Lucy said. 'We didn't catch that, Sarah. You need to speak as clearly as you can, because this is being recorded so that we can be sure we don't miss anything you tell us.'

The girl looked up through the loose strands of her fringe. 'I weren't abducted. I went with Seamus.'

Lucy nodded. 'Maybe you'd tell us in your own words what happened over the past few days? Yeah?'

'I knew Seamus was going away for a bit and decided to go with him.'

'Why?'

The girl paused. She picked off the laminate strip, then muttered an apology and tried to reapply it to the table's edge.

'I wanted to get away. I thought Seamus was going to Manchester. That's what he'd told Mum. But he weren't. I didn't know until I heard the van stop. I thought we were at the boat. When I got out, we were in the middle of the countryside. I'd nowhere else to go.'

'Did Mr Doherty know you were in his van?'

She shook her head. 'I took some money from the post office and packed my bag. I thought if I got to the boat, I'd hide out and get a lift somewhere else.'

'Why?' Lucy asked.

'I wanted to get away.'

'Did this have anything to do with "Simon Harris", Sarah?' Lucy asked.

The girl glanced up quickly, tears swelling in her eyes. Just as quickly she looked down at her lap again, sniffing. A tear dripped onto the floor from her bowed head. 'I don't know who that is.'

'We found your phone, Sarah,' Lucy said. 'We know who "Harris" was.'

If Sarah realized the significance of the past tense she didn't show it. Meanwhile, Lucy realized an incongruity in her story.

'You said you didn't get out of the van until Mr Doherty stopped at the house on the Glenshane?'

Finn nodded.

'But we found your phone in a lay-by along the Glenshane Road.'

The girl nodded again. 'Seamus took it off me the next day and dumped it somewhere. He didn't tell me where.'

'Why?

'The messages.'

'"Harris"'s messages?'

Finn nodded again, the tears coming more freely now.

'Did you not want to get any more messages from him?'

Finn shook her head, sniffing loudly. She raised her head, her hair sticking to the dampness of her cheeks.

'I told Seamus that he'd given me the phone in the first place. He'd "Find a Friend" set up on it.'

'What?'

'It's a thing where you can see on a map on your phone where all your friends are. It meant he knew where I was if he wanted to find me. I told Seamus. We switched it off, but I didn't think it was enough. So he took the phone away.'

'You don't have to be afraid of "Simon Harris", Sarah,' Lucy said. 'He's dead.'

The girl momentarily brightened, then at once, her expression seemed to darken and she began twisting one hand around the other. 'That wasn't his real name,' she said.

'We know,' Lucy said. 'He'd loads of names he used on Facebook. We know he targeted other girls, too.'

The girl straightened a little. 'You're sure he's dead?'

Lucy nodded. 'I watched him drown myself.' She managed a smile, which was reciprocated by Sarah Finn. 'So you don't need to be afraid any more,' Lucy said. 'You can tell us everything.'

'Can I get a drink?' Finn said. 'And can you let Seamus out, too? He's been looking after me.'

Lucy glanced quickly at Robbie who raised his eyebrows sceptically.

'We'll certainly manage a drink,' Lucy said. 'Let's see what you have to say first before we worry about the other thing, eh?'

Chapter Forty-three

'It started out OK,' Finn said, sipping from the can of Diet Coke she'd been brought from the Mace across the street from the station.

'We'd meet in town sometimes. I knew the first time I met him that he was older than he'd said in his profile. He said he preferred the company of teenagers 'cause we always told the truth. We weren't phonies, he said.'

She glanced up at Lucy, then quickly to Robbie. 'I tried to stay away from him, but he seemed harmless. He'd talk about music and that. But he had some really cool bands I'd never heard of. He'd let me listen to some. And we always met in the town where there was people about, so it was never weird or anything.'

She paused, sipping again at the Coke. A little dribbled as she lowered the can and she lifted her hand and wiped at her mouth with the back of her wrist.

'There was this one band I'd never even heard of. A singer. Jessica Hoop. He let me hear some of her songs. He said he thought I'd like it.'

She paused again, staring down at her hands. 'I bet if you asked my mum what music I liked, *she* wouldn't be able to tell you,' she snapped. 'She'd not have a notion. She'd not care.'

'But he did,' Lucy said softly. The girl needed to justify what had happened as a result of her trusting 'Harris'. She needed to know that Lucy understood. And she did.

She nodded. 'He told me he'd put it on a disc for me. Then, when we met the next time, he gave me a phone with a whole load of stuff on it. I didn't want to take it, but he said it was an old one he didn't need any more; he'd got a new one on contract and was just going to dump it anyway, he said. He'd put all this music on it for me. I didn't want him to think I wasn't grateful. He'd gone to all that effort.'

She finished her Coke, pressing on the two sides of the can, pinching with her fingers until it bent double in her hands.

'He phoned me and said he was going to a party. Did I want to come with him? They'd be loads of people – girls my own age and that, so I'd not to be worrying.

'I told my mum I was going out with my friends. She didn't give a shit anyway. Half the time I was there she didn't know it anyhow. She'd not care. Her and Seamus were out all the time when he was here.'

She placed the can on the table, moved it slightly until it sat just in the position she wanted it, a small act of control to compensate for the fact that the events she was describing would soon involve those over which she had had none.

'He picked me up at the bus depot. Me and another girl. I didn't know her. He said he would drop us off then he had to collect a friend. The other girl seemed to know him really well. He handed her a bottle of cider.

She took some and gave it to me. I wasn't going to drink it, but she looked at me like I was just a kid, like I was too young to drink. I'd had some before, at parties and that. So I took it.'

She swallowed. 'When we'd finished that bottle he handed us back another one.'

'Where was the party?' Lucy asked.

Sarah shook her head. 'I don't know. It was dark outside of the car. And the cider was making everything weird. It was in the country somewhere because I asked him to stop. I thought I was going to be sick and he pulled in along the road. There were no street lights or anything. I could see cows watching me from the field beside where we stopped. They were just staring at me. I thought I'd be sick, but I wasn't. Not then anyway. Later.

'We arrived at this old house. It smelt bad, like it wasn't being used all the time. There were loads of men in the house, all older than us. And a few girls sitting in the living room. I knew one of them to see, from about town. They were all drinking cider and beers. We went in with them and starting drinking.'

She paused again, moved the can again.

'I didn't notice that they were being taken out of the room. One at a time. Then "Simon" appeared. He was smiling. Said he had something to give me. A present. He didn't want the other girls to see, in case they were jealous. We went into one of the rooms by ourselves. He took out something in a packet. Said it would give my drink a kick. He put it in the drink, gave it a swish around and then took some, to show it was OK. Except … except I don't think he took any at all.

'I drank it because I knew he wanted me to. Then he started kissing me. I felt like I had to – he'd been so kind to me.'

The girl lowered her head, her tears coming freely now.

'I don't remember what happened after that. Only what had happened when I woke up again.'

She glanced at Lucy, scouring her face to see if she was being judged. She ignored Robbie completely.

'What he had done. What he done to me.'

She shuddered now and she spluttered into sobs. Lucy moved from her seat, round to where Sarah sat, put her arms around the girl and held her while she cried.

'Ssh,' she said finally. 'He can't do anything to you any more.'

She looked up at Robbie, who was sitting, his hands folded in his lap, his expression studiously neutral. 'Let's take a break, shall we?'

Chapter Forty-four

As they sat again after a toilet break for Sarah, Lucy sensed that something had changed about the girl, that in the telling of what had happened, and perhaps in the knowledge that 'Simon Harris' – as she knew him – was dead, the girl had found some degree of comfort, a modicum of solace in knowing she had been heard and believed.

'Will I start where I left off?' the girl asked, sitting.

'Please,' Lucy said.

She brushed her hair from her face. Her cheeks were dry now, but the skin still flushed, the eyes red rimmed with crying, the whites of her eyes threaded with veins. She looked somehow younger than her fifteen years.

'It happened a few times after that,' the girl said. Lucy realized that far from Sarah feeling relieved at what had passed, she had instead simply been steeling herself for the rest of the story. 'He'd invite me to a party. He'd pick me up with some other girls and we'd get drunk. Most of the time it was in the same house. A couple of times it was somewhere different. A bit nicer. Further away, though. Near the sea, I think. There was a room with an old pool table in it. We'd all hang around in there until he came back with more drink and … whatever it was.'

'Did he always rape you?'

The girl hesitated a moment before answering. 'I didn't know if it was rape or not. Because I'd had the cider and that. He said I'd agreed.'

'You can't agree, Sarah,' Lucy said. 'You're too young. He knew that.'

The girl flushed, her eyes brimming again. She inhaled, held the breath a moment, then let it go. 'Sometimes others did it. I woke one time and there was someone leaving the room that I didn't know. It wasn't "Simon". But I knew what he'd done.'

Lucy pulled a handful of tissues from the box on the table. Sarah took them and rubbed at her nose. She raised her head a little, as if to stymie her tears.

'How often did this happen?' Lucy asked.

'Every week,' Sarah said. 'We'd go every week.'

'Always to the same house?'

She shook her head. 'Two different places. It was like taking turns week about week; one week in the smelly house, the other in the place with the pool table.'

'Were the men there always the same?'

She shook her head. 'Some.'

'And what about your mum? Did she not wonder where you were all night?'

Sarah shrugged. 'She'd be out of it when I got home. She'd not even know I'd been out to start with.'

Lucy paused as she considered how best to word the next question without sounding accusatory. 'I don't want you to take this the wrong way, Sarah, but I need to know. Why did you meet with him again, after the first time he raped you, Sarah?'

'He said if I didn't, he'd hurt my mum.'

'Did you ever try telling your mother about what was happening?'

The girl shook her head. 'He said if I told her, they'd kill her. He said he knew who she was. They'd ... he said he'd ... shoot her.' Though the girl paused as she spoke as if to give the impression that she was too upset to speak freely, Lucy wasn't wholly convinced.

'What did he really say, Sarah?'

The girl stared at her, her mouth hanging a little open. 'He said he knew who sold her stash to her. That they'd put something in it if I told. She'd just not wake up again, he said.'

'But you told Seamus? Your mum said you didn't get on.'

'We didn't,' the girl conceded quietly. 'I didn't mean for him to find out. I just wanted to hide in the van. But I'd no choice. He wanted to take me back to my mum, but I knew Simon'd think I'd told her when I hadn't answered his messages and that.'

Lucy considered what the girl had said. 'Did Seamus ever try anything on with you?'

'God, no,' she replied. 'He made me up my own room. I didn't know he'd another house.'

'Did he tell you why he lied about going to Manchester?'

Sarah shrugged. 'He said Mum's using got to him. She was fun to be about for a while, then she started all that shit and he needed to get a breather from her for a few days. I know how he felt.'

'Why now?'

Sarah rubbed at her nose, balled the tissues in her hand and buried it deep in the pocket of the hooded top she wore. 'What?'

'Why leave now? What happened? Why not run away weeks ago?'

Immediately, she saw the girl glance at the doorway, as if to reassure herself that there was a way out. She licked at her lips. 'Can I get another Coke?' she asked.

'Why now?' Lucy persisted. 'Tell me that and we can take another breather if you need to.'

Sarah Finn seemed to consider the offer. 'The girl the first night. The one with the cider. I saw her a few times after that. At the parties. She was a nice girl. She looked after some of the others when they were hurting after … you know. She took care of them. Even when she was being hurt herself.'

Lucy could feel something gnawing at her insides, sensing already where the conversation was headed.

'There was a party at the weekend. All weekend. I was there just on Saturday night. But she was there. She'd been there for a few days. She was out of it, completely. It was like she didn't know where she was or what was happening. Well, I saw her again after the party.'

'Where?'

'She was the girl they found dead on the train tracks. Karen was her name, I think.'

They left Sarah to have her Coke while Lucy went to the main office and called through for the Strand Road to fax through pictures of both Karen Hughes and Carlin himself. Though the quality of the faxes wasn't ideal, both were still recognizable. 'Is this the girl you met?' Lucy asked, handing Sarah the image of Karen Hughes as she re-entered the room.

The girl looked at the image, her eyes flushing once more. She nodded. 'That's her.'

'One more question, Sarah,' Lucy said. 'This man.' She handed Sarah the page with Carlin's picture on it.

'I know him,' the girl said, dropping the page on the desk as if it had scalded her simply to hold it. 'He was one of them. He was at the parties.'

'One of them?' Lucy said. 'He was "Simon Harris".'

Sarah Finn's eyes widened, her face paling under the harsh fluorescent glare of the strip lighting in the room.

'That's not "Simon Harris". That's nothing like him. Is he the man who died? This man?'

Lucy glanced at Robbie, before nodding lightly.

'Jesus Christ,' Sarah Finn keened, backing into the corner, balling in on herself, wrapping her arms around her knees. 'Jesus. He's going to kill me.'

'No one's going to kill you, Sarah,' Lucy said, moving to the girl. 'I promise.'

The girl looked up at her from where she sat, her face a mask of disbelief. Lucy could think of nothing to say that might convince her otherwise.

Chapter Forty-five

Despite their best efforts, neither Lucy nor Robbie could convince Sarah Finn that she was safe from 'Harris'. Eventually Robbie agreed that her mother be allowed to spend some time with her in the interview room, though under his supervision, in the hope that her presence might help settle the girl a little. Lucy took Sinead Finn's arrival as an opportunity to check how the interview with Seamus Doherty was developing.

Burns was leading the interview with Doherty in Interview Room 2. He glanced round with some irritation when Lucy first tapped on the door, but upon seeing who it was, rose and came out to her.

'Has she said anything we can use on him?' he asked. '*He*'s saying nothing.'

Lucy shook her head. 'She claims that she hid away in his lorry. She got out when she felt it stop, thinking she was on the ferry. Instead, he was parked up at the house. She was at a party with Karen Hughes the night before she died, during the time Karen was missing.'

'Does she know if Carlin killed her?'

Lucy shook her head. 'She says Carlin wasn't "Harris". He was one of the others.'

'What others? Maybe she's confused. Give her a breather and try again.'

Lucy raised a hand to silence him, then realized the inappropriateness of the gesture to her superior.

'She was groomed by "Harris". They met up a few times in town. He eventually gave her the phone with some music on it, made a show of saying it was nothing too big. After a while he invited her to a party. He got her drunk, slipped her something in a drink and raped her. She says it happened several times after that, at other parties. Then, when she was passed out, she thinks other men raped her too. She recalls seeing at least one leaving her room as she came round from whatever "Harris" had given her.'

'Was Carlin one of the ones who raped her?'

Lucy nodded. 'He was at the parties. We can assume if he was there, he was involved in some way. I need to get pictures of Gene Kay, too, to see if he was there. But she says "Harris" definitely isn't Carlin. I think we're looking for someone younger.'

Burns swore softly under his breath. 'We *need* to connect Kay. After the prick burning to death over it.'

Lucy said nothing for a moment, guessing that his need to connect Kay had more to do with expediency than justice. 'She says Karen had been at the last party for most of the weekend. She saw her there on the Saturday. I think she went missing on the Thursday because she was taken away to a house party for the weekend.'

'Why did they kill her?'

'Maybe she recognized someone she shouldn't have,' Lucy suggested. 'But if she'd been there all weekend – been at the parties before – she'd presumably have encountered whoever it was before that.'

'She was seen alive on the day before her death? On the Saturday?'

Lucy nodded.

'Then what happened on the Sunday that would have caused someone to kill her?'

Lucy thought about it. She had done the press releases about her being missing, but that had been on Friday and had been in the Saturday press.

'Her father,' she said suddenly. 'The Sunday papers – one of them ran a story about her father. They'd connected her with Eoghan Harkin somehow.'

'Whoever had her knew her father then?' Burns offered.

'Maybe,' Lucy said. 'Or maybe they were just afraid of what he'd do if he found out. Sarah said that "Harris" said he'd kill her mother if she told. That threat might have been a little harder to use about Eoghan Harkin.'

'It couldn't have been a message to him? Retaliation in some way?'

Lucy shook her head. 'The body was set up to look like she'd killed herself on the train tracks. If someone wanted to send a message they'd want him to know she'd been murdered. In this case, they wanted to kill her and cover it up. Make it look like suicide.'

'Which would only be believable if she was the type to kill herself.'

'She was depressed,' Lucy said. 'She was struggling with self-esteem issues. She was the perfect candidate for it. And the perfect candidate for grooming, too. Lacking in confidence, open to flattery, unstable home life.'

All of which applied equally to Sarah Finn, Lucy reflected. 'The question is, how did the groomer know that they were perfect candidates for it?'

'Ask the girl, see if she knows. See if he gave her any hints about where he first saw her. And get a description.'

Lucy stopped at the main office again to phone through for a picture of Gene Kay. It took all of thirty seconds for Sarah Finn to confirm for her that Kay was not 'Simon Harris' either, nor indeed had she ever seen him at any of the parties.

'You're sure?' Lucy asked. 'Look again at the image. He might have been dressed differently.'

The girl studied the image, examining the eyes and mouth, covering part of the face with the flat of her hand to better focus on particular features. Finally she shook her head. 'I've never seen him before. I'd remember any of the people there if I saw them again. He wasn't there.'

'And the other man I showed you earlier, he was there but wasn't "Simon Harris"?'

Finn nodded her head. 'I remember his face. Simon was younger than them, in his twenties maybe. Thin faced. Short dark hair. He wasn't an old man.'

'But this guy was definitely not involved?' she asked, pointing to Kay's picture.

'I never saw him. Not once.'

If that was the case, Lucy realized, then how had the collection of images, taken from the parties, ended up in Kay's house, after Fleming had checked it and found nothing there the day before.

Chapter Forty-six

Robbie eventually agreed that Sarah Finn be allowed home with her mother, though only with the understanding that they would be visited daily and that Sinead Finn was to agree to enter an addiction programme. The woman announced that Seamus Doherty was no longer welcome in her home, having lied to her and kept her daughter from her for so long. Having been the only person Sarah felt able to confide in, Doherty now found himself excluded from the girl's life.

Lucy drove back to the PPU struggling to make sense of all that had happened. Gene Kay had clearly been used as a distraction, a scapegoat on whom could be pinned the killing of Karen Hughes. The fact that he had died in the house fire prevented him being able to argue his innocence.

When she reached the unit, instead of going into her own office, she cut across to Cooper in Block 10. He was working on a laptop, scrolling through a series of spreadsheets, when she came in, one of his colleagues having allowed Lucy into the block as he was leaving.

'That looks interesting,' Lucy said.

'Serious or sarcastic?' Cooper asked, leaning backwards to see who was talking to him. 'Oh, hi, Lucy,' he said, when he saw her. 'Sarcastic then.'

'That's very cynical,' she commented, pretending to be offended.

'But probably very accurate,' he countered. 'I hear you found the girl. It's been on the news. How is she?'

'Useful,' Lucy said.

'Well, I'm sure that'll be a relief to her parents.'

'After "Harris" had won the girls' trust, he took them to a house party and got them either drunk or high. They were raped while they were out of it.'

'This is why I work with numbers,' Cooper said. 'Tax fraud doesn't make you want to kill someone.'

'The important thing is she saw "Harris". And "Harris" is not Carlin.'

'Really?' Cooper asked, sitting up. 'What about Kay?'

Lucy shook her head. 'She'd never even seen him before. Carlin, at least, she'd seen at the parties. She thought he might have been one of the men who raped her. Kay, though, drew a complete blank.'

'That doesn't mean he wasn't involved.'

'Perhaps. But it does mean he wasn't "Simon Harris" and, therefore, not "Paul Bradley" or any of the other sock puppet identities.'

Cooper pushed back from the desk he was working at and rolled his seat across to the opposite bench, propelling himself with his feet. He reached the large iMac and began clicking through folders.

'What are you after?' Lucy asked, joining him.

'"Bradley" or "Harris" or whatever he was called was definitely using the free Wi-Fi in the Foyleside the day you went in. Kay was there obviously, but if he wasn't "Harris", then someone else in the restaurant must have been.'

'What, and it was just a coincidence that Kay was there too and we went after him?'

'Maybe,' Cooper said. 'Or maybe not. Maybe Kay was set up. Maybe "Bradley" got wind that we were on to his account after Karen's death and made a point of going on the accounts somewhere public, where we would find Kay. Regardless, we do know that whoever was on the accounts was in the restaurant, right?'

'OK,' Lucy said, pulling over a chair and sitting.

'I had the CCTV footage for the day sent across after I couldn't retrieve anything off Kay's phone. I wanted to satisfy myself that he had been online. If Sarah Finn has seen "Harris", or "Bradley", then she might recognize him as one of the other customers.'

'She might,' Lucy said, approvingly.

Cooper finally found the folder he wanted and opened up the footage. He played it through at half-speed, allowing them time to examine it in more detail, looking for possible candidates.

'Do you remember anyone standing out, apart from Kay?' Cooper asked.

Lucy shook her head, but, as she considered it, she recalled a man she'd put in his twenties sitting by the window. He'd been with a woman and child though.

She assumed that the perpetrator would be alone. She told Cooper as much.

'If he was at the window, this camera angle will be no good,' Cooper commented. He closed the image he was looking at and picked another from the folder. This time, the view was of the seating area, the main concourse of the Foyleside visible through the window beyond.

Cooper forwarded the footage until the time counter in the corner read twelve, then continued at half-speed. Sure enough, some time later, a young man with thinning black hair appeared in the image, bearing a tray with a burger and drink on it. He sat alone at the window and, taking out his phone, spent some time seemingly texting on it. After ten minutes a woman and child arrived. Though there was no sound, Lucy could tell that the woman was asking if they might share his table. He agreed without even looking at them, his attention focused on the phone he held in front of him.

Some minutes later, those in the seats all around him stood quickly, their attention directed off screen to where Lucy knew Kay had been. Sure enough, in the subsequent images, Kay could be seen running down the concourse outside the window, pursued by several officers, Lucy included.

Those inside watched as the events unfolded. Rather than following the events unfolding outside the restaurant, the man quickly put away his phone and continued eating. A few minutes later, a uniformed officer appeared at the table, paused for a few moments, clearly taking the names of all those there, then moved on. After a further minute, the man balled up the wrapping of his food, gathered his stuff and left, pulling the hood of his top over his head as he did.

'Can you run me off the best picture of him you can find?'

'The best? It's all relative,' Cooper offered apologetically. 'I could try sourcing footage from outside, but with the hood up, he'll be even more difficult to identify.'

He moved back through the footage slowly until he found the best image he could. He was right about it being relative; the image was grainy, the man's features blurred. Still, it would hopefully be enough for Sarah Finn to at least be able to confirm whether or not he was "Simon Harris".

Lucy drove straight up to the Finn house, having thanked Cooper for his work. Sinead opened the door, the action soundtracked by raucous laughter from the living room beyond. Sinead wore a black dress, low cut enough to provide Lucy with a view of her cleavage.

'Is Sarah free for a moment?' Lucy asked, stepping inside. In the confines of the hallway, she could smell the spirits off Sinead's breath, sweet and sharp.

'We're having a party, celebrating her safe return,' Sinead explained. 'Sarah?' she shouted.

A moment later, Sarah appeared from upstairs. It seemed she was the only one not attending the party being held in her honour.

'All right, love,' Sinead said, rubbing her daughter's arm a little too vigorously, smiling through the haze of her drink, a rictus that lacked all warmth. 'Come in for a drink if you want one,' she added to Lucy. 'Or are you on duty?'

Lucy wondered at the mentality of the woman, inviting an officer in for a drink hours after being told she would need to enter an addiction programme if she wanted to keep her daughter at home.

When the door to the living room closed, Sarah seemed to slump against the wall.

'Are you OK?' Lucy asked.

'I ... I don't want to be here any more. Being away with Seamus, even for those few days, was so easy. There was no shit, no drugs or drinking or parties. It was like a normal life.'

Lucy nodded. 'That's understandable,' she said.

'But how do you come back to this shit? At least before I didn't know any different. I thought this was normal.'

'I can ask them to leave if you'd like,' Lucy offered.

Sarah shook her head. 'They'll leave in a bit anyway, once the carry-out is finished.'

Lucy nodded, the folded picture in her hand, suddenly reluctant to ask the girl to look at it.

Sarah, though, had already worked out the purpose of the visit. 'Is this another picture to look at?' she asked, gesturing towards the sheet.

Lucy nodded. 'Do you mind?'

The girl shook her head, taking the page and opening it. She hissed a sharp intake of breath as she looked at it, then, handing it back quickly to Lucy, said, 'That's him. That's "Harris".'

'You're sure?' Lucy asked.

Sarah Finn nodded her head. 'I think that's him.'

Chapter Forty-seven

'This is "Simon Harris"?' the ACC asked. She was sitting in Burns's office, having been called by the Chief Super.

'According to Sarah Finn,' Lucy said. 'He was in the Foyleside at the time we picked up Kay. He was using his phone.'

'He could be anyone,' Burns said. 'The image is so grainy, it doesn't really help us move forward.'

'It at least necessitates that we do move forward,' Lucy said. 'We know Carlin was involved in this ring, but we don't have the ringleader. I think this is him.'

Her mother held the picture at arm's length, lowering her glasses to see if doing so aided her examination of the image. Finally she nodded, laying the picture on the desk.

'So, what's your next move, Superintendent?' she asked.

Burns was leaning against a filing cabinet to her right, biting on the skin around his finger, angling his hand to facilitate the process. He spat the small bit of skin he had removed from the tip of his tongue. Lucy watched the exchange between her mother and her lover with distaste.

'If the girl says he was the one who groomed her, then we need to follow it up. I still think Kay is involved, though, regardless of what the girl said. Why would he have had pictures of her?'

'Why would she not remember having seen him take them if he had?' Lucy asked.

'You said yourself she was drugged,' Burns retorted. 'Even she's not sure if she said she *thinks* it's him.'

'What if he played us?' Lucy said, pointing towards the picture lying before her mother. 'What if he knew Kay would be a suspect with his history and he set him up, going online somewhere public where we'd find Kay. He's been offline since, as far as we know. Maybe he saw Kay as the perfect fall guy. Then planted the pictures in his house after he'd been lifted.'

'What? Do you think he set the house alight too?' Burns scoffed.

'It's possible,' Wilson said.

'I don't think so,' Lucy began. After all, she suspected she knew who had been involved in lighting the fire. Gavin Duffy. 'I think Kay's burning was in retaliation for Karen Hughes's death. But we do know that uniforms took the names of all those who were in the restaurant at the time. Maybe we could follow up on any single men listed in that.'

'That's all been done already,' Burns said. 'Nothing showed up from it.'

'If whoever was interviewing thought Kay was our man, they may not have been too thorough,' Lucy objected.

'Careful, Sergeant,' Burns said. 'I seem to remember it was PPU who missed Kay's paedophile collection when you searched his house.'

'Maybe we didn't miss anything. If this is how it went down, maybe there was nothing to find when we searched the house,' Lucy argued. 'In which case what about Inspector Fleming?'

The comment was greeting initially with silence, her mother glaring at her as she lifted her glasses and put them on, the skin around her mouth tightening. Finally she spoke. 'That's not your concern, Sergeant. Leave it at that.'

'But the stuff in Kay's might have been a set-up, to put Kay in the frame for Karen Hughes,' Lucy began. 'It's not fair if Tom —'

'That's enough, Lucy,' her mother warned. Then she turned to Burns. 'Would you give me a moment, Mark?'

Burns lingered a second, as if in protest at yet again being ask to leave his own office, before pushing himself off the cabinet with his rump and padding out of the room.

Wilson stared at Lucy a moment before speaking. When she did speak, it was not what Lucy had expected.

'What happened to your face?'

'I was hit.'

'By whom?'

'A suspect.'

'I see.' She rubbed at the bridge of her nose, then removed her glasses again. 'These bloody things are new and they're leaving me with sores on my nose. I should have stayed with the old ones.'

Lucy watched her, aware of the tactic, the circling around small talk as she worked out the best angle for attack.

'I heard there was an incident at Alan Cunningham's family home last night.'

'Really?'

Wilson stared without speaking this time.

'If you heard that,' Lucy queried, straightening herself up in the seat, 'then why are you asking what happened to my face?'

'I just wondered if you were really so stupid as to go to that house alone.'

'No one else is interested.'

Wilson shook her head, smiling ruefully. 'The martyr role doesn't suit you, Lucy. Is that what you think? You're the only one who cares? That we should take every case personally, make it our mission?' She widened her eyes on the final word to emphasize its grandness.

Lucy shrugged. 'I think we should at least give a shit.'

'But no one feels as deeply as you do, isn't that right?' Wilson replied, sitting back now. 'Because that's what we should do. Invest everything in our work. Care so deeply that we forget about everything around us.'

'Well, I learnt from the master,' Lucy commented, holding her mother's stare.

Wilson accepted the comment with a light laugh. 'Always the answer, Lucy.'

Lucy folded her arms, waiting to see what the next angle would be. Again, it was not what she had expected.

'The Kellys in Petrie Way. How do they fit into this case you're working?'

Lucy shook her head, once, briefly. 'I don't know who you're talking about.'

'The Kelly family. You've been parked outside their house, watching them three or four times now.'

'Twice,' Lucy corrected, then regretted speaking.

'My mistake,' Wilson replied. 'And they connect to Karen Hughes, how?'

'They don't,' Lucy said, softly. Then she straightened herself again and, clearing her throat, repeated the comment. 'They're connected to something else.'

'They are the family who have adopted the Quigg child, is that right?'

'Again, if you already know that, why ask?'

'How did you find out?'

'How did you?' Lucy retorted.

'Officially,' Wilson snapped. 'Not through the back door. Not off a cheating ex-boyfriend.'

'He's not a cheat,' Lucy said.

'You told me he cheated on you.'

'I said we disagreed on monogamy. I didn't say he was the one who cheated.'

'Of course he was the one who cheated; you're not the type, Lucy,' Wilson said.

'So says the expert on commitment,' Lucy replied.

Wilson shook her head, as if appraising her daughter anew. 'I've had my fill of the cheek, Lucy. And the chip on your shoulder.'

Lucy blushed in spite of herself, but did not respond.

'If you really cared as much as you say, you wouldn't be putting other people at risk. If this comes out, about you stalking that family, what would happen to your boyfriend? Giving out details of foster families? Is that you caring deeply?'

'He can fend for himself,' Lucy snapped. 'I didn't ask for it.'

'I'm sure you didn't have to.'

'I wanted to make sure he was OK. Joe Quigg.'

'And when you did? The first time you went you must have seen that he's in a good home. A home vetted by people who actually know what they're doing. What took you back the second time?' she added scornfully.

'I don't know,' Lucy muttered.

'They've reported your car registration number,' Wilson said.

'How did it come to you?'

'Never mind,' Wilson said, glancing at her desk. Lucy knew that such a small matter wouldn't make it to the ACC unless she was keeping tabs on Lucy.

'Are you checking up on me?' Lucy asked suddenly.

'I'm your mother, Lucy. I've a right to be interested in how you're getting on. God knows, talking to you gets me nowhere. I worry about you.'

The baldness of the comment caught Lucy off guard. She shifted in her seat uncomfortably. 'Well, you don't have to. I'm just doing my job. You were the one who put me in the PPU because of my "affinity for the vulnerable", wasn't that what you said?'

'Having an affinity with them doesn't mean becoming one of them,' her mother said. 'I know how you feel. I used to— look, Lucy, you can't take every case personally. Because some things don't get solved. Killers walk the streets every day – even ones we caught and jailed. We have to see them back on the streets because an agreement was made. Should we all *feel* that?'

'At least you'd know you could feel.'

'Don't be so melodramatic, Lucy,' her mother snapped. 'Look at where feelings got Tom Fleming.'

'He's a good man.'

'He's responsible for you!' Wilson said suddenly, standing now. 'He should be looking out for you. If he's drinking, he can't do that. His drinking puts you at risk and I won't tolerate that.'

'Don't pretend you're looking out for me,' Lucy said, standing, feeling suddenly unsteady, the room seeming to shift beneath her. She could feel her face flush with heat.

'Of course I am, Lucy,' Wilson said. 'I worry about you.'

'Like you did when you walked out on me? Left me with a father who liked teenage girls? I preferred you when you didn't give a shit. At least then we knew where we stood.'

Her mother opened her mouth to speak, then seemed to swallow back her words. Instead she moved back behind her desk and sat, putting on her glasses again. 'You have one chance left, Lucy,' she said finally. 'You're making mistakes, putting yourself and others at risk. Your stalking the Cunningham house could be used against us if we ever do get him and try to convict. Police victimization. You should be taken off the case immediately. I'm giving you one last chance. Do the job you're expected to do. That's all. No personal vendettas. Before someone gets hurt.'

Lucy remained standing, struggling to find something to say.

'And leave that family in peace.'

'Alan Cunningham's or Joe Quigg's?'

'Both,' her mother said.

Chapter Forty-eight

Tara Gallagher was sitting in the incident room working on a report at her PC. The remains of her dinner sat on the desk next to her: an empty crisp packet and an opened can of Diet Coke. She leaned close to the screen as she typed, stabbing one-fingered at the keyboard.

'Thinking of someone?' Lucy asked.

Tara glanced up. 'Oh, hey,' she managed, then turned her attention to the screen, swore softly and deleted the mistake she had just made.

Lucy pulled across a seat and sat next to her. 'Everything all right, you?'

'I'm stuck with bloody witness reports,' Tara said. 'Everyone else is working on other things and I'm stuck writing up this crap. I can hardly read half of the notes.'

'Where's the rest of the team?'

'Reassigned. There's been a spate of beatings in the town. A young lad got a battering this evening on his way to his work do.'

'Christmas parties week,' Lucy said. She realized that she'd not given it much thought.

Tara nodded. 'You know. I thought you'd made the wrong choice, going with PPU. But at least you're working stuff. This is mind numbing.'

'Burns?'

Tara nodded again, lowering her voice as she spoke, glancing furtively towards his office door lest she be heard. 'It's like an old boys' network. Your face needs to fit. And mine doesn't.'

'That's 'cos you're too good-looking,' Lucy said, laughing. 'How could this face be fitted in a frame?'

Tara laughed, thumping Lucy lightly on the leg. 'Bitch,' she said.

'You know I mean it,' Lucy replied, glad that whatever uneasiness she'd felt over Tara reporting her to Burns following the scrapyard had been passed. She knew Tara was finding it hard to make her mark in CID. There was little point in holding a grudge. 'So what are you working?'

'Door-to-door statements from the Finn abduction.'

'Sure we've got her back now,' Lucy protested.

'Tell that to him,' Tara said, sulkily. 'All Ts need to be crossed apparently.'

Lucy began shifting through the paperwork piled on the desk. 'The day we got Kay in Foyleside. Someone went round taking the names of everyone else in the restaurant afterwards. Do you have that here?'

'You're messing it up,' Tara said, slapping Lucy's hand away. 'It's in reverse order.'

'Reverse order? Do you want to feel challenged?'

Tara laughed. 'I lifted it out of the box like that. The newest stuff went on top. The Kay arrest was before the house-to-house.' She sorted through the pages, eventually pulling out handwritten lists of names and contact details stapled to handwritten statement sheets.

'Bingo,' she said. She laid them on the desk and began leafing through each page. 'Mickey did the checks,' she said. She read through the first brief statement, then flicked to the next. 'Jesus,' she muttered. 'Look at the state of this.'

Lucy leaned across and began reading the statement. The first was taken from a fifty-five-year-old school teacher who had been in the restaurant with his wife and children for lunch.

> *The interviewee reported first being aware of the suspect's presence when the suspect assaulted an officer and fled the scene. The interviewee saw officers pursue the suspect along the central concourse of the shopping centre.*

When Lucy turned the page to the next statement, she understood Tara's reaction, for that statement was exactly the same.

'Look at the time he recorded for each statement,' Tara said. Lucy glanced at the details on the bottom of the page. Each statement was separated by at most ten minutes.

'He interviewed them by phone,' Lucy said. 'And copied the same statement over and over.'

Tara beamed. 'The lazy bastard! Wait till I tell Burns,' she added, gathering the sheets.

Lucy raised a placatory hand. 'Would it not be even better if we could show that the actual perpetrator had been interviewed by Mickey and he'd not picked up on it?'

She knew it was a low shot at Mickey, with whom she had no particular gripe. Nevertheless, having got this close to the list of names, the last thing she needed was for Tara to hand them over to Burns before she had a chance to look at them.

Tara hesitated, clearly torn between her desire to land Mickey in it straight away and the possible increased kudos she'd gain if she could only delay gratification for a few hours.

'Let's just take a look at the men he spoke with, eh? See if anything stands out,' Lucy suggested.

A little reluctantly, Tara sat again, laying the pages down flat.

'Have you the list of names first? We know that the possible suspect was sitting with a woman and child. Let's see if we have any groupings of three, with the man having a different surname from the woman and child accompanying him.'

It was not quite so simple, for the names were listed continuously, so that the size of each group could not be determined. Still, there were, in the end, only eight men listed who did not share surnames with any of the family groups.

'Have we statements for these eight?' Lucy asked. 'We can check their dates of birth, see if that helps eliminate some of them.'

Comparing names against statements, they were able to identify two of the men as being over forty-five.

While it didn't exclude them completely, Sarah Finn had suggested that 'Simon Harris', as she knew him, was in his twenties. Four of the men listed were, in fact, teenagers, ranging in age from fourteen to eighteen. The elder ones certainly would have to be considered. Of the final two – Peter Bell and Gordon Fallon – Fallon's date of birth put him at twenty-nine, while the other, Bell, did not have a date of birth listed.

'He didn't speak to him,' Lucy said. 'He filled out the statement sheet without talking to him.'

Lucy could understand entirely. Kay had been caught, a paedophile with history. Why waste time taking witness statements from people who were all saying the same thing?

'Let's check the driving licences,' Lucy suggested. 'See if their pictures match the image ICS pulled from the CCTV footage.'

Tara contacted Licensing while Lucy made them both tea. By the time she'd come back, the images had been emailed through. Both men were in their twenties; Bell was twenty-five. Both were relatively slim in their picture, both had dark hair, though the shadows on the images made it impossible to tell whether this was natural or a trick of the light.

According to the addresses on the licences, Fallon was a local, born and bred in the Creggan, while Bell's address was actually listed for Belfast. Despite this, he had given the officer in Foyleside an address in the Waterside.

'Do you fancy a run out?' Lucy asked. 'We'll try Mr Fallon first, shall we?'

Chapter Forty-nine

Fallon's driving licence details placed him in Westway, in Creggan. They took an unmarked car, planning on speaking to Fallon simply to ascertain whether he had remembered anything further following his initial interview with Mickey.

Fallon lived in a row of houses opposite the local boys' school.

Tara nodded across at the building as they pulled up in front of Fallon's house.

'Significant?' she asked.

'All the victims we know of were girls,' Lucy said. 'That doesn't mean we should dismiss it entirely.'

They knocked at the door of the house, aware that in both houses abutting Fallon's, neighbours had appeared at the living room windows, watching their approach, one more surreptitiously than the other.

The door opened to reveal a girl, in her late teens, standing in the hallway, a baby nestled against her hip.

'Yes?' the girl asked.

'Can we speak with Gordon Fallon, please?'

'Who are you?' the girl demanded, hoisting the child from one hip to the other. The child watched them both with wide-eyed wonder, a baby's bottle of orange cordial clenched in her tiny fist.

'We're with the PSNI,' Tara said. 'We'd like to speak to him about an incident he witnessed last week.'

'The paedo in the Foyleside?' the girl commented. 'Come on in, then.'

The house was small, the lower floor constituting a living area, giving way to a kitchen. The wall separating them carried a breakfast bar and a hatch in the wall through which food could be handed between one room and the next. The girl led them into the living area, then opened the hatch.

'There's two cops to see you,' she called. 'About the paedo.'

'What age is your child?' Lucy asked.

'Fourteen months,' the girl replied. 'She should be walking by now but she's too lazy. She wants to be carried everywhere.'

Fallon appeared at the doorway, looking in. 'All right?' he asked. 'Do youse want a drink of something before I sit down?' he added to Lucy and Tara.

'I'll have a can,' his partner said.

'I'm already in,' Fallon replied. 'I was asking them.'

'I'll take some of yours, then,' the girl commented.

Fallon scowled, moving into the room, handing the girl his beer can and taking position in the armchair opposite the TV. 'What's up? I already talked to the guy on the phone about this. I told him I didn't see anything.'

'Maybe you'd talk us through it again,' Lucy offered. 'Just in case something had bubbled to the surface of your memory between then and now.'

Tara glanced at her, incredulously. For his part, affecting an air of boredom, Fallon ran through a description of the incident that was, in fairness to Mickey, very close to the cut and paste job he'd done on all the witness statements.

'Do you drive?' Lucy asked, when Fallon was finished.

'What's that to do with anything?'

'I'm just wondering,' she offered, nonchalantly. 'I noticed there's no car outside, even though you have a licence.'

'Got repossessed, didn't it,' Fallon said, glancing across at the girl who stood watching proceedings, sipping from the beer can while the child hefted against her side reached out to try to take it from her.

'I told him not to buy it. It was too dear for us. Now I have to take the bus everywhere, wi' a pram and everything.'

'We'd have kept it if you'd stayed working,' Fallon snapped.

'I had to have me baby, didn't I?' the girl retorted.

Aware that long-simmering tensions had been brought quickly to air by the comment, Lucy changed the topic. 'Who were you with when you saw Kay's arrest?' she asked.

'A couple of people from work,' Fallon replied, glancing quickly at his partner again.

'Can you give us their names?' Lucy asked.

'Fiona Doherty, Sharon McMenamin, Kayley Gallagher.'

Though he said nothing further, Lucy could see from the looks they exchanged, that at least one of those named was not someone Fallon's partner was happy to have sharing lunch with him.

'Did any of them have their children with them?' The man in the image had been sitting at a table with a woman and child.

'They've not got kids. Any of them,' Fallon replied.

'Yet,' came the muttered comment from the corner.

'No car,' Lucy said as she and Tara climbed back into their own, having left the couple to whatever fight was brewing between them.

'No hope either,' Tara commented. 'That poor kid.'

They drove down through the town to head across to the Waterside. The streets were busy, people heading to staff parties, some already stumbling along in a manner which suggested that the party, for them at least, had started some hours earlier. Part of Bishop Street was closed off by a police cordon.

'That must be where the beating happened,' Tara said.

They cut down Shipquay Street and waited, halfway down the hill, while a girl tottered across the road, her arms stretched outwards to help her maintain balance on a pair of shoes several inches too high for her own safety. Her dress, meanwhile, was both several sizes too small and several inches too short for her not inconsiderable frame. She held, in one hand, a tiny clutch purse, in the other a bottle of WKD. Despite the cold, and the paucity of material on her dress, she did not carry a coat.

'Jesus, there's someone who got dressed without the three Ms,' Tara said, watching her cross. 'No mother, no mates, no mirror.'

Lucy tried unsuccessfully not to laugh. The girl, glancing up mid-crossing, saw them doing so and loosened the grip on her clutch bag enough to offer them a one-fingered salute.

'Pure class,' Tara commented.

They reached the address listed for Bell a few minutes later. He lived on Bond's Hill, a steep incline running towards the railway station in the Waterside. While most of the buildings along it were businesses, the lower few were residential. The house they stopped at was in darkness. They knocked several times, without response. Finally, Lucy knocked at the door of the neighbouring property.

'We can come back,' Tara said.

'He clearly didn't answer Mickey's call, nor is he answering his door. We don't even know if this is his real address.'

'In that case, we don't even know if Peter Bell is his real name.'

'I think it is,' Lucy began, but was interrupted by the shunting of a dead bolt of the door at which she now stood. The neighbour who answered was an elderly woman. She opened the door a fraction, a thick security chain obscuring a clear view of her face.

'Yes?' she asked.

Lucy held up her warrant card for the woman to see. 'My name is DS Black with the PSNI's Public Protection Unit. We're looking for your neighbour, Mr Bell. Have you seen him lately?'

'What's he done?' the lady asked, the door not moving, Lucy's warrant card clearly not sufficient to engender trust.

'Nothing. He witnessed an incident a few days back and we wanted to check some details on his statement.'

The woman nodded, the gesture clear only through the slight rise and fall of the wisps of grey hair Lucy could make out.

'He keeps strange hours,' the woman said. 'I never know when he's coming. Sometimes I hear him playing music, but that's about it.'

'Do you know what he does?' Lucy asked. 'Does he work locally? We could maybe call with him at work tomorrow?'

'I don't know,' the woman said. 'I think he works with computers.'

Lucy rummaged in her pocket, pulled out the sheet taken from the CCTV footage. 'Mrs ...?'

'Sinclair.'

'Mrs Sinclair. If I hand you in a picture, would you mind looking at it and telling me if it's Mr Bell? In case we've got the wrong person.'

'What was your name again?'

'DS Black,' Lucy said. 'Lucy.'

A thin hand emerged through the gap, the fingers impatiently flicking at the page, taking it and withdrawing back through. Lucy watched as the small figure, her back hunched over, shuffled to beneath the meagre light being thrown off by the ceiling lamp in the hallway. Lucy could understand the woman's reluctance to open the door even to two girls. She was less than five feet tall, her arms narrow, her calf muscles carrying little flesh. Lucy imagined the fear that each knock on the door at night must produce in the woman.

Finally, she shuffled back towards the door. The page was pushed through the gap.

'It could be him,' the woman said. 'It's hard to tell. It could be.'

Chapter Fifty

'If it is our guy, what makes you think it's his real name?' Tara asked, as they pulled away from the front of the house.

'When we raided the restaurant, he was online. He'd been using each of his accounts, updating things. When we arrived, if he did think we were after him, he couldn't be sure which identity we'd uncovered. Working on the assumption that the only identity he hasn't used online is his real one, it would make sense that that would be the only one he'd give to police. Besides, that was the only name he had an ID for, if it was needed: his driving licence.'

'I think that's logical,' Tara said. 'You lost me at "online".'

Lucy raised an eyebrow and smiled. 'I've one other stop I want to make,' she said. 'There's a young lad in care, he was with Karen and saw her with someone in the weeks before she died. I want to check this picture with him. Are you in a rush to get back?'

Tara looked at the clock on the dashboard. 'I'm on shift till ten,' she said. 'You have me for another hour and a half.'

'You're a star,' Lucy said, patting her leg. She took out her phone and called through to the unit.

'Robbie,' she said when he answered. 'Is Gavin there? I wanted to call up and see him for a moment.'

'Sorry, Lucy,' Robbie said. 'Gavin's not come back to the unit yet. The grandparents don't know where he is either.'

'We're in the Waterside,' Lucy said. 'I'll take a quick check around the shops, see if he's hanging around there again. I'll let you know.

'Is that OK?' she asked Tara, who had overheard the conversation. 'It'll only take a few minutes.'

'Is that the boyfriend?'

'Ex,' said Lucy.

'What happened?'

'He snogged one of his co-workers on Hallowe'en night.'

'You broke up with him for that? That's a bit harsh,' Tara said. 'Mind you, he must be a dick, cheating on you,' she added, glancing across at Lucy, holding her gaze.

'I don't take well to people messing me around,' Lucy said.

They pulled up in front of the block of shops, looking around for Gavin or the gang of kids who seemed to habitually congregate there. Tara stayed in the car while Lucy moved around to the rear of the block, but the place was deserted. Finally, she went into the shop. A different assistant was working, a young girl, a student, Lucy guessed, by virtue of the fact she sat behind the till, a lined notebook on her lap, filled with neat blue

301

copperplate script, a copy of 'The Pardoner's Tale' in her hand.

She placed the books on the stool and stood as Lucy approached.

'Sorry,' Lucy said. 'I'm just ...' She scanned the sweet selection in front of her, lifted a bar and offered it to the girl, hunting through her pockets for money. 'No youngsters hanging around tonight,' she asked, handing the girl a pound.

'You get three for one fifty,' she replied. 'The bars. They're eighty pence each, but you get three for one fifty.'

Lucy glanced down to the sign, which stated this, hanging off the shelf. 'Of course. Great. I'll do that, then.' She lifted the other two bars and handed them to the girl. 'Thanks.'

The girl waited while she hunted again for fifty pence. 'No kids ...' she repeated.

'They're all in the local youth club tonight. It closes at ten.'

The girl stood patiently, waiting for Lucy to continue. Something in her features, the sharpness of her nose, thin and aquiline, made Lucy think she had seen her before.

'Are you looking for Gavin again?' the girl asked and Lucy realized why she recognized her: she had been standing with Gavin the night she had first picked him up from behind the shops.

'Yes.'

'Is he in trouble?'

Lucy shook her head. She glanced at the girl's name badge, which read 'Elena'. 'I needed to ask him something, Elena. Are you and he ...?' She left the question open-ended.

Despite this, the girl blushed. 'Kind of,' she said.

'You're not at the club, then? Too busy working?'

Elena nodded. 'I miss all the *craic*. They all went away paint-balling a few weeks ago to Magilligan for the weekend and I had to work then, too. They stayed over and had a party and everything.'

'It'll be worth it in the long run,' Lucy said, suddenly aware as she said it that it was the typical platitude that an adult might come out with. 'Though it's crap missing stuff like that. Where did they stay?' she added, for she did not remember Gavin being away. Of course, she reasoned, she and Robbie had broken up by then; there was no reason for her to know.

'Jackie has an old house there. They all stayed there, in sleeping bags and that. The youth club supervisors went too, but they were sound about them partying.'

'I'll take a run down to the club and see if Gavin's about,' Lucy said, taking the bars and turning to leave. She turned back and handed one of the bars to the girl. 'For when you're having your break,' she said.

The girl flashed her a smile. 'Thank you,' she said. 'Exam tomorrow,' she added as explanation for the books.

'Good luck,' Lucy offered.

* * *

303

Tara agreed to take her to the Oaks Youth Club in return for the other chocolate bar. The youth club was actually an annex off one of the local factories, a low, stucco block, flat roofed, with metal grilles on the walls. While the grilles were marked with dried splatters of various colours of paint, the walls of the building, though not freshly painted, were clean of all graffiti.

Two younger lads stood in the entrance way, one trying to strike a match to light their cigarettes while the other sheltered him, his coat a makeshift windbreaker.

Beyond them, Lucy saw a figure appear and advance towards the double doors in front of which they stood.

Jackie Logue pushed open the door. 'Not in front of the door, lads,' he said. 'Go on off the grounds if you're going to insist on smoking.'

One of the lads straightened and, for a second, Lucy expected him to challenge Logue. Instead, hiding the cigarette behind his back, he said, 'Sorry, Jackie. We can't get a light out in the wind.'

Logue nodded, signalling that they could continue. 'You shouldn't be smoking at all, you know that. It stunts your growth.'

The boy, now successfully puffing on his cigarette, standing almost a head higher than Logue, laughed good-naturedly. 'Is that what happened you, Jackie?' he asked.

'Bugger off, you cheeky git,' Logue laughed. Then, he must have seen Lucy standing on the pathway to the club. 'Let the lady through, lads. And no smoking on the grounds. Off you go now.'

Logue stepped back, holding open the door, which Lucy took as an invitation to come in. To do so, she had to pass by the two smokers who stood, almost as a guard of honour, on either side of the doorway. Lucy passed so close to one she could smell the stale sweat off his football top, ripe beneath the cigarette smoke.

'Mr Logue?'

'DS Black, isn't it,' Logue said. 'Gavin told me about you. What's he done now?'

'Vanished. He wouldn't be in here, would he?'

'I don't think so,' Logue said. 'Come on in. We'll go through to the office.'

The city had a number of such youth clubs, set up in community centres by the local people to keep the youths off the streets and out of trouble. Lucy followed Logue through the building, which was mostly a single open-plan area. The centre of the room was dominated by two snooker tables. A handful of fellas stood around them, stacks of twenty pence pieces sitting on the cushioned ledge of one showing that they would be playing for sometime. The crack of the balls carried in its wake a collective groan at a missed pocket.

In the far corner was an old-style TV. Another group sat around it, two at their centre gripping the controls of a games console as they steered the two cars racing each other on screen.

As she passed through, Lucy saw a small tuck shop, being staffed by one of the teenagers and, against the back wall, a row of PCs, all of which were in use. At the furthest end of the block was a small room partitioned from the rest of the building. Though it was this that Logue had called his office, it was, in fact, a small kitchen, leading off to a toilet.

'How's Gavin getting on?' Logue asked, as they came into the room. 'Tea? Coffee?'

'No, thanks,' Lucy said. 'He's doing OK. Apart from the gang he's running with.'

'They'll keep him out of trouble,' Logue said, lifting a mug down from the cupboard above his head. 'And I keep them out of trouble. You sure you don't want a brew?'

'I think he was involved in the burning of Gene Kay's house,' Lucy said, studying Logue's face for any flicker of reaction.

He set down the mug and turned to face her. 'Have you any reason for thinking that?'

'He arrived back in the residential unit smelling of petrol.'

Logue shrugged. 'He was probably part of the petrol bombing.' He raised his hands, as if anticipating argument. 'I'm not justifying it. But we both know that they all engage in a bit of recreational rioting on occasions.'

'He was back before the rioting started.'

Logue leaned back against the counter. 'I'm assuming that you've kept this to yourself for now. Or else he would've been lifted long ago for it.'

'He's had his problems,' Lucy said. 'I'm not keen on complicating things for him.'

'He's very lucky then,' Logue said. 'I knew his father. The apple's not fallen too far from the tree there.'

'Was he a killer?' Lucy asked.

'Apart from serving time for the murder of Louisa Gant,' Logue said, confused.

'Of course,' Lucy said. 'But before that, I mean. Did he strike you as a killer? As capable of killing a child.'

'You never really know someone,' Logue said. 'But he was troubled. He was part of the old guard. Hated your crowd for a start. He ruled this area with an iron fist. Had kids kneecapped for thieving, drugs, the whole bit.'

'Whereas you offer them snooker and games consoles?'

'I offer them a roof over their heads and a bit of respect. There's always one or two who are beyond the pale, but most of them are just looking to test the boundaries. That's all. You see this place – no litter, no scrawls on the walls. Set high expectations, and they'll meet them. Bully them and they become bullies.'

'You know a lot about teenagers,' Lucy said. 'Experience?'

Logue shook his head. 'I lost my own boy when he was a teenager,' he said.

'I'm very sorry,' Lucy said, caught off guard by the comment.

Logue shrugged. 'These things happen.'

'How do you find Gavin? Like his father, obviously,' Lucy said, steering the conversation to safer topics.

'He's troubled like Gary. They both struggled with anger. Like they're angry inside and can't deal with it. Gavin might learn from the other kids here how to handle things better.'

'Or those in the residential unit,' Lucy suggested.

Logue nodded. 'Though they've all got their own problems, too, haven't they?' he said.

'Do you think he did burn Kay's house?'

Logue shrugged. 'He was angry about the Hughes girl. He might have, to be honest. I'd hope not. Still, if Kay did kill her, he got what was coming to him. I make no apology for saying that.'

'If,' Lucy agreed.

'You think Kay didn't kill Karen?' Logue asked. 'I assumed it was him. From what was said on the news and that.'

Logue's use of her Christian name struck Lucy as odd, though she did not comment on it. 'The investigation is ongoing.'

'I see,' Logue said. 'I'll ask some of the lads where Gavin is.'

Logue moved out of the office and whistled sharply through his teeth. 'Jimmy, lad. Come 'ere.'

The boy in question slouched into the kitchen, his shoulders hunched, his hair hanging over his face.

'Gavin's missing,' Logue said. 'Any ideas where he's at?'

Jimmy shook his head, the hair flicking across his brow with the movement.

'You don't know who he'd be with? Tony?'

'Tony's here,' the young lad said. 'He's playing "G. T. A".'

Logue repeated the call, this time for Tony.

'Any ideas where Gavin is this evening?' Logue asked.

Tony looked at him, then at Lucy, then back to Logue.

'It's OK. He's done nothing wrong,' Logue reassured him.

'I don't know,' Tony said. 'He had class earlier.'

'School?' Lucy asked.

'Nah. Here.'

'There are after school classes run for the kids here,' Logue said. 'Homework clubs, first aid, basic IT, literacy and numeracy skills, the like of that.'

'Was Gavin here for that?'

Tony nodded. 'He left after six. He's going out with a girl over in the Bogside. He might be away to her.'

'What about Elena?' Lucy asked. 'Is he not going out with her?'

Tony smirked, lowering his head and wiping at his nose with the back of his hand. 'Off and on,' he said. 'Know what I mean?'

Lucy thanked him. Eventually, she figured, Gavin would return to the residential unit. She could drop Tara back, then head to the unit to wait for him there. It might also, she reasoned, give her a chance to talk with Robbie.

As Logue walked her out of the centre, Lucy asked, 'Just as a matter of interest, did Louisa Gant live around here too?'

'Just a few streets across,' Logue said, indicating the direction with the half-empty mug he carried. 'Her father's still there. The mother died a few years after the wee girl. Hanged herself. He found her in the garden. They'd planted a tree with the wee girl in the yard. She hanged herself off it.'

'Jesus,' Lucy whispered. 'I'd not heard that. I remember the case, but I didn't hear what happened afterwards.

'That's always the way, though,' Logue said. 'All the attention at the time. It's them that have to live with what's happened that have to go on in secret. Knowing what they know. What they can't forget.'

Chapter Fifty-one

After leaving Tara off at the Strand Road, Lucy collected her car and headed back to the unit. Before doing so, though, she took a detour via her own house in Prehen for a quick shower. She'd bought Robbie a shirt and a bottle of aftershave for Christmas a few weeks earlier, the two gifts hanging in a plastic bag over the ornamental carving at the bottom of the banisters, mocking her for having thought of him. Still, she wrapped them now, figuring that it might be the last time she would see him before Christmas. Besides, it was the week before Christmas and she was alone. Not that that was good enough reason to reconcile. But it was, she decided, *a* reason.

Robbie looked pleased to see her when he answered the door to her an hour later. 'Come in. You look great. Off on a night out?'

Lucy shook her head. 'I wanted to see Gavin,' she said. 'I just freshened up. Am I normally so bad looking?'

Robbie smiled. 'You know that's not what I meant. Come on in. Gavin's just back. He's in his room.'

Lucy sat on the sofa and placed the plastic bag containing the present on the floor, pushing it slightly beneath the seat so that it wasn't immediately obvious. She realized with some embarrassment that Robbie may not have bought her anything, that he would be embarrassed himself if she gave him a gift without anything to offer in return.

Gavin arrived down a moment later, dropping onto the end of the sofa sullenly, folding his arms across his chest. 'What?'

'I was looking for you,' Lucy said. 'Where have you been?'

'Out.'

'Out where?'

'Just out. What do you want?'

Lucy knew better than to push it. If Gavin felt he was being compelled into telling her where he had been, it could make him more uncooperative as a result. 'I need you to look at something,' Lucy said, taking out the folded sheet on which was printed the image of the young man from Foyleside. 'The guy you saw Karen with a few times? Remember? Was that him?'

Gavin took the sheet from her, studying the page. His mouth seemed to move, as if he were silently forming words to speak, but lacked the ability to do so. Finally, he handed the sheet back.

'I don't know him,' he said.

'Is he the man you saw with Karen?'

'Jesus,' he snapped. 'I said I don't know him. All right?'

'Fine,' Lucy said, putting the page away. 'If you remember anything, let me know.'

Gavin pushed himself up from the seat again and made as if to head back to his room. He stopped, though, and turned to face her.

'I thought Kay killed her,' he said at last.

Lucy shook her head. 'I don't think he did,' she said. 'I think he was set up.'

Gavin stared at her, his shoulders curving into a slight crouch, his hands balling into fists, which he lodged in his trouser pockets. He raised his head interrogatively. 'By who?'

'Possibly by this man,' Lucy said. 'You're sure you don't know who he is?'

'I told you already,' he said. 'I'm going to bed.'

He slouched back towards the rooms, his hands still in his pockets, his gait like one defeated.

'He'll be all right,' Robbie said, though Lucy had not commented.

'If the petrol on his clothes didn't come from petrol bombs, he's probably struggling with whatever it was he did the morning Gene Kay died now he knows Kay didn't kill Karen.'

Robbie moved across to the kitchen. 'Do you want a cuppa?' he asked.

Lucy followed him, leaving her bag on the sofa, Robbie's gift still sitting beneath the seat. 'Have you nothing stronger?' she asked.

Robbie opened the top cupboards, using the small key from his key ring to undo the lock. Inside were bottles of red wine, which a grateful parent had left to the unit months earlier. Lucy remembered it well; Lorna, another member of staff, had told her all about it, proudly showing her the bottles that same evening.

'We don't often get those,' Lorna had commented.

'Bottles of wine?' Lucy had asked.

'No. Grateful clients.'

Robbie lifted down a bottle now. 'Do you fancy a glass?' he asked. 'I've only red.'

'Red's fine,' Lucy said. 'I'll have just the one.'

'I'll maybe join you,' Robbie said. 'A very small one, though.'

They moved back to the sofa, the TV playing soundlessly in the corner. Robbie sat at one end of the sofa, Lucy at the other. He tapped at the bag lying on the floor with his foot. 'Is this mine?' he asked.

'That's very presumptuous,' Lucy smiled. 'It could be for Gavin.'

'Is it?'

She shook her head. 'Happy Christmas.'

Robbie leaned down and, lifting the parcel, weighed it in his hands, as if that might give him some hints as to the contents. 'Clothes?'

'Duh.'

'Can I open it now?'

Lucy shrugged. 'It's up to you.'

Robbie stood and moved back across to the locked cupboard. This time, though, he lifted down a small box, gift wrapped, and carried it across to Lucy.

'And Happy Christmas to you too,' he said, handing the box to her.

Lucy took it sceptically. 'Is that another present from a grateful client you've just given to me?'

Robbie pantomimed offence. 'I bought it before, you, know, it all … you know.'

Lucy shook the box lightly, heard the rattle of a chain against the inside of the box.

'Not clothes,' she guessed.

'You'll have to open it to find out.'

She peeled back the tape from the folds of paper at the bottom of the box, pulling off the ribbon tied around it, which had clearly been applied by the woman in the shop who had sold the gift to Robbie, for such wrapping skills were well beyond his abilities. Or Lucy's if she was honest, as she glanced at the sloppily wrapped gift Robbie was tearing open.

She opened the small jeweller's box. Inside was a fine gold chain, at the end of which was small gold square framing a golden heart.

'It's beautiful,' Lucy managed, unclipping it from the fitting in the box and putting it on.

'I'm glad you like it,' Robbie said, pulling out the shirt, atop which sat a bottle of aftershave. 'Lovely,' he said, nodding with approval to emphasize his apparent satisfaction.

'It's a bit crap now I see it,' Lucy said. 'Sorry. The aftershave's nice, though.'

Robbie opened it, sprayed some onto his neck.

'How do I smell?' he asked, leaning across, offering her neck to sniff.

Lucy smiled. 'Thank you for the necklace. It is beautiful. Happy Christmas.'

'And you,' Robbie said, angling his head, moving closer, until they kissed.

* * *

When she woke, just after five the following morning, it took Lucy a moment to realize that she was not in her own bed. She was in the spare room of the residential unit, her clothes lying in a pile on the floor next to the bed. Her mouth felt thick and heavy. One glass of wine had segued into one bottle, the kiss had developed to more than just a kiss. Now though, the duvet was flicked up on the other side of the bed, Robbie was nowhere to be seen.

She heard the thudding of his footfalls, then the door opened and he was standing in the doorway, half blocking the hallway light beyond, dressed in his underwear and T-Shirt.

'Gavin's gone,' he said.

Lucy pulled the sheet around her, aware of her nakedness. 'Shit! How long's he been gone?'

'I was sleeping,' Robbie said, shrugging sheepishly. 'He's done a runner.'

Lucy sat up in the bed, too quickly, the room starting to spin with the movement. She swung her legs out of the bed, hoped the solidity of the floor beneath her bare feet might provide her with some semblance of stability.

'I'll head out and see if I can spot him about,' she said. 'He might have headed back up to where those kids hang around.'

'You've drunk too much,' Robbie said. 'I only had two glasses. I'll drive you.'

Lucy pulled on her clothes, suddenly aware of the coldness in the room. 'It's bloody freezing,' she said.

'Gavin left the back door open,' Robbie explained.

'Where did he get the key?' Lucy asked. The children in the unit had to be locked in at night.

Robbie reddened. 'I left it hanging in the cupboard door last night when I got your present out. I meant to take it out, but I got distracted,' he added.

Lucy rubbed her face, lightly slapping her cheeks to wake herself up. 'Have we time for coffee?' she asked.

Robbie lifted his jeans and shirt off the floor. 'I'll stick some on,' he said.

Lucy heard him rattling about the kitchen as she padded down to the toilet. She threw some water on her face to freshen herself up a little, but could do nothing to take the taste of red wine from her mouth.

When she came into the kitchen area, the fluorescent lights seemed unnaturally harsh. Robbie was finishing his own mug of coffee. He handed her a steaming cup. 'Give me your keys,' he said. 'I'll start the engine up and get the car heated. There was fairly heavy frost last night and the windows'll need cleared.'

Lucy rooted through her bag, handed him the keys, then began drinking the coffee, after blowing on it to cool it down. Finally, to speed up the drinking of it, she moved across to the sink, turned on the tap and poured in cold water to cool it, then drained the cup.

She was just at the door when the windows shivered. She heard the dull thud of the explosion outside, saw the blast of light from the car, felt the thick buffet of air from the blast, as the glass rained around her.

Friday 21 December

Chapter Fifty-two

It took Lucy a moment to regain her balance. The room filled with a high-pitched whining and she tugged at her ear, as if to loosen whatever obstruction she felt was there.

Finally, recognizing the noise as an after effect of the explosion, she hauled herself through the doorway, struggling to pull her phone from her pocket. She could see flames ballooning in the darkness beyond.

Her car sat in the driveway, though had shifted several feet sideways from where it had been parked. The side panel around the wheelbase of the driver's side was shorn open, the under carriage of the car exposed. The tyre of the front wheel, deflated now, was alight, the metal wheel itself sitting askew. The driver's door hung at an angle from its upper hinge, the glass of the window shattered in pieces on the ground beneath. The windscreen, while still intact, was a mesh of cracks and fractures, which made it impossible for her to see in to Robbie. All she could tell, through the black smoke of the burning rubber and the thick cloud of dust in the air, thrown up by the blast, was that he was no longer sitting upright.

She managed to key in 999, screaming as she did for Robbie, hoping that, perhaps, he had not been in the car at all, scanning the shrubbery bordering the driveway lest the force of the blast had blown him onto it. She heard the emergency operator respond to the call and managed the salient details, before dropping the phone, still connected to the operator, onto the ground

As she approached the car, the flames from the burning tyre were building now, licking across the side panels, scorching the metal. Grabbing at the handle to pull the door open, she could see now, through the shattered window, that Robbie lay across the two front seats. She could see blood on his shirt and face.

She tugged at the door, but the twisted metal of the frame had caught somehow and, try as she might, she could not pull it free. She suddenly realized that the flames had caught her jacket, the bottom of which was now alight. She shrugged it off, pushing her way around to the passenger side of the car.

She tugged open the door and clambered into the car, reaching for Robbie's head, desperate to check if he was, at least, still breathing. She leaned in as close as she could, shaking him by the shoulder, calling his name. Finally, a soft moan formed on his lips. She noticed that his face carried a deep gash on the side that had faced the blast, perhaps a result of the flying glass from the window. She also knew that, as the fire spread on the other side, there was a much greater chance that the petrol tank, which had not yet seemingly been affected by the blast, could ignite. She needed to get Robbie out quickly.

She reached across his body, spidering her way along his trunk until she felt the hard edge of the seat belt. Tracing along its length, she finally was able to stretch far enough to feel the metal clasp. She fumbled in the half-light of the flames beyond, trying to find the release latch which would loosen the belt. As she did so, she was acutely aware that she did not know the extent of Robbie's injuries. Leaning any weight on him might only exacerbate any internal damage already done. Still, leaving him here was not an option.

At last, the clasp gave and the seat belt recoiled across his body. Lucy pushed it out of the way, then, gripping him beneath his armpits, she hefted him across, away from the building flames.

A groan escaped his lips as she pulled, though he himself did not seem conscious. 'Robbie,' she cried, as she tugged at him, dragging him towards her. Her left hand slipped, causing her to lose her grip and, looking down, she saw it was slick with blood from the right-hand side of his face. Wiping it on her own top, she tugged at him again, but he would not move, as if caught on something. She shifted over the top of his body, pulling at his legs, but they seemed free of obstacles. Then she realized that the handbrake had caught his belt, preventing movement. She had to angle herself in order to push him back towards the flames in the hope that, in doing so, it might free him from the lever. As she did so, she heard the metal frame of the car keening as it warped beneath the heat.

In the end, she had to twist him slightly before pulling once more, finally hefting him across onto the passenger seat and out of the car. She dragged him away from the car, back towards the unit, managing as far as the doorstep before she lost balance and fell back into the hallway. She scrambled back to the step, pulling Robbie towards her, cradling his head in her hands as his blood seeped onto her jeans.

The air popped as the petrol tank caught, the force of the subsequent blast throwing Lucy and Robbie onto their backs on the step, scattering flame onto the trees at the edge of the garden from whose branches now dripped flame onto the frosted grass below.

Then, through the thickening smoke, Lucy noticed the flickering blue of the ambulance lights in the distance, dancing along the fronts of the houses opposite where, one by one, lights were coming on.

Chapter Fifty-three

Lucy was examined in one of the ambulances while Robbie was receiving attention in the other. The closeness of the hospital to the residential unit meant that they had been on the scene within minutes. After the paramedic had checked her over and offered her a foil blanket against the pre-dawn chill, she moved across to where Robbie lay, still inert.

'Is he going to be OK?' she managed.

'He's alive,' the man tending him commented. 'He's not awake yet, but he's alive. He has a fairly deep leg wound. We need to get him into surgery. Do you want to come with?'

Lucy nodded. For a moment she thought she had blood on her face, for her skin felt suddenly chilled. She smeared her hand across her cheek and was a little surprised to find that she had been crying.

'Climb in,' the man said, offering her a hand.

She steadied herself. 'I'd best wait here. They'll want to know what happened,' she said. 'I'll be straight up then.'

In fact, it was almost an hour before Lucy was even able to leave the scene. Soon after the first patrol cars arrived, her mother appeared, her face drawn, her mouth a pale line.

'What happened?'

Lucy nodded towards the wreckage of the car. 'A bomb by the looks of it. Robbie went out to defrost it and it went off.'

'Your car was here all night then?' her mother asked.

Absurdly, Lucy could not discern if she was asking in a maternal or professional capacity. 'Yes. It was here all night. As was I.'

'Who would have known that?'

'Gavin Duffy,' Lucy said. 'The kid in the unit. Gary Duffy's boy. I came up last night to see him, to see if he recognized the man from the Foyleside CCTV image. He'd told me before that he saw someone with Karen Hughes matching the description Sarah Finn gave me.'

'Did he recognize him?'

'He said he didn't,' Lucy replied. 'But he's done a runner.'

Her mother pantomimed bewilderment.

'I think Gavin was part of the gang that torched Kay's house. I think when he found out that Kay might not have been responsible for Karen's death, it pushed him over the edge. He helped kill the wrong man.'

'You think he knows who the man in the picture is?'

Lucy nodded.

'And Duffy told him that you were here?'

Again Lucy nodded.

'How's Robbie?'

'I don't know,' she said. 'I'm not —'

She felt her eyes fill, felt the tears brimming. Her mother stood, looking at her a moment, then leaned in towards her and put her arms around her, hugging her lightly, shushing in her ear. Lucy accepted the embrace.

'You can say I told you so,' Lucy managed. 'It's my fault he was hurt.'

Her mother shook her head sadly. 'You know that's not what I meant,' she said.

'But it *is* my fault,' Lucy said.

One of the technical officers who had been examining the now smouldering car came across to them. They moved apart. Lucy daubed her eyes dry with the sleeve of her top. Her mother held her other hand, clasped tightly.

'Ma'am,' he said, nodding lightly to the ACC. 'Sergeant.'

'Did you find anything?' Wilson asked, glancing quickly at the wreckage.

'He was very lucky,' the man began.

'Lucky?' Wilson repeated, incredulously.

The man blushed, aware of the insensitivity in the statement. 'It was a rushed job, ma'am. They placed it under the engine block, which absorbed most of the blast. If they'd had it a foot to the other side of the wheel bay, it would have taken a fair chunk out of the whole side of the car. They'd not have stretchered him away from it.'

Robbie was still in surgery when Lucy reached the hospital. Her own hands having been scorched while she'd tried to open the driver's door, she was sent to A & E where they applied salve to the already blistered skin and dressed it with light gauze. She returned again to the theatre ward to see how Robbie was, but was told instead to wait at the café for word.

She sat alone, drinking a cup of hot chocolate from the vending machine, so tepid and watery that neither part of its name seemed wholly accurate. The foyer was in semi-darkness, the only illumination coming from the padlocked fridge which, during the day, would hold sandwiches and plastic dishes of salad. In the half-light, she stared at her reflection in the windows. The sky beyond was still dark.

She reflected back on all that had happened. On Kay. Carlin. Louisa Gant. Karen Hughes. Sarah Finn. All of them featuring in Kay's collection. A collection that, she believed, had been planted by whoever was actually responsible.

Louisa Gant. She had planned to go back to the start, to see where the groomer had crossed paths with Karen and Sarah. She remembered that the information she had requested from the schools would be in her office in the Public Protection Unit in Maydown. However, perhaps she needed to go back further, she reasoned. Louisa Gant was actually where it started; she was, in reality, the first victim who had found their way to Carlin's house.

She took out her mobile and called Tara. The phone rang out three times before she eventually answered, her voice little more than a whisper.

'Lucy, is everything all right?' she managed.

'Did I wake you?' Lucy asked.

'It's fine. Is everything all right?'

'The Louisa Gant murder. Has anyone been looking back at the files?'

'We all have,' Tara said. 'Why? What's wrong?' She sounded a little angrier now and Lucy realized that she had woken her without explanation.

'Someone put a bomb under my car this morning,' she said.

'Jesus. Are you okay?'

'Fine,' Lucy said, her mouth dry. 'Robbie was the one in the car. He's in surgery.'

'Is he ...? Will he be ...?'

'He was alive when I pulled him from the car. I think his leg is injured. They've not told me.'

'Do you want me to come up to you? Are you in the hospital?'

Lucy was touched by the offer. Her own mother had asked an officer to bring her across while she went back to the station. While Lucy could understand that, had the ACC accompanied her, it might have drawn attention to the fact that she was taking a personal interest in Lucy, at the same time she couldn't help but feel a little annoyed that she'd been left on her own.

'I'm OK, thanks,' Lucy said. 'I wanted to know about the Gant killing though. Was it definitely Gary Duffy? Was there any suggestion that someone else might have been involved?'

'Why?'

'Louisa Gant's body was buried at Carlin's farm, supposedly by Gary Duffy. Except Duffy's dead now and yet the house is still being used, by Karen's abductor for his house parties. Maybe Duffy didn't kill Louisa Gant. Or maybe he had help and the person who helped him then is the one grooming these girls now. Was there any suggestion of other people being involved in Duffy's file?'

'I don't know,' Tara said. 'The file was full of gaps.'

'Why?'

'Because Duffy was who he was. His being connected with the paramilitaries, it seems that Special Branch took over the case. A lot of the files contained intelligence material apparently. Names of informants that couldn't be revealed.'

'Said who?'

'Burns. He said the ACC told him herself.'

'Mr Gant lives locally, doesn't he?' Lucy asked. If the files couldn't offer new light on the girl's killing, perhaps her father might still recall something from that time. Whether he'd thank Lucy for reopening old scars was a different matter. Though, Lucy reflected, if her feelings over Mary Quigg's death were any indicator, those old scars might not have healed anyway.

'I don't know. I'm not sure,' Tara said. 'Look, maybe you should take—'

'He does,' Lucy said. 'Thanks.' She hung up. Leaving her cup, she crossed to the main desk where a night porter was playing Temple Run on his phone.

'Can I borrow your phone book?' Lucy asked.

330

Chapter Fifty-four

Just after nine, a doctor came down to tell her that Robbie was out of surgery. He'd lost a significant amount of tissue and muscle from his right leg and had required stitching to his side and face. That said, he was, she argued, lucky to not have been more badly hurt.

'Is he awake?'

'He's coming round,' she said. 'He'll be on morphine for the day though, so he'll be out of it. You can see him briefly if you want to.'

She stood by his bedside, watching him drifting in and out of consciousness. At one stage she thought he recognized her, for he smiled lightly, his lips moving as if he were trying to say something.

Before she left, she leant over and kissed his cheek, wiping away the tears that dripped from hers onto his. She noticed, where he lay, that he had a small scar on his neck she'd never noticed before. She traced its outline with the tips of the fingers of her bandaged hand.

She took a taxi to Gant's house. The phone book had only listed one in the immediate area and Logue had told her the previous night that the man still lived in the vicinity, so she took a chance that it was the right address.

The house was neat and clean looking from the front, the small lawn trim and tidy. Lucy knocked on the door and waited. The man who answered was in his fifties. He wore brown corduroy trousers and a loose-fitting white shirt, which did little to disguise the fact that he stooped slightly as he walked.

'Yes?' he asked.

'Mr Gant?'

'Yes.'

'I'm Lucy Black from the PSNI's Public Protection Unit.'

The man attempted to straighten himself a little. 'Yes?' he repeated, more slowly this time.

'I'd like to talk to you about Louisa,' she said.

He raised his head, glancing up and down the street. Finally he nodded lightly and stepped back. 'You may come in, so.'

She followed him down the darkened hallway.

'Do you want something?' he asked. 'I'm making breakfast.'

'I'm fine,' Lucy said. 'Thanks.'

'You'll have an egg,' he said, shuffling into the kitchen.

He moved across to the fridge and removed two eggs from the shelf. A saucepan of water was already coming to the boil on the cooker. He placed the eggs in the water then, reaching up, opened a cupboard above his head and lifted down two egg cups. As he did so, Lucy saw a small plastic mug with the image of Ariel from *The Little Mermaid* on it. Beneath the image, the name 'Louisa' was written in multicoloured lettering.

'You found her then?' he asked suddenly, not facing her. 'They told me they think they found her.'

'It's not confirmed yet,' Lucy said. 'I'm sure someone will be in touch as soon as they know for sure.'

He nodded. 'So why are you here?'

'I don't know,' Lucy said. 'I wondered if, maybe, the right man had been caught.'

Gant nodded lightly. 'I heard he died.'

'That's right.'

He nodded again. 'I hope he suffered.'

Lucy cleared her throat, beginning to regret having called with the man. She feared that, far from helping her, the visit would only serve to reopen old wounds for Louisa's father.

'*She* suffered,' he said. 'Louisa's mother. 'She suffered every day for eight months after Louisa went.' He raised the spoon he held and pointed out through the window to where a single hawthorn tree stood in the centre of his back garden. 'I found her hanging off that.'

Lucy felt sudden shame for having intruded on the man's grief.

'Do you want to see Louisa? She was a beautiful child. I've pictures here.'

He turned, leaving the saucepan bubbling, and led her into the front room. Against one wall stood a dark wooden bookcase. A range of pictures, each in small silver frames, sat on the shelves. With a pang, Lucy realized that the images were not photographs of Louisa as a child. They were the police mock-ups of how she might look, released each year after her disappearance in the vain hope than she might still be alive.

'That's how I watched her grow up,' Gant said. 'Just like that. In pretend photographs.'

Lucy remembered vaguely some of the images being released. Despite Duffy being charged with her murder, in the absence of a body, the family had issued a picture each year, in hope. Lucy realized now that it was Mr Gant himself who had done it, for when Louisa had been taken from him, so too had the rest of his family. Only he had remained, to carry the hurt alone. It was no wonder, she reflected, that he had bent beneath its weight.

'That was taken the day she went,' he said, pointing to a picture sitting on the mantelpiece.

Lucy moved across to lift it. 'May I?' she asked.

'Please,' he said.

In the photograph Louisa Gant wore the same clothes in which Lucy had seen her remains pictured. The girl was not smiling in the picture, but looked past the camera, as if ignoring its presence. Around her neck, she wore a leather necklace on which hung a round, green decoration.

'What is that?' Lucy asked.

'One of those hologram things that were all the rage back then,' Gant said. 'An eye. One of her friends bought it for her. She never took it off.'

Lucy tried to remember if she had been wearing it in the images she had been shown at Carlin's farm, but could not recall its presence.

'You never thought of leaving here,' Lucy asked, replacing the photograph exactly where it had been. Despite this, Gant moved past her and shifted it a fraction. Lucy suspected that he simply wanted to touch it, to maintain his connection with the child who never came home.

'No,' he said. 'I couldn't have done that. What if she'd made her way back and we were gone. What if she thought she'd been forgotten?'

Lucy nodded. 'Of course,' she said.

'Even if she had ... if she wasn't coming back ... wherever she is, she needs to know that I have not forgotten her.' He spoke so earnestly that, for a moment, Lucy could not reply.

'That sounds stupid, perhaps,' he said.

Lucy shook her head. 'I understand completely. While we remember, they are never truly lost.'

Gant smiled at the comment and nodded, once, satisfied that Lucy shared his belief. 'I'll show you her room,' he said. 'I never changed it either. Whatever time they tell me for definite that it's her, I'll maybe need to redecorate then.'

He moved up the stairs. Lucy could hear the sizzling as the pan spat water onto the cooker. She went into the kitchen and removed it from the hot ring before following the man up the stairs.

As he had claimed, Louisa's room remained unchanged since her disappearance. The walls were painted a shade of pink, but the girl had perhaps felt the colour too babyish for the bedclothes on her bed were a paisley pattern.

On a chair next to the bed, a small black top had been placed. Lucy moved across, afraid to touch anything in the room, as if in the presence of relics. Gant followed her, lifting the garment from the chair, holding it to his face, breathing in.

'You can still smell her off her clothes,' he said. 'Sometimes. Sometimes I can't catch it any more.'

Lucy nodded, not trusting herself to speak. On the bookcase, a small photo album sat, its spine decorated in pink feathers. 'Can I—' She cleared her throat, tried again. 'Do you mind if I take a look?'

'Go ahead,' the man said, smiling gently. 'We bought her a camera for Christmas that year. She loved taking pictures. She said she'd be a photographer when she grew up.'

Lucy lifted the book and opened it gently, so as not to disturb its contents.

'You look like her,' the man said.

Lucy felt a shiver wash through her. 'Excuse me?'

Gant smiled mildly in a manner that made Lucy wonder whether his survival technique all these years had been drug enhanced.

'The first officer. When Louisa went. There was a woman officer too. She stood where you're standing. Looked at that book too. You look like her. You remind me of her.'

Lucy felt something tickle at the back of her throat, had to cough several times to clear it. The photographs in the book had been taped in. In some cases, the tape had dried, leaving a brown line on the page, the picture itself lying in the folds of the book at the spine. Most were of Louisa and her parents. Lucy was surprised to see how young Mr Gant appeared in them, how significantly he'd aged in the intervening years.

One set of photographs, towards the end, was taken on a beach. Louisa was pictured sitting on the sand. Her head was bowed slightly, her eyes lowered, as if embarrassed by the picture.

'She didn't like getting her picture taken as she got older,' Gant said, moving closer to Lucy to point to the photograph in question. Lucy could smell something, almost like infection, off his breath in such close proximity. His stomach rattled with wind.

'Excuse me,' he said. He moved away from her, rifting lightly to clear the wind from his gut. 'Pardon me.'

Lucy flicked through the album. Towards the end she saw a picture of a young boy, perhaps a year or two older than Louisa. He wore a black T-shirt, emblazoned with a Guns and Roses logo. His black hair hung over his eyes. His dress seemed out of place for a trip to the beach.

'Was this your son?' Lucy asked. There had been no other pictures in the house, so Lucy could not be sure if Gant even had a son.

'God, no. He was a friend of Louisa's,' Gant said. 'Peter. He was a bit old for her. Not age wise – I think he was only a year older than her – but in other ways. She insisted on him coming with us that day.'

'What happened to him?'

'He moved away after she died. With his mother. I think the family broke up. He went to Belfast, I think.'

Lucy nodded.

'He was the one bought her that necklace you'd asked about. The eye. The eggs should be done,' he added. 'Will you come down?'

Lucy nodded, placing the album back on the shelf where it had been, then followed him out of the room.

'I'm sorry if my calling has been difficult for you —' she began.

Gant stopped on the steps and turned, snapping his fingers, his face alight with remembrance. 'Bell,' he said.

'Excuse me?'

'I've been trying to remember his name. It's Peter Bell,' he said.

'Who?'

'The boy at the beach. Peter Bell.'

Chapter Fifty-five

A team was already at Bell's house by the time Lucy managed to get a squad car to pick her up from Gant's. A uniform was banging on the door, but without response from inside. Despite this, Lucy noticed that the curtains had now been pulled closed.

Lucy introduced herself to the Senior Officer.

'Chief Superintendent Burns will be here shortly,' the man said. 'Must be important for the Super to come out.'

Lucy nodded then glanced next door to where the lace curtains hanging on the windows shifted incrementally at her gaze.

She knocked on the door. A moment later, she heard the light click of the lock and the door opened fractionally. The elderly neighbour, with whom she had spoken the previous night, peered out at her through the gap. She wore a thin net over her hair, her cheeks sunken in a manner that suggested she had not yet put in her teeth.

'Good morning, Mrs Sinclair. I'm sorry we've bothered you. Do you remember me? From last night?'

The woman tutted as if the question had offended her.

'We're looking for Mr Bell now, Mrs Sinclair. A bit more urgently. Has he been home since I called last night?'

The woman nodded.

'Can I come in, Mrs Sinclair?'

'No,' the woman said.

Lucy tried to glance behind her, wondering if perhaps Bell had hidden out in his neighbour's house.

'Is everything OK?' Lucy asked. 'Is there someone in the house with you?'

The woman glanced across at where other officers had gathered on the roadway. She said something, her voice faint and dry.

'I'm sorry?' Lucy said.

'I'm not dressed,' the woman replied. As she spoke, she pointed towards where the male officers stood.

'I understand. Of course. Has Mr Bell been home since I spoke with you?'

The woman nodded lightly. 'He came back late. I didn't get a chance to speak with him about you calling.'

'That's fine,' Lucy said. 'Is he still in his house, Mrs Sinclair?'

'I don't know. I heard shouting though. It woke me up. Around four o'clock.'

'Shouting?'

A brief nod. 'Thudding and shouting. Then I heard his front door slam. It makes my windows rattle. I've asked him not to do it. He normally doesn't.'

'But you heard signs of fighting in the middle of the night?' Lucy repeated, loudly enough for the Response Team officers standing around to hear her.

The woman rolled her eyes, repeating it louder herself lest Lucy was hard of hearing.

'Thank you, Mrs Sinclair. Keep your door closed. We're going to check on Mr Bell.'

Lucy called over the man who had been banging on Bell's door. 'The neighbour says she heard a fight in there at four in the morning, then someone leaving. For all we know, Bell could be lying dead in there.'

'We should wait for the Chief Super,' he replied. 'To be sure.'

'We can't wait,' Lucy said. 'She said she heard a violent struggle.' She moved across and pushed at the door, shoving it with her shoulder. The man with whom she had spoken took out his radio and contacted the station. The other three officers stood watching her as she tried to force the door, without success. Two of them began to laugh at her efforts. The third however, a younger uniform, came across to her. 'Do you need a hand, Sergeant?' he asked.

'A shoulder would be more useful,' she said, smiling.

Between them, on the second shove, they managed to crack the frame of the door jamb sufficiently to push the door open.

'Mr Bell?' Lucy called, entering the house. 'PSNI. Are you here, Mr Bell?'

The man who had helped her moved in behind, the others following them in through the open doorway.

'Mr Bell?' Lucy called. 'We've had reports of a fight, Mr Bell. Are you here?'

341

The house was silent. Lucy moved in through the living room. 'Check upstairs,' she said to the man behind her. 'I'll check the kitchen.'

She moved through into the kitchen area. A scattering of dishes lay on the worktop. Beyond that, nothing seemed disturbed. She checked the back door into the yard, which was locked.

'Sergeant,' she heard one of the men shout from above.

Taking the stairs two at a time, she came into the room from which the call had come. The young uniform stood in what had presumably been a bedroom that Bell had converted into a workroom. An old piece of kitchen worktop had been screwed into the wall. Along it sat three different computers. A tangle of cables snaked beneath the worktop and down to a wall socket.

Lucy took out her phone and called through to ICS. The call went to answering machine, though the recorded message listed a mobile number for emergencies. Lucy scribbled it onto her hand as she listened, then redialled the new number. David Cooper answered.

'Are you free?' she asked.

'Now there's a question I don't get every day,' he replied. 'What's up?'

'I followed up on the names from Foyleside when Kay was lifted. I think I've found something. One of them works with computers. Can you come across?'

'What's the address?' Cooper said. 'Give me ten minutes.'

* * *

Burns arrived before that. His initial anger at the fact that the team had entered Bell's house was tempered somewhat by learning that the neighbour had provided them with a cause for concern regarding the health of the person inside.

'I heard about this morning,' he said to Lucy when he saw her. 'Are you sure you should be working today?'

'I wasn't the one hurt,' Lucy replied, disingenuously.

'Regardless,' he said. 'No one would think less of you for needing a break.'

Lucy shook her head. 'Gavin Duffy has vanished,' she said. 'I showed him the image of the young guy from the Foyleside and, a few hours later, he'd gone. I think he knew who the man in the picture was. I think he's gone after him, because of Karen.'

'I see,' Burns said. 'Do you think the Duffy boy was involved in placing the device under your car?'

Lucy shook her head. Gavin could be difficult, but she'd sensed that they had got on well. She didn't believe that the youth would want to kill her, or, more particularly, Robbie. She told Burns as much, adding, 'Maybe he caught up with Karen's killer and revealed that he'd identified him from an image I had. Peter Bell, if he is the groomer, might have panicked.'

'If that's the case,' Burns said, 'we need to find Gavin, in case Bell has hurt him too.'

'I've asked David Cooper from ICS to come across and look at the machines here to see what he can find. It might help us locate Bell.'

Burns shook his head. 'Not without cause, he won't be examining them. You broke in because you heard there had been a disturbance. There being no sign of anyone injured, we have no excuse to start searching the man's computers.'

'He was in the Foyleside when Kay was arrested. He was best friends with Louisa Gant before she died. It can't be just coincidence that he crosses both cases.'

'Possibly not,' Burns said. 'But you can't check his computer. You'll need to call ICS off. We'll set officers outside. If Bell returns, we can bring in him for questioning. But we can't start checking his PCs. Without a warrant.'

'That's —' Lucy began.

'The law, Sergeant,' Burns snapped. 'What would you do? Fuck up a prosecution because you stormed ahead and ignored procedures. Let's say he is the one who killed Karen Hughes. Will it help us if he gets off because we didn't follow procedures? We arrest him, get cause, then we get a warrant. OK?'

Lucy grudgingly nodded assent.

'I suggest you either return to the PPU or go home, Sergeant,' Burns said. 'But either way, you're not staying here.'

The officers from the Response Team, who were standing in the living room below, watched silently as Lucy passed them and moved back out of the house. She knew they had heard everything, knew that it would be the station gossip for the next day or two.

As she stepped out into the weak mid-morning light, she remembered she didn't have a car. She was damned too, though, if she was going to go back inside and ask for a lift now. She was taking out her phone to call for a taxi when a black Avensis pulled to a stop outside the house and Dave Cooper waved out.

'Where do I start?' he asked, climbing out of the car.

'Giving me a lift back to the PPU would be a great place,' Lucy said.

Chapter Fifty-six

'I know it's him,' Lucy said, after explaining to Cooper why he was no longer needed at the scene.

He was driving back down the Limavady Road, slowing as they approached the roundabout at the Foyle Bridge. 'Burns is right, you know,' he said.

'That doesn't make me feel any better,' Lucy grunted. 'We're this close to catching him. We just need something to fall into place.'

'Take a step back from it,' Cooper said. 'Forget about it for a while. It'll sort itself out in your head when you're not trying so hard. Have a night off.'

Lucy scoffed, assuming he was joking. 'Gavin went after him,' she said. 'I'd bet money that's what the fight was. He went and faced him down.'

'How did he know who he was?' Cooper asked.

'What?'

'How did Gavin know who he was?'

Lucy shrugged. 'I dunno,' she said. 'He knew Karen was with someone in the weeks before she died. Maybe she told him Bell's name.'

Cooper nodded. They passed Gransha Hospital to their right as they drove. Lucy glanced back, feeling a pang of guilt that she had yet to go back and see her father again.

'What happened to you?' Cooper asked. He lifted his own hand off the gear stick and gently touched Lucy's bandaged hand to indicate what he meant.

'I had an accident,' Lucy said, flushing as she wondered why she hadn't told him the truth. Told him about Robbie. She felt a further pang of guilt that she hadn't contacted the hospital since to see how he was doing.

'You're pushing yourself too hard,' Cooper said, his hand remaining lightly on top of hers a second longer, before he had to change gears again. 'You need to take a breather.'

'I need a cup of tea,' Lucy said.

'I have no milk,' Cooper said. 'Unless you have some in PPU?'

'Possibly,' Lucy said. Fleming was the one who usually bought the milk and biscuits. Lucy didn't even know if he did so out of his own pocket. Had never thought to ask.

'Then tea you shall have,' Cooper said, pulling in through the main gates, waving to the officer on duty at the entrance checkpoint.

The Unit seemed cold, less inviting without Fleming's presence. The lights were off, the rooms gloomy. Lucy turned on the main light and directed Cooper towards the kitchen.

'I'm expecting a fax,' she said, remembering that the schools had said they would send through a list of events prior to Karen and Sarah's first contact with 'Bradley'. Or 'Harris'. Or Bell.

When she went up to her room, Mary Quigg stared at her silently from her space on the wall. The fax machine in her room was still on, several pages of text lying on the tray at its base. She flicked through them. A number were Missing Persons posters from other districts: most were children who had run away from care, foster parents, or their own homes. Requests to be on the lookout. While many of the notices were from England or Scotland, one was from An Garda Sciochanna, in the Republic. A fifteen-year-old, Annie Marsden, had gone missing from the care home in which she was placed in Stranorlar. Something about the girl's name seemed familiar, though Lucy could not place it. Regardless, she marked the fax to remind herself to send out a BOLO to all local cars, considering the proximity to their own jurisdiction.

Lucy eventually found the lists from the two schools. Karen's had already given her a list of the events of the week prior to 'Bradley' contacting her, but had now sent through details of each event and the people involved. The secretary had noted at the bottom that all appropriate background checks had been done on anyone coming into contact with the children. Besides, Lucy knew that someone in CID had done checks on Karen's school and would have checked such vetting had been completed.

She flicked through to Sarah Finn's school's list next. It was significantly longer, seemingly a calendar of events for the entire term rather than just the week before she'd first been contacted online. As Lucy

348

scanned through it, one name stood out. A name that had also appeared on the list from Karen's school: Country Photographers.

Lucy sat at her desk and phoned through to the school, asking to speak to the secretary. If schools were anything like police stations, the people in the front office would have a better sense of what was happening in the school on any given day than anyone else.

After Lucy introduced herself the woman on the other end, who'd called herself Rose, interrupted her. 'I sent you through the list already.'

'I know. Thank you,' Lucy said. 'I wanted to ask you about Country Photographers.'

'Yes?' the woman replied slowly.

'Are they a new company to the school?'

'God, no. They've been coming into us for years. Why?'

'And they'd have done vetting and background checks, presumably.'

'Of course,' Rose replied. 'What's this about?'

'Where could I find them?' Lucy asked.

'Have you not got a phone book?' Rose snapped. 'Or a computer.'

'I've got a pen,' Lucy asked. 'Ready to write down the address which I'm betting you know by heart.'

There was silence for a moment, then the woman rattled off the address once, before hanging up.

Cooper was sitting in the Interview Room on the sofa, drinking his tea. A second mug sat on the table, blobs of cream gathering on its surface.

'I'm not sure about your milk,' he offered when she came down the stairs.

'Do you fancy giving me another lift?' Lucy asked, handing him the faxes. 'My car's out of action.'

Chapter Fifty-seven

Country Photographers was operated by a man named Niall Hines, out of the ground-floor unit of a block on Spencer Road. The shop itself was small; the walls cluttered with wedding and graduation pictures, displayed to show the range of Hines's craft. In fact, Lucy thought, they all looked remarkably similar. What scope there was for originality in an image of someone in a cloak holding a scroll, Hines seemed not to have explored it.

An older blonde woman was sitting at the reception desk when they came in. She looked up and smiled at them. 'How are you? Wedding photos is it?' she asked.

'No,' Lucy said, glancing at Cooper to see him struggling to conceal his smile. 'We're a little past that, I'm afraid. We were hoping to speak with Mr Hines. I'm DS Black of the Public Protection Unit. This is Officer Cooper.'

The woman's smile faltered. 'Oh. I'll see if he's available.' She stepped in through the gap in a curtained partition. Cooper moved across to where she had gone and peered through.

'The master's at work,' he said.

Lucy followed him and they stood looking into a small studio space. The back wall had been painted white. Three coloured beanbags of varying sizes were placed in the middle of the floor. On one a young boy sat cross-legged. Next to him, on a bigger red bag, lay a girl whom Lucy took to be the boy's sister. She was lying flat on her stomach, propping herself up on her arms. Hines himself was standing next to a camera on a tripod. He was a small man, thin framed, with wiry grey hair. Despite standing erect, his back seemed to arch outwards, as if he was so used to hunching that even when he stood straight, his back retained the shape.

'Give me a smile, young man,' he said. The boy obliged, smiling brightly, in doing so revealing the gap where his two front teeth had once been.

'And now, you my pretty? Can you give me a smile, like your brother?'

The girl nodded with such vigour, her pigtails wagged wildly on either side of her head.

'Haven't you the prettiest eyes?' he said.

The girl beamed at the compliment and, in that instant, a flash illuminated the ceiling as the camera shutter clicked.

'And now one of the two of you. Nathan, can you lie next to your sister and both of you look at me?'

Lucy looked across and saw the clearly proud mother of the two children standing at the far wall, absurdly using her phone to take pictures of the pictures being taken.

The boy did as he was directed and, after a few minor adjustments to positions, the final few shots were taken in quick succession, each image preceded by a compliment from Hines to the children.

After the children had been led out by their mother, Hines came across to them.

'Wedding photographs, is it?' he asked, smiling. 'Such a beautiful couple.'

'I'm afraid not,' Lucy said, glancing at Cooper who, again, couldn't resist grinning. 'I'm with the PSNI Public Protection Unit. I'm investigating a case involving two school children.'

Hines's expression darkened. 'I've been completely vetted,' he said.

Lucy raised a placatory hand. 'I'm simply following up on connections between the two girls,' she said. 'You visited the schools of both in the days before they were first targeted.'

'What schools?'

Lucy told him. The man muttered to himself, his hand to his mouth, his eyes downcast, as if searching the studio floor for an explanation. 'Are you sure I even took pictures of the children?'

'I'm not,' Lucy admitted.

'What were the dates of the shots?' he asked, moving across to a small anteroom set off the studio. In it a single computer hummed on the desk.

Lucy offered him the date of the visit to Karen's school. The man scrolled through folders, finally hitting on one for that date. He opened the folder and a series of images of girls, numbered from 001, all seated in front of faux bookcases, appeared.

He began scrolling down through the images. 'Tell me if you see her. I have no names with the images here.'

As he scrolled, Lucy scanned the pictures. Eventually, at image 098, she saw the picture of Karen Hughes.

'That's her,' she said, pointing.

'Where are images 96 and 97?' Cooper asked. He pointed to the screen. Lucy noticed now that the image of a child before Karen was number 095 and yet Karen was 098.

Hines peered closely at the screen. 'Those shots were spoiled. She might have blinked, or looked at the floor, or something. What was the second date?'

As Lucy told him, he closed one folder and opened another. Again he scrolled through the images. This time, when Lucy saw the picture of Sarah Finn, a copy of the one she had seen in Finn's house the day she vanished, she noticed that there were three shots of the child. In the first two, she was glancing downwards.

'You see,' Hines said, pointing to the picture. 'This folder hasn't been cleared yet. She kept looking at the floor.'

'Why? The flash?'

Hines shook his head. 'The flash doesn't hit them directly. I angle it to the ceiling. I always tell the girls that they have pretty eyes. It makes most of them smile. A handful can't take the compliment and they look away. When that happens, I usually just have to get them to say "Cheese". They get embarrassed by it.'

'Why?' Cooper asked.

354

'Low self-esteem,' Lucy said, reflecting on how she had described Karen Hughes to Burns on the day she had been found.

'You can spot them a mile off,' Hines admitted. 'But what can you do? They hear me telling the others how pretty they look. I can't very well not say it to them.'

'Maybe not say it at all,' Lucy suggested.

The man shrugged, unconvinced. 'I've been doing it twenty-five years,' he said.

'How many people work here?' Lucy asked.

'Just me and my daughter, Julie,' Hines said. 'You met her at the front desk.'

'And you've both been vetted?'

Hines nodded. 'Of course. I've been in schools for twenty-five years doing this,' he repeated. 'Whatever happened to these girls, my being in the school is coincidence.'

'No one else would have access to these images?'

Hines shook his head, though a little slower now, less certain.

'Who?'

Hines scratched the side of his head. 'I have someone who handles my online stuff. Orders and that. He designed the website and keeps it updated. He would see them. He helps me out at times if we're busy. The start of the school year and that, it can get a bit hectic.'

Lucy felt the hairs on her arms rise. 'Who is he?'

'He's a good fella.'

'Who is he?' Lucy repeated.

'Peter Bell's his name,' Hines said.

Chapter Fifty-eight

On the way back to the Strand Road, Lucy called through to the Press Office and asked them to send out details of the child from Donegal, Annie Marsden. She had called through to the incident room to be told that Burns was in a meeting, but would be free shortly. Lucy hoped that if she could convince him about the need to examine Bell's PCs they might get a warrant quickly and Cooper could get started straight away.

When she came into the incident room, Tara immediately ran across to her and hugged her, quickly. 'Are you OK?' she asked.

Cooper looked at Lucy quizzically.

'Fine,' Lucy said, a little flustered.

'Why are you in work? You should have gone home.'

'I'm OK,' Lucy said, quietly, hoping Tara might take the hint.

'You were in a bomb,' Tara said. 'That's not OK.'

'You were in a bomb?' Cooper repeated, turning to Lucy.

Lucy shrugged. 'I was *near* a bomb. This is Dave Cooper from ICS Branch, Tara.'

'Hi.' Cooper smiled. Then to Lucy: 'How near?'

'Her boyfriend was in the car,' Tara said to Cooper, then she asked Lucy, 'Any word?'

'Your boyfriend?' Cooper repeated. 'Was he injured?'

Lucy nodded. 'Leg injuries,' she said. 'I've not had a chance to find out how he is since,' she added to Tara. It wasn't entirely true. She could easily have phoned from Cooper's car, but had been reluctant to do so in front of him. 'Is Burns here?'

'In his office,' Tara said. 'Just.'

'Can I borrow a computer?' Cooper asked. 'While I'm waiting?'

Burns was fixing his tie when he called Lucy into the office. 'I thought you were going home,' he said, watching her in the mirror as he straightened his collar.

'I went back to the Unit,' she said. 'I discovered the connection between Sarah Finn and Karen Hughes. Both had their photographs taken by Country Photographers in the weeks before they were first contacted online.'

Burns nodded curtly, angling his head to examine that his tie was sitting right. 'We did all the background checks on them,' he said. 'They'd been vetted.'

'Peter Bell was their web designer. At times he helped out with processing the photographs when they were in a busy period; like the first weeks of school term for example.'

Burns turned and stared at her a moment, before sitting behind his desk. 'Was he vetted?'

Lucy shrugged. 'Possibly not. He never came into actual contact with any of the kids. But his name keeps cropping up in connection with these girls. I think I know how he picked them too. Sarah and Karen. When they were having their pictures taken, Hines the photographer told the students that they had pretty eyes or smiles or whatever. To get a reaction. Both Karen and Sarah reacted in the same way.'

Burns shrugged. 'How?'

'By staring at the floor. Embarrassed.'

'So?'

'I think that as Bell worked through the images from the schools, he realized that the kids who stared at the floor were shy, lacking in self-esteem. That they were vulnerable.'

'How would he have got their contact details? To find them online?'

'Bell processed orders for Hines through his website but, during busy periods, helped out with the ones coming in through schools, too. Maybe they thought because he wasn't in direct contact with the kids, it didn't matter. But he had access to their images and their names.'

Burns considered what she had said. 'I'll need to speak with the ACC before we do anything,' he said. 'Though this might be enough to get a warrant to examine his house.'

There was a brief knock at the door and, as it opened, Tara peered around. 'Sir, there's something you need to see.'

They moved out into the incident room where Cooper was working at one of the PCs. 'I've found something,' he said.

He clicked on the mouse and a website for Country Photographers appeared on the screen. A range of images decorated the main page, including wedding shots, children posing on the beanbags they had seen on their visit to Hines's studio and staged portraits. One of the images was a close-up picture of a daisy. The individual stamens of its head could be seen, encircled by a white crown of petals.

'I've found a tiny key here,' he said. 'On the fifteenth petal around.'

He moved the mouse in a slow circular motion. They could see the arrow on screen moving across each petal. Sure enough, as it reached the fifteenth petal, the arrow changed to a pointing finger, suggesting that it was hovering over a web link. Cooper clicked on it and the screen changed to a plain black screen with a single white text box at the centre.

'What's that?'

'A password,' Cooper said. 'The rest of the site is word protected. This part of the site is hosted in a different place from the rest, too,' he added. 'We've been taken to a different website.'

'How do you know?'

'There's no IP address as such,' Cooper said. He typed a few keys and pointed to a piece of text at the bottom of the screen: a series of numbers ending with the word 'onion'. 'It's a darknet site.'

Lucy shrugged. 'And that means?'

Cooper sighed, then raised his hands, laid flat one above the other. 'This,' he said, moving his upper hand, 'is the ordinary internet that we all use. Google and Yahoo and that. OK?'

'If you say so,' Lucy said.

Then, moving the lower hand, he said. 'This is the darknet. Instead of a range of servers hosting sites, which can be traced, it's created by file sharing between users. It means its completely untraceable.'

'Why is that allowed?'

'No one can prevent it,' Cooper said. 'Besides, it does have advantages in, say, a dictatorship where people can't express political views openly. It just also is used for all kinds of online criminal activity. And paedophiliac websites, obviously.'

'How would users know how to enter this site?' Lucy asked.

'They'd get the address through a forum or personal recommendation,' Cooper said. 'I'm guessing too that there's a common password for getting through this level of the site to whatever's behind this. You'd have to be given the password to go beyond here, in case anyone stumbled on it by accident. You'd probably find that there's then a second level of password protection to go beyond the next page, probably personalized from then on in.'

'Can you break the password?' Burns asked.

Cooper shook his head. 'No. But, if it is a common password, there's a chance that we might find it on some of Bell's PCs in his house. My guess is that it will be something obvious, something significant to the type of people attracted to that type of site. Humbert, Lolita, Wonderland, something along those lines.'

'Get across to Bell's house,' Burns said. 'I'll have a warrant sorted by the time you get there.'

Chapter Fifty-nine

Cooper told Lucy that he wanted to return to the unit first to collect some of his equipment, which might make working through any encryption on the machines easier.

While she had waited in the car, she reflected on what they had found. Peter Bell had been a childhood friend of Louisa Gant when she died. Now he appeared to be involved in, or running, a paedophile website and was grooming teenage girls to be used for sex at house parties he organized in Peter Carlin's house, next to where Louisa Gant's body had been buried. Somehow, Gavin had recognized Bell in the picture and had clearly gone after him. He must have told Bell that Lucy had his picture and that she was in the unit, allowing Bell an opportunity to plant the device in her car. She had to assume that Gavin had been coerced into giving this information. Unless he had been involved in Karen's death himself. Lucy found that hard to believe, based on her experience with the boy. Still, she could not fully dismiss the thought, even after Cooper got back in the car and began speaking to her.

On the way from the unit to the house, Cooper finally raised the subject of the car bombing. 'So, you didn't think it was worth mentioning then?'

'It was nothing.'

'It left your boyfriend hospitalized.'

'He's not ...' she began. 'It's complicated,' she managed finally.

'I assumed as much, considering you're still at work and he's lying in hospital,' Cooper commented. 'In fact, I'd say "complicated" is an understatement.'

'I need to borrow your car,' Lucy said. 'The kid from the residential unit vanished after the attack. I need to see if I can find him.'

'I'd also say that was a neat change of subject, but it wasn't,' Cooper commented. 'Can you drive with a bandaged hand?'

Lucy smiled. 'Is that concern for me or for your car?' she asked.

'Are you mad? My car, obviously.'

By the time they reached Bell's, the house was cordoned off and teams were already beginning to conduct a search of the rooms.

Cooper went straight upstairs and booted up the three PCs. Lucy, for her part, drove on up to Gobnascale. She phoned the school first, already guessing that Gavin would not have turned up. The person she spoke to explained that they had closed early for the Christmas holidays and that attendance had been very poor.

She continued round to the youth club. Jackie Logue was standing in the middle of the hall, directing several of the kids where to pin up Christmas decorations.

'DS Black. We're having a party tonight. A Christmas disco. Do you want to come?'

'I'm looking for Gavin,' Lucy said, without preamble.

Logue shrugged. 'He's not here. I've not seen him all day.' He called to the kids. 'Anyone seen Gavin?'

There were murmurs from the kids as they worked, all in the negative.

'Will you contact me if he appears?' Lucy asked.

Logue nodded. 'I hope you weren't badly hurt,' he said.

Lucy stared at him. 'What?'

He pointed towards her hand, thick in bandages. 'Your hand,' he said. 'I hope it wasn't anything serious.'

'No,' Lucy said. 'Not serious.'

As she was leaving, she met Elena coming up the path to the hall.

'Hi,' she said, though did not raise her head to look at Lucy.

'You haven't seen Gavin have you?' Lucy asked.

Elena shook her head. 'He was meant to meet me after my exam this morning. He never showed up. Not even a text.'

'How did it go?' Lucy asked.

The girl glanced up briefly. 'Shit,' she said.

'I know how that feels,' Lucy commented.

She stopped at the hospital on her way back to Bell's. Robbie was in a room of his own, dozing quietly. She came across and lifted the chart at the end of his bed, scanning it, while all the time aware of the futility in so doing for it meant nothing to her. When she glanced up, she saw he was awake and watching her.

'Hey, you,' she said.

He smiled, his lips dry, and winced as if the slight movement had hurt the stitches in his cheek.

'I wondered where you were,' he said. 'When I woke. I thought you'd be here.'

'Sorry,' Lucy said, putting the chart back. 'I think Gavin went after whoever killed Karen. And I think he told them I was with you.'

'Why?' Robbie managed.

'Maybe he was forced into telling. If that's the case, he may be in trouble. I hoped if I could find Gavin, I could find the person who did this.'

'That's not what I was thinking about when I woke,' he managed, pushing himself up in the bed. Lucy moved across and, lightly gripping beneath his armpits, helped him shift. In doing so, she was reminded of having done something similar to pull him out of the burning car hours earlier.

'What?'

'I wasn't thinking about catching the person who tried to blow you up. I was thinking about you.'

Lucy nodded. 'I'm sorry,' she said. 'How are you feeling?'

'Like I've just been in a bomb,' Robbie commented, smiling wryly.

Lucy smiled. 'That sounds about right,' she said. She moved closer to him, laid her hand against his face. 'I'm sorry it was you in the car, Robbie. I'm so sorry.'

'I'm not,' Robbie said, placing his own hand over hers.

Lucy leaned down and kissed his lips. They felt dry and cracked, his breath stale behind the kiss.

She felt her phone vibrating in her pocket. Embarrassed, she straightened and took the call. It was Cooper calling from Bell's house.

'You need to come back here. Now.'

'I was able to bypass the password,' Cooper said, when Lucy arrived. He was standing at the front door of Bell's, waiting for her return.

'All in one piece,' Lucy said, handing him the keys. The parking ticket she'd been given for not paying and displaying at the hospital car park, she kept in her pocket.

'Thanks,' Cooper said, looking at the keys but seeming not to realize the import of her comment. 'I was right.'

'I thought you said you couldn't break the password,' Lucy said, following him up the stairs.

'I didn't. I traced his history on one of the PCs. He had used it to access the site. The computer had automatically remembered the password through to the next level. You need to see it.'

They went into the small room. Lucy could see one of the PCs displaying a web page very similar to the main Country Photographers' website. On it were a number of pictures, all of school children, all taken by Hines. In each, the girl, for they were all girls, was sitting in front of the faux library of books that Hines used as his backdrop.

Lucy leaned in and examined the screen. She felt her throat tighten as she recognized one of the pictures as that of Karen Hughes. The next one was the image of Sarah Finn that she had seen before.

'That's not quite what I was expecting,' she said.

'It's like a stud wall into the site,' Cooper said. 'Let's just say someone does accidentally make it through the first level, they reach this, it's innocuous looking. Click on one of the individual pictures, though, and you get this.'

He clicked on the image of Karen Hughes and a pop-up box appeared requesting a username and password.

'You register for membership here,' Cooper said, pointing to a small text box at the bottom of the page he had shown her, where viewers could sign up for a newsletter. 'Again, it looks innocuous. Presumably, though, once you request a newsletter, Bell has your details and sends you a password and username. Then you get to whatever he's hiding back there.'

'It's definitely him,' Lucy said.

'Look at this,' Cooper said, pointing to the bottom picture of a schoolgirl. Lucy stared at the girl's face a moment before she realized where she had seen her before. Immediately she also realized why the name had seemed familiar. The recently reported missing Annie Marsden had commented on a Facebook posting by one of the suspected sock puppet accounts, 'Liam Tyler'.

'The girl from the Missing Persons fax,' Cooper said. 'Annie Marsden. I think he's got her.'

Chapter Sixty

Lucy contacted An Garda to tell them about her concerns regarding Annie Marsden's safety. The Inspector with whom she spoke, a softly spoken man, promised that he would visit the Marsden house and check whether Liam Tyler was a real friend of Annie's, or whether the account was simply another sock puppet.

Cooper had been busy working at Bell's PC with a black external hard drive which he'd connected through a USB. He muttered to himself as he worked.

'What are you doing?' Lucy asked.

'Deciphering Bell's password,' Cooper said. 'The website will have a memory of his password, so that, when he logs in, it knows it's him. I can access the database of the site for his password. It brings up the text as a series of hashes. This device tries to decode them by cycling through every possible letter, number or symbol for each hash.'

'Like breaking a safe?'

'Pretty much. It guesses each letter at high speed. Because we're using his own computer, it will automatically complete his username.'

'Impressive,' Lucy said.

'But slow,' Cooper countered. 'How's your boyfriend?'

Lucy nodded. 'He's OK,' she said, feeling her face flush. She couldn't understand if it was at the thought of Robbie or because it was Copper asking about him.

On the device, the series of six hashes flickered as the first one converted to the letter L.

'It's a start,' Cooper said.

A few seconds later it flickered again and the second hash converted to 'o'.

'Now we're moving,' Cooper said. 'Anyone any good at crosswords?'

Lucy stared at the word: Lo ####. Some of the other officers had moved across and were standing behind Cooper, watching.

'Lovers,' one suggested. Cooper tried typing it in, but the screen simply returned to the empty password box.

'Louisa,' Lucy said.

Cooper glanced at her and nodded. He typed in the word. For a second, nothing happened, then the screen changed and a series of folders appeared on the screen. Each folder had a different name. One was marked 'Karen'.

'Open that one,' Lucy said.

She recognized some of the images that the folder contained as being part of the collection that had been found in Gene Kay's house. There were others, though, where the perpetrator was clearly visible. Lucy wanted to reach out and cover Karen in each image, cover her from the watching eyes of the officers who stood in silence as Cooper quickly scrolled through the images.

'Do we need to look at these?' she asked.

'There were two houses, you said,' Cooper replied. 'I'm trying to see if there's anything to help us find the second one.'

Lucy nodded. 'Try Sarah,' she said. 'She told us that she remembered being in two different houses.'

Cooper went back and opened the second folder. The images contained in there were of similar quality and content to those featuring Karen. In one, Lucy recognized the man with her as Carlin. Any possible misgivings she'd had about his drowning in Enagh Lough were swiftly dispelled.

'There,' Cooper said, quickly.

He stopped at one image in particular and, double-clicking, enlarged it. It was clearly taken in a different room from the bulk of the other images. It was brighter, the bed on which Sarah Finn lay placed next to a window. What Cooper was pointing to was something visible through the window, in the middle distance.

At the far right of the window frame, almost moving out of sight, was a silver four-by-four.

'It's facing onto a road,' one of the uniforms said.

'No,' Cooper commented. 'Look beside it.'

Sure enough, the rest of the surrounding space was the slate grey of water, the white heads of waves just visible.

'So how would a four-by-four go on water?' Cooper asked.

'On a car ferry,' Lucy said. 'And there's only one car ferry within driving distance of here.'

'Magilligan Point,' Cooper said.

Chapter Sixty-one

The light was beginning to fail by the time the Response Teams were on their way. Magilligan lay about twenty-five miles away from the city, along the Sea Coast Road that skirted Lough Foyle. At its narrowest point, between Magilligan and Greencastle in County Donegal, the Foyle was only 2 kilometres wide and it was at this point that the ferry crossed, taking cars between the Republic and Northern Ireland.

Having studied the maps that they had, which, due to the location there of Magilligan Prison were fairly detailed, they had worked out approximately where the house must be, based on the angle at which the ferry had been viewed through the window.

The wind that carried up the lough buffeted the sides of the cars as they travelled the coast road, the cold draughts of air pushing through the gaps in the doors at the rear of the Land Rover.

Lucy glanced out through the viewing slits along the side of the vehicle. To her left, bright against the starless December night, the illuminated shape of Magilligan Prison stood out. Somewhere inside, she realized, Eoghan Harkin would be passing his final night in prison. She wondered, in fact, if his daughter, Karen, had ever been in the Magilligan house where Sarah Finn had been photographed, whether she had realized her proximity to her father.

They trundled along the roadway until, after a few moments, Lucy heard Burns speaking from the front where he was sitting. She looked up to see him pointing out to the right. Moving across, she looked out through the opposite side of the vehicle and saw, set against the darkness, the squat shape of a small house about a mile down a laneway. By its angle, its rear would have looked out onto the lough, facing the path of the ferry.

Burns twisted in his seat, his face pressed against the mesh that separated them from the front seats. 'This is us, folks,' he said. 'Our priority is to get any children out first. We can round up any adults in the place. And obviously, Peter Bell is our target.'

They felt the Land Rover turn sharply to the left, Lucy almost losing her balance with the suddenness of the movement. A moment or two later, they pulled to a halt and the back doors were flung open. In addition to the CID team, there were several uniforms to assist. Further Land Rovers, behind, had been brought to carry any suspects lifted in the raid.

The house was a low-set dormer style. Lights shone from almost all windows, their glare deadened by the thin scraps of curtains that hung over the windows themselves. Even from out here, above the sharp whistling of the wind against the visors of their helmets, they could hear the raised voices inside, the sounds of laughter.

The uniforms approached the front of the house and positioned themselves with the small blue metal battering ram. Two swings were sufficient to force in the front door. Lucy thought of Cooper, brute-forcing his way through the website, as she watched them work.

Then, at a word, they poured in through the open doorway, immediately splitting in all directions, moving into the body of the house. Almost at once, the noise inside increased, people shouting and screaming. Lucy filed in through the door, the clumsiness of the riot gear helmet she wore obscuring her view. She glanced across and saw, in one room, several men sitting, cans of beer in their hands. She saw at least two young girls sitting among them, fully dressed at least, their faces drawn in bewilderment at the source of the intrusion, their eyes glassy. Whoever they were, neither looked like Annie Marsden.

Across to the other side was smaller room, with a pool table sitting in the middle of it, just as Sarah Finn had described. A number of younger people stood around in here, boys and girls. Some of them were loudly remonstrating with the officers who had entered the room, shouting in their belligerence that the raid was an invasion of privacy. Lucy scanned the group for either Annie Marsden or Gavin Duffy but could see neither.

Instead of entering either room, she quickly pushed her way upstairs, using the banisters to help her pull her way upwards. Mickey shoved past her on his way up, immediately cutting left at the top of the stairs and pushing open the door of a bedroom. Lucy glanced across to see an older man standing, naked, twisting to see the source of the intrusion. A thin pale figure lay prone on the bed in front of him. Mickey shoved his way into the room and Lucy saw him grab the man and shove him face down onto the floor.

The door of the room facing Lucy was closed. She turned the handle and pushed it open. In the half-gloom, she could make out two figures lying on the bed, both in a state of undress. Lucy reached across and clicked on the light. Gavin Duffy, stripped to the waist, turned to look at her, his eyes wide and red rimmed. Beneath him lay a young girl, still in her underwear. She too stared up at Lucy, her face drawn in terror. The side of her face, and the hair which clung to it, seemed matted with vomit.

Lucy pulled off her helmet. 'Gavin?' she said.

'Lucy?' Gavin asked, his face draining of colour. He stumbled off the bed, struggling to keep his footing. 'Lucy?' He moved across to her, his hand extended, touching her arm. 'Are you OK?'

At such close proximity, Lucy could smell the haze of alcohol that surrounded him. His eyes were wide, the whites threaded with burst blood vessels, the pupils little more than pinpricks of black at the centre of each iris.

'Are you OK?' he slurred. The words bubbled into sobs which broke from him.

'I'm so sorry,' he said. 'I didn't know he'd do it.'

'Where's Peter Bell?' Lucy managed, struggling to control her anger.

'Not Peter. Tony. I didn't know he'd do it. The car.'

'Tony?' Lucy asked. She remembered the tall youth who had seemed to run the gang in Gobnascale. 'Tony who?'

'I don't know. I told him you'd shown me Peter's picture. He asked where you were. I didn't know he'd do that.' Gavin nodded, then straightened, as if aware that he was drunk and trying very hard to appear sober. Lucy suspected he'd taken more than just alcohol.

'Tony planted the device in my car?'

Gavin nodded 'I didn't know,' he said. 'I swear. But you're all right.' He gripped her arm, forcefully. 'You're all right,' he repeated.

'Robbie was in the car,' Lucy said. 'He was the one who caused it to blow. He is in hospital.'

'Jesus,' Gavin said, the tears streaming now, bubbling round his lips as he spoke.

'You set him up, Gavin,' Lucy said, shoving him roughly backwards, towards the bed. The girl who had been lying there was trying with difficulty to sit up, pulling at the bedclothes, searching for her top.

'I didn't,' Gavin said. 'The picture you showed me. I knew who it was. I went and told him and he said he'd take care of it. He asked where you were and I told him.'

'You told Tony?'

Gavin shook his head. 'Jackie. I told Jackie.'

'Jackie Logue? Why?'

'Peter took a computer class run by the youth club. I went and told Jackie that he had killed Karen. Jackie said he'd take care of it.'

'Bell taught in the youth club? Did Karen know him?'

Gavin shook his head. 'No. He didn't teach *in* the club. He worked in a place across the town. Jackie only allowed some of us to go. Karen didn't do the class.'

'What about Sarah Finn?' If Sarah had known Bell already, Lucy wondered why she hadn't told them his name when they'd interviewed her?

'I don't think so. It was just me and a few other fellas.'

'Where is Bell now?' Lucy asked.

'He went to get drink,' Gavin said. 'Him and Tony. And the new girl.'

'Annie?'

Gavin nodded. 'I think so. Maybe. They said we needed more drink. I came up for a sleep.'

Lucy pointed at the girl sitting up now. She looked little more than fourteen.

'A sleep?' she asked.

Gavin glanced at the girl, then back at Lucy, his mouth hanging open. 'I don't ... I can't remember if—'

He did not finish the sentence for Lucy struck him across the face with such force, he lost his balance and stumbled, having to put out his hand to arrest his fall.

'You better hope you didn't,' she said, moving past him to reach for the girl. 'Are you OK?' Lucy asked her, putting out her hand to help the girl up off the bed.

Chapter Sixty-two

As they came downstairs, Burns was standing in the hallway, his hands on his hips, glancing between the two rooms as officers in both dealt with those who had been arrested. He smiled when he saw Lucy.

'Is this Annie?' he asked. 'Is she all right?'

Lucy shook her head. 'Annie's been taken out with Bell and a youth called Tony. He runs a gang in Gobnascale. Under Jackie Logue's watch. Bell taught a computer class apparently that some of the youths attended.'

'We'll put out descriptions,' Burns said. 'Someone will spot them. This is a great result.'

'They've gone for drink,' Lucy said. 'They'll have to come back this way. If they see the Land Rovers outside they'll either turn back or drive on round the point. We should send a car up as far as the prison. It can close in behind them when they pass. They'll not see the activity here until after that anyway and we can maybe sandwich them in.'

Burns considered the suggestion a moment, then nodded. 'Take a team with you,' he said. 'A few uniforms in case Bell gets heavy handed. Eh?'

* * *

In the end, they sat at the entrance to the prison for almost an hour before they saw the headlights of a car bouncing along the roadway towards them. They had parked about two miles from the house, on the verge at the prison gates; no one would think a police car outside a prison odd, even at that time of night, Lucy reasoned.

As the car passed, Lucy glanced across, keen not to be too obvious lest Tony recognize her, even through the tint of the police car windows. She was fairly sure that the vehicle that passed had three people in it. Certainly, there were two men in the front and a further figure sitting in the back seat.

Once the car had rounded the bend past the prison, they pulled off the verge and followed them along the road, keeping their own headlights off, using the overspill of light from the prison to help make their way. The last thing they wanted was Bell to spot them and take off around the point.

Instead, after a few hundred yards, they saw the bright red blinking of the brake lights on Bell's car as he realized that there were Land Rovers parked outside the house. Instantly the lights on the car went out, save, however, for the reversing light to the rear of the vehicle as Bell tried reversing back along the roadway he had just driven down.

Lucy radioed through to the waiting Land Rover sitting outside the house to move up the road towards them, effectively sandwiching Bell's car between them.

When Bell's car appeared at the end of the stretch of roadway on which they now sat, Lucy leaned across and switched on their headlights and told the uniform driving to speed up.

The car ahead of them stopped abruptly. For a moment, nothing happened. Then the two front doors flung open and Bell and Tony spilled out onto the road and set off, one in each direction, down the incline into the fields bordering the road.

'Get after them,' Lucy snapped, already opening her own door. She sprinted the distance to Bell's car, pulled open the rear door and reached it. A young-looking girl sat in the back seat, her expression one of shock.

'Annie Marsden?' Lucy asked.

The girl nodded.

'I'm DS Black of the PSNI. You're safe. OK?'

The girl glanced around her, then nodded.

'Have they hurt you in any way?' Lucy asked.

'No,' Annie replied quietly.

'They haven't tried to make you do anything?'

The girl shook her head.

'Stay here,' Lucy said. 'I'll be back in a moment. Don't get out of the car until I come back, do you understand?'

Annie Marsden nodded. She wore a light vest top and a denim skirt, her legs bare, save for streaks of fake tan. Lucy shrugged off her coat and handed it into the girl. 'Wrap that around you,' she said.

Standing, she looked across to the field where Tony had run. She could see the bobbing of torch beams as the two uniforms pursued him as he zigzagged in and out of the edge of the light from Magilligan. Finally, he seemed to lose his footing as he turned, and instead he slid, hitting the ground an instant before the uniforms were on him.

Lucy turned towards the opposite field where Bell had run and began the descent down the incline from the road. The ground was little more than marshland, and she could feel it seep around her feet as she stepped onto it. As she moved she could feel the mild tension of the mud sucking at her boots, the squelch as each foot was lifted.

To her left, she could see the uniform scouring the gorse that bordered the field, moving along it slowly, his torch angled at a height, the beam focused down to offer as wide an illumination as possible, searching for Bell.

Lucy pulled her own torch off her belt and, flicking it on, ran it along the length of the field. She could hear, beyond the shouting of Tony in the field opposite and the terrified lowing of cattle, the gentle rushing of water and she realized why the uniform had stopped where he had: the field abutted a stream, running down towards the lough. The edge of the field ended in a slight rise, where the stream, when it had burst its banks over the years, had pushed the earth along its edges upwards, creating a natural levee. She assumed that either Bell was hiding along it, or indeed had crossed the stream beyond in making his escape.

She slowly shone her torch along the length of the earthen levee, even as she moved closer to it. At its far end, away from where the uniform was moving, it merged with a thin copse of trees and low-lying bushes. It was for here that Lucy set off, assuming that Bell would have headed for cover.

She tried to increase her pace, constantly slowed by the sucking mud of the field, her feet sinking deeper as she moved closer to the stream itself, the land now water-logged, the surface reflecting the bounce of her torch beam.

As she approached the tree line, she could see a thin mist gather in loose clouds just beyond the levee, as if someone's breath was condensing in the chilled night air. She assumed that Bell was lying just on the other side, panting hard from his own exertions, his breath condensing above his head, marking out his spot. She tried to step more carefully as she approached, aware that the dull sucking of mud around her feet would alert him to her proximity.

Gun in one hand, torch in the other, she crested the earthen embankment, moving over the top quickly, expecting to see Bell on the other side. Instead, the wide eyes of a cow rolled towards her as it struggled to raise its heft off the sodden ground in which it was trapped. The sudden movement of the creature caused Lucy to start and she lost her footing a little, sliding down the embankment towards the stream.

Suddenly, from among the trees to her right, Bell appeared, launching himself at her. He made to grab at her hair, managing only a loose grip. It was enough to pull her off balance, though not enough for him to retain hold of her as she fell.

She scrabbled along the ground, reaching for his feet, even as he kicked out at her to shake her loose. She grabbed one leg and tugged as hard as she could, effectively pulling Bell over the top of her and forcing the two of them to roll into the freezing water of the stream.

Lucy fell awkwardly, the motion of the roll resulting in Bell lying above her, pinning her down beneath the surface. She could taste mud in her mouth, her ears filled with the rush of the water, her hands grappling with the slimed stones of the stream bed in an attempt to gain purchase enough for her to push upwards and dislodge Bell from where he lay on top of her.

She could feel again his hands gripping at her hair, the back of her neck, trying to force her head downwards, further into the water. Bell shifting his position now, straddled her, his knees either side of her body as he tried to drown her, leaning his weight onto her. She managed to shift a little, onto her side, moving her head enough to manage a gasp of air, before Bell pressed harder, scraping the side of her face against the rocky stream bed.

By angling herself, however, she'd freed her hand a little. Scrabbling along the ground, she managed to find a solid enough surface to press against to lever herself. She pushed as hard as she could, her lungs feeling as if they would burst, her body suddenly aware of the chill. She bucked her body upwards, unseating Bell sufficiently for her to repeat the manoeuvre a second time, more forcibly. Bell, reaching out to arrest his fall, lost his balance sufficiently that Lucy was able to drag herself from under him. Gripping a rock from beneath her, she turned sharply in the water and swung upwards. The rock connected with the side of Bell's face, stunning him enough momentarily for Lucy to push herself away from him and struggle to her feet.

Bell, too, was rising to his feet, cursing in the dark. He lunged for Lucy now, but she sidestepped him, swinging the rock a second time, connecting with his temple.

The lunge, combined with his weight and the slippery surface on which he stood, conspired against him and he fell into the water. In an instant, Lucy was on him, straddling him now, holding his head into the water. She gripped the back of his hair, pulled his head upwards sharply then slammed it downwards, his face connecting with the stones beneath the water with each strike.

She felt something rising inside her, felt a rage she had not felt since the night Mary Quigg died. She tightened her grip, holding his head under now with both hands as he thrashed in the water beneath her.

Suddenly, she was being lifted up and away from him. She felt arms constricting across her chest and she realized that the uniform had arrived and was pulling her away from Bell.

'I'm all right,' she said, twisting to look at the man. Only when she saw his expression did she understand that he had dragged her away for Bell's protection, not for hers.

She stepped quickly away from him, holding her hands aloft to indicate she would not touch Bell again.

For his part, Bell rolled onto his back. He struggled to pull himself out of the stream and lay on the embankment, retching as he brought up the water Lucy had forced him to swallow. His hair was plastered to his scalp, his face smeared with dirt, his nose and lips oozing fresh blood and saliva down over his mouth and chin. He lay back finally, his breaths coming in laboured pants in between fits of laughter.

Lucy leaned over him, the movement causing the uniform to step towards her. Around Bell's neck he wore a leather necklace on which hung a green holographic pendant. Shining her torch on it, Lucy saw, at its centre, an eye.

'Get up,' she said, pulling him by the shoulder.

'I want to speak to my father,' he said, not to Lucy, but to the uniform, twisting his head to look past her at the man. 'Call my father. Call Jackie Logue.'

Saturday 22 December

Chapter Sixty-three

Bell and Tony were bundled into the back of the police car, the other uniform and Lucy taking Bell's car, still blocking the roadway, in which sat Annie Marsden.

When she sat next to her, the girl offered Lucy back her coat.

'You're soaked,' she explained.

Lucy smiled, taking it and wrapping it around herself. After the initial buzz she had felt, first in overpowering Bell, then in his arrest and the revelation that Jackie Logue was his father, Lucy now began to feel the chill, the sodden clothing clinging to her with a damp heat that she knew would eventually sap her energy. She rifled through her coat pocket and took out her phone.

Handing it to the girl, she said, 'You should phone your parents. Tell them you're with us.'

The girl hesitated, her hand stretching out towards but not touching the phone. 'What should I tell them?' she asked, unconsciously pulling at the hem of the skirt she wore.

Lucy looked across at her, smiling a little sadly. 'Tell them you're safe. That's all that they'll care about for now.'

* * *

An hour later, Lucy sat before her own mother. A Response Team had brought with them a change of clothing and Lucy now wore one of the unit's boiler suits.

'I'm fine,' Lucy reassured her, as her mother asked for the third time how she felt.

'That'll need stitched,' Wilson said, touching the gash on her face with the tips of her fingers.

Lucy shifted her head away sharply from her touch. 'You knew about Bell, didn't you?'

Her mother raised an eyebrow quizzically. 'How would I have known? You only made the connection yourself today.'

'Not about now. About Louisa Gant. He killed her, didn't he?'

Wilson stared at her a moment. They were sitting in one of the upper bedrooms, the one in which she had found Gavin Duffy. She moved across and closed the door softly, then turned and leaned her back against it. Lucy, sitting on the edge of the bed, stared at her, waiting for her to speak, determined to stay silent, determined not to allow her a way out.

Her mother coughed to fill the silence, then pushed herself off the door with her rump and moved towards her daughter. She sat next to her, their bodies not touching, both staring straight ahead.

'He never admitted to it, but I knew Bell had been with her on the day she died,' her mother said, finally. 'I found a picture of him with her in an album she kept.'

'I saw it,' Lucy said.

Her mother turned. 'You visited Gant's? How is he?'

'Broken,' Lucy said. 'How would you expect him to be? So you knew?'

'I started investigating. Bell was only fourteen at the time. His mother was still with Logue at that stage. Once I connected his name to Bell, Special Branch took over.'

'Why?'

Wilson shrugged.

'Don't pretend to be stupid. Why?'

Wilson took a deep breath, held it a moment, then released it slowly. 'It was the new age of policing. They needed to be sure they had some support in those communities that hadn't backed the RUC before the change. Gary Duffy was set against the Peace Process and especially against the police, even with the changes. He was threatening to target Catholics who joined, the whole bit. Logue was known to be more sympathetic to policing change.'

'By the police covering up the fact that his son had killed a child, he became even more sympathetic, I'd imagine.' Lucy had been told Gary Duffy had been a hawk. He'd never have supported the newly formed PSNI and, as a community leader, would have ensured that the residents in the area would not cooperate with them either. From her searches for Cunningham, Lucy knew just how damaging that lack of cooperation could be to an investigation. If Duffy could be discredited in the community's eyes, and a more sympathetic community leader, like Jackie Logue, put in his place, the PSNI would find policing the area much easier. By covering up for Jackie Logue's son, the PSNI had managed to make Logue a puppet himself, she reflected.

Wilson nodded. 'I'd assume so.'

'And Gary Duffy was put in the frame to take him off the picture?'

'Arresting him for terrorist activity would simply have strengthened his reputation, strengthened his position in the community.'

'Label him a paedophile, though, and he'll be ostracized,' Lucy said.

'Presumably.'

'Why not give Gant back his daughter's body?' Lucy asked.

Her mother remained silent. Lucy studied the circling floral pattern of the carpet beneath her feet, piecing it together. 'Because then there'd have been forensics that Gary Duffy could have challenged in court, that would have implicated Logue's son,' she said, turning to look at her mother.

If the woman heard the comment, she did not react.

'So what role did you play in all this? Was this how you were groomed for success? Turning a blind eye?'

'No,' Wilson said, looking at Lucy directly for the first time. 'The case was taken off me. I was a young officer, told to hand over what I had. I simply did as I was told.'

'And what happened to Bell? Jackie Logue told me he'd had a son that he'd lost when the boy was a teenager. I assumed he meant the child had died.'

Wilson shook her head. 'He and his mother were forced to move away and change their names to Bell. In the hope that he wouldn't reoffend.'

390

'Because that's worked so well in the past,' Lucy spat. 'You knew —'

'I knew nothing for certain, Lucy,' Wilson said sharply. 'Nor do you.'

'You. You and your ... secrets.'

Wilson's mouth tightened as she sat more erect. 'We all have secrets, Lucy. That's what happened. Doing deals with bad people to try to do some good. On all sides.'

'And that justifies it?'

'That Finn girl went missing and you could go into that community to investigate it, without fear of being shot. Because of those deals. That's the price we pay for peace.'

'So what will happen to Jackie Logue now?'

'If he was involved in this ring, he'll face charges,' Wilson said. 'If he wasn't, he won't.'

'About Louisa Gant, I mean?'

'Nothing. He didn't do it. Peter Bell will face charges if any forensics taken from her remains implicate him.'

'Jackie Logue's an accessory.'

Wilson dismissed the statement. 'So too is Special Branch then. And every officer who benefited from our having Logue on the ground, arguing on our behalf.'

'That's rubbish,' Lucy muttered.

'Don't you judge me. Not until you're able to make the hard decisions too.'

'John Gant deserved to know the truth about his daughter. That's not a hard decision. The man's living in a museum,' Lucy said, aware as she said it that Gant was not the only one refusing to let go of past grief. Was the picture of Mary Quigg, pinned to her office wall, any different from Gant looking at E-FIT images of the girl his daughter might have grown up to be? 'He deserves the truth,' Lucy repeated.

'Well now he'll get it. Some of it at least,' Wilson said.

'A father deserves to know who killed his child,' Lucy stated. 'It doesn't matter the cost.'

Wilson shook her head and stood. 'Go back to Derry and get changed. Get that wound on your face checked.'

Lucy borrowed one of the squad cars that had come down from Derry. It was after ten in the morning by the time she left the house. She reached the front of Magilligan and parked up on the verge where she had sat the night before when they had waited for Bell.

Just after 10.45 a.m., the front gates swung slowly backwards and a single figure stepped out into the watery sunlight, his hand raised above his eyes as he glanced up and down the roadway. A little distance down the road, there was a bus stop and he started walking towards it, hefting his bag onto his shoulder.

As he drew abreast the car, Lucy leaned across and opened the door. Eoghan Harkin leaned down.

'Officer,' he said. 'Whatever it was, I didn't do it. I've only just got out.'

'I thought I should give you a lift,' Lucy said. 'We should talk.'

Harkin looked up and down, as if judging whether there were any potentially better offers, then nodded and, pushing his bag over the shoulder rest onto the floor of the back seat, got in.

Tuesday 25 December

Chapter Sixty-four

Lucy went to first Mass on Christmas morning. The air was sharp with the promise of coming snow, despite the sky being clear of cloud. The other parishioners smiled at her and offered her a Happy Christmas. She returned the wishes, even as she struggled to feel the joy they should have carried with them.

After Mass, she drove to see her father. She had dug out a picture of the garden with the fountain from the laneway behind Prehen and had it framed. When he unwrapped it, he smiled and thanked her, but she could tell from the blankness in his expression that he did not recognize the place. Another of his memories had passed beyond him forever, the wisps of her childhood diminishing one by one with each day his illness progressed.

'What's this for?' he asked.

'It's Christmas, Daddy,' she said.

'I've not got you anything,' he said, his eyes rheumy.

'That's OK,' she said.

She sat next to him, her hand on the arm of her chair, his hand, soft and warm, lightly balanced on top of hers.

'Are we having dinner?' her father asked suddenly.

'No, Daddy,' Lucy said. 'I've got to go soon.'

'Where to?'

'The cemetery,' Lucy said.

The man snorted, derisively. 'What's a young girl like you doing going to visit the dead?'

Lucy stared at him, surprised by the lucidity of the comment.

'You want to take Lucy somewhere nice today, love,' he said, winking against the light coming in through the window of his room.

'I am Lucy, Daddy.'

He squinted at her, then patted her hand lightly. 'Isn't that funny? I thought you were your mother for a minute,' he said.

As she was leaving, Lucy was surprised to see her mother's car pull into the small car park in front of the block where her father was being held. In truth, she had assumed that the woman did not visit her father. She moved quickly across to the squad car that she was using until her own was replaced, but struggled to get the door open, her movements clumsy because of the bandage on her hand. By the time she'd managed to pull it open, she had no choice but to speak to her.

Her mother approached, walking crisply across the scattered leaves that blew around their feet.

'Happy Christmas, Lucy,' she said.

'And you,' Lucy said. They leaned awkwardly towards one another, briefly pressing their cheeks lightly together.

'I didn't know you visited him,' Lucy said.

'Well, I do.'

'He's not well,' she said, unnecessarily.

Her mother nodded absently. She glanced around, pulling her coat tighter around her against the bracing wind. 'So, what are your plans for the day?'

'I'll see Robbie. Then Tom Fleming asked me to help out with a soup kitchen he works in for the homeless and that. Part of his Christian group.'

'You could call for some dinner later with me, if you wanted,' her mother said. 'I'm having some friends around. But you'd still be welcome.'

Lucy smiled. 'Thanks, but I'm OK.'

'You'd rather eat with the homeless?'

'I've things to do,' Lucy said, suddenly pained that she had inadvertently offended the woman.

'On Christmas Day?'

Lucy shrugged. 'It's just a day,' she said, feeling her eyes fill. The gash on her cheek, stitched up a few nights previous, throbbed angrily.

'I see,' her mother said. 'I'll go on.'

Lucy nodded and turned to fumble with her car keys again.

'Oh, we found Jackie Logue last night,' her mother said, turning on her step.

'Really?' Lucy asked. Logue had vanished soon after his son, Peter Bell, had been arrested in Magilligan. They'd assumed someone had tipped him off that the PSNI would be coming for him. 'Where's he being held?'

'The morgue. He'd been stripped naked and shot in the head. His body was laid out on the train tracks where they found Karen Hughes.'

'That's ... terrible,' Lucy said, aware of how insincere the words sounded.

'Yes. Eoghan Harkin gets out of prison, Logue goes missing, then he's murdered on the spot where Harkin's daughter was found. You'd swear someone had told Harkin that Logue was involved in Karen's death.'

Lucy felt the wound in her face throb again.

'And you were so moralistic,' her mother said.

'I don't know what you mean,' Lucy mumbled, her face flushing.

'You were spotted picking up Harkin outside the prison. What did you tell him?'

Lucy shook her head but said nothing.

Her mother stepped closer to her again. 'I put you in PPU because I didn't think you'd be able to handle the politics of CID. I thought you were better than that. It seems I was wrong.' She regarded Lucy a moment coldly, as if appraising her anew. 'You're more like than me than you want to admit.'

With that, she turned and strode off. Lucy stood watching her, her face so hot and sore, she felt as though she had been slapped.

Robbie was eating his own dinner when Lucy went in. He smiled as she entered the room, leaning towards her to accept her kiss.

'Merry Christmas,' he said.

Lucy smiled, sitting on the bed next to him. 'How are you feeling?'

'Sore,' he said. 'But I'll recover.'

Lucy took his hand in hers, was reminded in the gesture of the feeling of her father's hand earlier.

'I am sorry, Robbie. For this. And for us, too.'

He smiled sadly. 'I know, Lucy.'

'I'd rather it had been me,' she said. 'You didn't deserve all this.'

He shrugged. 'I'm glad it wasn't you,' he said.

'When do you get out?' Lucy asked, embarrassed by his comment.

'The next day or two,' he said. 'I'm going to go home for a while. To my folks.'

'Do you want me to give you a lift up? I'll check under the car before you get into it this time,' Lucy said.

'And so you should,' Robbie joked. 'No. My dad's going to collect me.'

Lucy swallowed, shifting on the bed. 'Will I see you over the holidays at all?'

Robbie looked at her, his eyes soft in their kindness. 'I don't know,' he said. 'I'm not sure what's happening.'

'With the holidays or with us?' Lucy said, trying to smile, pretending indifference.

'Both,' he said. 'Either. I'm not sure.'

Lucy patted his hand with hers, then lifted it again and, clasping it between both hers, drew it to her lips and kissed the skin between his finger and thumb.

'I am sorry,' she repeated.

She didn't go to the cemetery in the end. Instead she found herself once more on Petrie Way, glancing in the mirror at the wrapped gift that sat on the back seat of the car as she pulled up outside the house.

She sat, watching the house, wondering whether she should leave the gift at all. Perhaps wait until the sky darkened and then leave it on the doorstep. But she knew they would never give it to the child, not knowing whence it came.

Finally, she got out, clutching the gift in her hand. She made it as far as the driveway of the house before stopping. Through the large front window she could see, in the lounge, the Kelly family sitting on the floor. Joe sat at the centre of a scattered collection of new toys, his foster mother helping him play with a truck while her husband recorded it.

Lucy could see, for the first time, how happy the child looked, how content was the whole family. She knew that, if she knocked at the door, left her gift, she would have to explain how she knew the child and why she felt responsible for him. She would have to share Mary's sacrifice with them. She knew that the knowledge of what had happened to him would profit none of them. In the end, she turned to leave.

Across the street, a neighbour was standing at his car, watching her. 'Are you looking for someone?' he called over.

'No,' Lucy said. 'I've the wrong house,' she explained, moving back to her car.

Around four she went to the soup kitchen where Tom Fleming was working. She helped them to prepare the meals for the homeless. As she helped laying the tables, she watched out for Janet, the girl who had featured so prominently in Lucy's own father's past. The last time Lucy had seen her she had been living on the street, an alcoholic, abandoned by her own family. Lucy hoped and feared, in equal measure, that Janet might appear at the soup kitchen for food, but she did not.

After the dinner, she and Fleming stood in the kitchen of the church hall, drinking coffee.

'Pudding?' Fleming asked, offering her a dish.

Lucy shook her head. 'I'm stuffed.'

'I'm not allowed it,' Fleming said, putting the dish down a little ruefully. 'Because of the brandy. In case it sets me off on another bender,' he added with a smirk.

'How is it going?' Lucy asked.

'I'm OK,' he said, smiling lightly. 'I had to dry out for a few days. It was a little hairy, but ... it's done now.'

Lucy nodded. 'I did tell them you didn't miss that stuff in Kay's. I told them it was planted.'

Fleming patted her arm. 'I know,' he said. 'Your mother told me. But she was right, Lucy. I needed a break, to sort myself out. I wasn't doing anyone any favours, the state I was in.'

'Are you OK now?'

He nodded. 'I will be,' he said. 'I heard about the attack on your car. Are *you* OK?'

Lucy nodded, busying herself with rinsing her cup. 'Robbie was the one who was hurt.'

'You're not having dinner with your mum today?'

Lucy shook her head. 'No. I must feel more at home here, I guess,' she said, looking around at the ragged dinner guests sitting before her.

'You and me both,' Fleming said, putting his arm around her shoulders and briefly pulling her close. 'Happy Christmas, Lucy.'

'And you, Tom.'

She drove down through the Waterside on her way home. As she passed the shops at Gobnascale, she glanced across. They were closed for the day, their shutters pulled. Despite that, a group of kids still gathered outside them, standing in a loose circle.

As she slowed to glance across, Lucy saw a car sitting in the parking bay opposite, the door open, the owner sitting half out of the car, watching over the group, a cigarette in his hand.

When he saw her, Eoghan Harkin stood and moved across to the fence between the shops and the road.

Lucy rolled down the window as she pulled abreast where he stood.

'Have you no home to go to?' Harkin asked. 'It's Christmas.'

'I could say the same,' Lucy said.

'Someone needs to keep an eye on this crowd. Give them some direction. Now that there's a vacancy in the area, what with Jackie Logue in the wind.'

'Not any more. They found his body on the railway tracks last night.'

'Did they now?' Harkin asked. 'Imagine that.'

He smiled at her, his grin feral. Lucy tried to ignore the sickness gnawing at her guts.

'So what about Alan Cunningham? Any rumours on his whereabouts?' Lucy asked.

Harkin straightened, looking across the top of her car a second, drawing a final pull on his cigarette. 'I wouldn't know anything about that, now,' he said. 'Though wherever he tries to go from here onwards, he'll be getting a cold reception. He'll have no more bolt-holes. He'll have to resurface eventually. When he does, you'll need to be ready to grab him, Sergeant.'

Suddenly, two figures stepped out onto the road from the pavement opposite and passed in front of her. Gavin, his arm wrapped protectively around Elena's shoulder, his head held high, crossed in front of Lucy's car while she waited, staring in at her as he did so. Lucy held his stare until finally the boy had to turn away to step up onto the pavement where Harkin stood. At his arrival, the group of youths, who had been at the shop, moved towards him, their voices raised in greeting, as if to welcome a returning conqueror, encircling him the way they had once done for Tony.

Harkin smiled and raised his voice to be heard above the noise of the youths. 'That's the thing about your bad deeds. They'll always resurface eventually,' he added. 'You take care for now, Lucy Black. I'll be seeing you again.'

Lucy watched as he turned to lead the gang back to the shops, Gavin by his side, the youths trailing in his wake.

'I can promise you that,' she said.

Acknowledgements

Thanks to Finbar Madden and all my friends and colleagues in St Columb's College for their continuing support, and to Bob McKimm and James Johnston for their invaluable advice.

Thanks to all the team at Constable & Robinson, particularly James Gurbutt, Lucy Zilberkweit, Clive Hebard, Sandra Ferguson and Martin Palmer, and to Jenny Hewson of RCW and Emily Hickman of The Agency.

Continued thanks to the McGilloways, Dohertys, O'Neills and Kerlins for their support, especially Carmel, Joe and Dermot, and my parents, Laurence and Katrina, to whom this book is dedicated.

Finally, my love and thanks to my wife, Tanya, and our children, Ben, Tom, David and Lucy.

About the author

Brian McGilloway was born in Derry, Northern Ireland, in 1974, and teaches English at St Columb's College, Derry. He lives near the Irish borderlands with his wife and four children.

For more information, visit www.brianmcgilloway.com.